Temperance Lloyd

Hanged for Witchcraft in 1682

by
B. Chris Nash

Copyright © 2012 by B. Chris Nash
First Edition – October 2012

ISBN
978-1-4602-0427-6 (Hardcover)
978-1-4602-0425-2 (Paperback)
978-1-4602-0426-9 (eBook)

All rights reserved.

No part of this publication may be reproduced in any form, or by any means, electronic or mechanical, including photocopying, recording, or any information browsing, storage, or retrieval system, without permission in writing from the publisher.

Cover Photos: Julian Luxton and Alfred Boyd

Produced by:

FriesenPress

Suite 300 – 852 Fort Street
Victoria, BC, Canada V8W 1H8

www.friesenpress.com

Distributed to the trade by The Ingram Book Company

DEDICATION

To Roger Nash, my first and most constructively critical reader, my editor, my Poet. And to the Women's Legal Education and Action Fund (LEAF) "In the Hope of an End to Persecution and Intolerance" everywhere.

Rougemont Castle: Exeter

THE DEVON WITCHES
IN MEMORY OF
TEMPERANCE LLOYD
SUSANNAH EDWARDS
MARY TREMBLES
OF BIDEFORD DIED 1682
THE LAST PEOPLE IN ENGLAND
TO BE EXECUTED FOR WITCHCRAFT
DIED HERE & HANGED AT HEAVITREE

In the hope of an end to persecution and intolerance

PROLOGUE
1604

"*Many confessd under torture to having met with the Devil [who] had the witches dig up corpses and cut off different ... organs which were then tied to a dead cat and thrown into the sea to call up the storm that had nearly wrecked the King's ship*". (North Berwick Witch Trials 1590-92)

This heat. This too warm June day. The ninth day of June in the year of our Lord 1604, the record shall show. The record shall not show the heat, the stench. Our barge came on the fetid Thames. So thick it was with floating refuse and excrement it seemed to slow our progress through the haze. Inside our Palace of Westminster the smell of all those sweaty, fire-smoky robes assails my senses. I feel quite unwell. I must keep my royal comportment in the sight of the Lords and Bishops. I sit still. Beneath the elegant robes, none can see my hands that clench in fists so tight the blood flows from my palms. O God, let me not die this day I have awaited so long to make us safe from the evils that surround us. It's just the heat, the smoke.

I cannot breathe. God help me. I cannot breathe. I need air. I feel my throat closing up. The walls are fading. Dark shadows frame the windows. The sun pierces through mine eyes, bores hard into my head, blinding me. The Palace seems to close in on me. Think. I must think on the Act, the Statute that is my salvation. My triumph is so close. I must think not on past evils. 14 years have past. The past is past, yet sleep keeps it fresh in dreams. It comes to me even in this sunlit day.

I feel I will be sick. In my mind I am again on that terrible voyage to Copenhagen when the storm sent my ship to shelter in port in Norway. The floors beneath this throne are rolling as did the boat that awful night. I feel I shall vomit. I must try to breathe even the smoky air that makes my stomach heave. Think on the beauty of my then betrothed, and now my wife, the Princess Anne of Denmark. We prayed the wind to change. God answered.

I watch the red, the purple, the black robes sway as the Bishops, Barons, and lesser dignitaries listen to Mr Secretary Herbert. He intones,

> An Acte against conjuration Witchcrafte and dealing with evill and wicked Spirits — BE it enacted by the King our Sovraigne Lorde..."

"He that suffered the assails of witches 20 years back", mutters Viscount Montague to Viscount Budan.

"Witches or politics, the King's discontent was great and lasting. Fifteen years passed since the Scottish trial".

"And the King himself went there to witness the trial, to see those heads roll".

They sit so close beneath me. Think they I cannot hear their chatter?

"But ... Listen".

Aye. They should listen. For their pay, if not for love of their King.

> "... the Lordes Spirituall and Temporall and the Comons in the present Parliament assembled, and by the authoritie of the same ..."

Three times the Statute be before this Parliament, amended and amended till we found it right enough.

The Bishops of Bristol and Oxford look so piously heavenwards.

"Pray God this do be right".

> "... That the Statute made in the fifte yeere of the Raigne of our late Sovraigne Ladie of the most famous and happy memorie Queene Elizabeth, intituled An Acte against Conjuration, Inchantments and Witchcraftes be ... utterlie repealed
>
> AND for the better restrayning of saide offenses, and more severe punishings of the same, be it further enacted by the authoritie aforesaid, That if any ... persons after the ... Feaste of Saint Michaell the Archangell next comeing, shall

Temperance Lloyd: Hanged for Witchcraft in 1682

> *use practise or exercise any Invocation or Conjuration of any evill and spirit, or shall consult ... Employ feede or rewarde any evill and wicked Spirit to or for any intent or purpose; or take any dead man woman or child out of his her or theire grave ... or ... any parte of any dead person, to be imployed or used in any manner of Witchecrafte, Sorcerie, Charme or Inchantment ..."*

As did mine own cousins to the North that died as traitors for it. To bewitch a King, tis treachery of the highest. I turned away as their end came. I confess I smiled.

> *"... or shall use practise or exercise any Witchecrafte, Sorcerie, Charme or Incantment whereby any person shall be killed destroyed wasted consumed pined or lamed in his or her bodie or any parte therof; then that everie such ..."*

So now the Statute. Tis done. I feel the calm, the calm of our own voyage onward. I saw her standing there to greet me, my tall, my slender Princess, her hair a golden halo around her shoulders. It was worth the wait, worth the stormy passage. Now I knew all would be well.

The sea was calm again. We could ready to set sail for Scotland. I held my new bride in my arms. The crew set forth for home in good spirits. My love and I were so happy, walking the decks, enjoying the morning sun. The sickness comes again. I can barely see the Lords gathered before me down there. I feel the ship rising beneath me in the storm. That wind, pushing black clouds across the sky to darken the afternoon into night. I take my Anne to sit below decks. We try to breathe our way through the heaving waves. I was first to succumb to the sickness. Then she was heaving. We prayed God for salvation. How long before we reach harbour?

It seemed like days, though twas only hours, that took us to the coast. Dear Anne, she knelt on the quayside to thank God. I, the King, was loathe to be seen on my knees outside of the Royal Chapel. I thanked my maker more discreetly. I pulled Anne to her feet and presented her to my cousin, Francis Stewart, first Earl of Bothwell. If I had known ...

The Secretary's voice suddenly booms loud. He brings me back from the cold of Scotland past to the heat of the House of Lords present.

> *"Ayders, Abettors and Counsellors, being of saide Offences dulie and lawfullie convicted and attainted, shall suffer pains of deathe as a Felon or Felons, and shall loose the priviledge and benefit of Cleargie and Sanctuarie ... and if any person ... By Witchecrafte ... Tell ... In what place any treasure of Golde*

or silver ... or things loste or stollen be founde ... Shall suffer Imprisonment of one whole yeere"

Time was I knew little, nay nothing, of the powers that witches hold over nature itself. It was to Holyrood the horsemen from the coast brought reports from Berwick of the true causing of the storms. We were warm by the fire as I read the paper.

The heat grows more oppressive, that sweaty heat rising towards me as the sun warms still more the assembled heavy robes. Or is it thought that triggers that same sick panic in my belly I first felt reading of the confession of the servant girl, Gellie Duncan, of Tranent, the village so close to my beloved Edinburgh. It could not be true. And yet ... There it was, on the paper. Oh God, I see it again plain as this Statute I hold today.

The rack and other gaolers' instruments loosened Gellie's tongue and those of her damned accomplices. Messengers brought more news daily. It made me sick to read it, but I had needs know the depths of the trouble. Gellie had named them all. The local schoolmaster, Dr John Fian, was leader of a coven of some size. Other respected local folk, the midwife Agnes Sampson, Lord Cliftonhall's daughter, Euphemia MacLean, widow of Earl Archibald of Angus, Barbara Apier ... They were all within the coven. Under duress came still more, a wealth of informations, a babble of other confessions. Worst of all, pray God it not be so ... mine own cousin, Francis Stewart, was one amongst them. My own kin in whom I trusted so. It seems my Cousin Francis knew well how to achieve his own political ends by means of the foulest powers of darkness.

It was a fantastic tale but one, I was assured, that was confirmed under oath in the confessions of so many, of near seventy accused witches. And there was the proof. The storm would surely have claimed my own life had my prayers not been so steadfast, my God so merciful.

Twas terrible news to hear. Worse than the horrid details of the events, to uncover that I was not as beloved of my people as up to then I had no cause to doubt. And had I perished in that storm, who would gain the throne? Francis Stewart. What lengths would he not go to obtain the power over Scotland and England, perhaps over France? I had to know more. I had to send for the witch. Face the fear.

We watched the sun dip behind the horizon in my Palace of Holyrood. We feasted on venison and turnip, good Scots fare. I slept well that night in my own bed till we were awakened by the sunlight in the royal bedroom high above the ravines of our beloved Edinburgh. We broke our fast with fowl and strong ale. I commanded a servant to take me down to the dungeons below to see Witch Sampson. The stairs below the great hall smelled damp. Water dripped down the walls. The rail was slimy to my touch, the steps slippery underfoot. Still today I cannot enter dark dank spaces without my stomach turns.

A narrow passageway led into a lower chamber. There she was, an old woman standing close against the moss-covered stone wall, held from me by the witch's bridle. Sunken eyes gazed fearfully up at me from that haggard face. The guard held a lantern over her head casting the yellow light the better for me to behold her. Could this be the same Mistress Agnes Sampson that had approached the Princess Anne with such a pretty courtesey to offer her services as midwife, "Should she ever be in need of one in Edinburgh, Ma'am"? She looked too weak to be of any danger to me, but the evil she had done showed in her eyes. The devil was in her. The open weave helmet kept her at bay, the four sharp prongs inserted inside her mouth, two against her tongue, two against her cheeks drew blood at her slightest movement. Blood. Even the thought, the collection of it makes me faint.

In those first weeks after the executions, I lived over the trauma many times. I dreaded the night, not quite so often with the years gone by. Anne tried to comfort me, had the physician give me lettuce and opium seeds for sleep. She went out herself between Michaelmas and Lady Day to find woman's milk to mix with oil of violets from the apothecary and laid the cloth herself upon my head, murmuring so sweetly. Then as now she read me into sleep. Much good that it did.

The nightmares still came often in those autumn months. Old women with cats flew through the air, their filthy tattered clothing brushing my forehead as I struggled sick against a stormy northern sea. I called out in fear. My legs would not obey my wish to move them against the icy waters. No one on the ship heard my frantic shouts for help though they awakened the courtiers of the bed chamber and brought the guards running. I awoke night following night here in London shivering, my nightgown soaked in cold sweat, thinking myself once again on the eastern shore of my other kingdom, my beloved Scotland.

Secretary Herbert drones on.

> "Provided alwaies that if the ofender in any cases aforesaide shall happen to be a Peere of this Realme, then his Triall therein is to be had by his Peeres, as it is used in cases of Felonie or Treason "...

Budan and Montague have their heads together. Their voices rise with the smoke,

"As is right and proper "...

"Aye — but I know not what will become of it "...

"Then do not say so for safety's sake".

"So great his discontent, he wrote — or caused to be writ — his 'Daemonologie'. And now, he sits close with us".

"I be not ignorant that a fearful abounding of witches and enchanters moved our Lord the King to resolve any doubt in the hearts of many; that such assaults of Satan are most certainly practiced".

"And those practices merit most severely to be punished".

Had they any doubt? Are they not knowledgeable of the world? Montague is nodding,

"With this Act, the King himself doth publicly confirm for all to hear there are for sure divers and many practices of witchcraft by the companions of Satan".

"And he no mean scholar upon the object".

Montague is whispering,

"The effort will begin here, but it will require England to be involved at every level".

He is right. England must be, shall be, involved at every level.

As Secretary Herbert reads the words of the Statute I see some Members nod into sleep.

My fears faded from my dreams as I wrote them into my 'Daemonologie'. Sleep came back at night without aid of potions, needing only my bride, my lovely Anne, by my side in my bed. The words became a salve for my spirit. The writing of it made a way to mend my damaged faith in my divine right to rule as England's Lord and Monarch. Like other learned men of our day, my device was one of conversations. I spoke in the voices of Epistemon and Philomathes, their wisdom of Holy Writ and argument to banish from this land any doubts that the "assaults of Satan are most certainly practiced and that the instruments thereof" must be "severely punished".

For I, the King. have surely seen witchcraft for myself. I myself have seen those most well respected citizens, and my own cousin, wield the tools of Satan. Those that argue that "there can be no such thing as Witchcraft" must be silenced. There be learned men, even a German physician of great repute, that deny the existence of witches and do declare that therefore they should not be punished. Clearly, a man who can say such things betrays himself to have been one of that profession. My words are there for all to read, my mind calmed by the writing down of it.

Now I give England the gift of my Statute. She now can rest easy knowing we have the means to punish those servants of Satan that would destroy us in our beds as they did in my other kingdom.

The Lords Temporal and Spiritual are moving on to the other business,

> "An Act for Confirmation of certain Letters Patents, made to Sir George Howne, An Act to restrain all Persons from Marriage, until their former Wives and former Husbands be dead, An Act ... against the destroying of Hares with Hare-pipes and tracing Hares in the Snow ...

Twill be late in the day afore the Lords and Bishops step out of the Palace of Westminster on to the street. I have no further business there. I rise. The Lords rise. They bow as the I pass among them. My entourage follows me through the great door. The outside air feels fresh on my face. Even the stench of the Thames is better than the smoke-filled heat of the grand chamber. My duty is done. There is a long light summer evening to enjoy.

CHAPTER ONE

"THE feareful aboundinge.. In this countrie, of these detestable slaves of the Devill, the Witches, ... hath moved me ... to resolve the doubting harts of many ... that such assaultes of Sathan are most certainly practized, & ... merits most severely to be punished ..."

(The Preface: Daemonolgie, James R - VI of Scotland, 1597)

In Bideford, the River Torridge sparkles in the evening sun. Inside The Arms that stands high on the hill overlooking the bridge, the pewter ale-pots reflect the pink light as the sun sets above the fields over East-the-Water. Seamen, merchants, travellers, order up their ale or scrumpie and crowd onto the rough wooden benches set by tables to exchange views about the troubles of the day. Masters of merchant ships come in to find men to replace the mariners too sick from fever or the drink to sail on the next tide. Wages are agreed. The men leave. Against the rough brick wall under the small east windows on a raised platform, the backs of fixed benches form alcoves around the tables. Merchants and ships' masters choose these seats to deal more privately in port or pottery or butter.

Older men whose days at sea have passed, or perhaps never came, sit at the table in the northeast corner. The Welshman Sion seats himself there at opening time. He leaves to return to his chamber at the Almshouses when the bell rings for closing. Sion speaks when he's spoken to, offers an occasional comment, but mostly he sits and listens. When something peaks his interest, he leans forward to hear better, sometimes putting his hand to his right ear, sometimes nodding his head. He listens.

"Can't see nought, I can't, can I? Seen nought since I slipped from the Crows Nest that black stormy night off Rhosilli Point. Funny thing, when ye'm blind, tis like folk don't see ye. Oh, they buys me ale they do. Very polite they are with it. Say, Good Day, blind Sion, God Bless ye Sion, Nos Da, Sion, Good Night, John, that's what the English here calls me. Same difference. Then they leaves me be, sat in me corner up Th'Arms, day come, day go. Can hear it all, hear all of them, better than most, see. Tis blind I be, not deaf. So they gab and gab like I can't hear them. Can't see, can't hear, maybe some believe as I can't think nor speak neither. Well, don't say much I don't. Listens best with your mouth shut".

The voices grow louder in the square outside, not the soft Devon accents, harder, sharper, the sounds of strangers.

"London coach must be in this night, been coming right through to Bideford since they cut the Crediton cart trail through to meet Silchester road to Exeter. The strangers buy their ale and seat themselves. London folk all talking of King James and that lovely bride he brought from the Kingdom of Denmark. Saved him causing Wars by choosing twixt all tother ladies he could woo, queens of Spain, France, Germany, they say. And they say the Princess Ann be fair of face, hair like gold, a rare beauty".

In the summer months, more and more London folk alight outside the Ship Inn on the quay.

"Come to do their trading, see their ships be solid and goods in the hold. Watch them sail down river on the night tide. Their work done, they stroll up to The Arms and sit themselves down by the fire to tell their tales".

Sion listens, a faint smile on his wrinkled face.

"Them London folk thinks us knows nothing. Or thinks them knows all. They say ... Tonight tis all talk of our Scottish King, Good King James, he that brought all ken of witchcraft and phantasms from up his north country. They say he were troubled in his mind, so troubled he did sit every day in his chamber writing a learned journal of his personal ken of witches and their powers. Could not rest till he have a Statute to punish the phantasms that came with him from Scotland. More force be needed to stem the evil all around. They say "...

Sion shrugs and drinks his ale.

"Oh they say lots them folk from London town. Sits themselves down by our fire and tells us their tales. Now they say the King be well pleased with his new Statute. Mind you, sat here they be quick to say as greater minds (of which they count themselves) might see talk of witchcraft as but foolish superstition. Seems wisdom like that be only whispered up

Temperance Lloyd: Hanged for Witchcraft in 1682

London way. Here in Bideford up The Arms, they'll say their piece to all that will listen, thinking to impress us ignorant country folk. With us proper enlightened they can't hardly wait to leave on the next coach back to Town. There in their coffee houses, they praise the Lord and the Lords for their wise protection of the people from such evils as the King himself had personal ken... Our Scottish King".

The talk from London was reassuring as to the King's state of mind. The perfection of his Statute, it was reported, laid to rest the sovereign's demons. Knowing he need take no more time in the pursuit of witches, he could turn his mind to other matters of state. By Corpus Christi, word was spread across the country. The Broadsheet came to Bideford on the London coach. Sion listens as Master Hibberd read it out in The Arms,

> "Many Englishmen, and Scotsmen need no convincing that the blessings of the Church carry the price of responsibility. They only need to hear a call to action. The calls that have come should be picked up by Mayors, Sheriffs and Lieutenant Governors".

Who would dare to disagree? Certainly not the old seamen chatting over their ale in The Arms. Master James Puddicombe is always quick to support the law, being himself a Constable years past.

"Right it be, a matter of 'security' of King and Country, and a Christian duty to boot. Can leave the witch-hunting to all that now have the means to do it. For sure such fine upstanding citizens as the Mayors and Aldermen of country towns, that serve as Justices in Bideford, must answer the call. Tis their sworn duty. Bideford Justices be proper educated for it. Not like them up Barnstaple way. They can read and take up the taxes".

"True enough. Well ... they do keep account of fees for the Bridge holdings. Though there be some as say Mistress Jarrett do help with that by candlelight late of a night when Christian folk be abed".

"And as to the reading ... They can read the charges well enough".

"That 'em can. Us do hear them of a Sunday read from the Prayer Book".

"Oh they do that — just half a word behind the Clergy".

"Still, Master Johns heard 'em after Matins asking what's to do with this witchcraft. They knows to settle petty thievery and use of scales giving low measure by pillory or the stocks. An' when tis an inconvenient coming with child blamed on a serving woman's betters, they do deal well in private with quick betrothal to some lower manservant. Thievery and lust be temporal matters to judge on".

The Constable whispers to Sion,

"Us 'eared quite a to-do over that Witchcraft Statute this day down Town Hall. 'Em 'ad Mistress Corning write the County Sheriff up Exeter askin' how shall they call on matters of supernatural evils. How shall they serve justice on the witches that must certainly be in our very midst? How could they know them? Sheriff say one thing be certain, to deny witchcraft be to deny God himself".

Sion nods.

"So, tis a religious matter then. But what religion? Roman church or new church, folk don't know what to follow".

"Reverend James says tis best do what Rector say. He knows of good and evil, his preachings of a Sunday should guide them".

"Aye. If he can be found sober, he can aid the Court of a Monday".

Constable knows all about that. No matter. The Lord High Justice do decree it. The Broadsheet do report it.

> "The rooting out of witches be something all citizens could accustom themselves to, and grow to love. The law must be enforced".

*****

Decades later, Blind Sion gazes sightlessly at his empty tankard. He feels a draft on his face as the outer door opens, and hears clogged feet on the taproom floor. Every night The Arms is packed tight with seamen. Bideford is a thriving port, the Torridge so afloat with ships, there's hardly room to turn about to catch the tide. Jim Crouch tells Sion,

"London bark be tied up down the quay. Nigh fetched up on Lizard rocks in that great storm out the Channel, blew up past Bude and found safe moorage down our quay".

"Well, I woulda known it from the voices ordering up Fremington ale, all of them telling that fears of witchcraft be travelling south fast from the northern wilds. Still savage up close to Scotland whence came King James, he that been dead and gone these many years, the good Lord rest his soul in death, as his Statute did for him in life. Didn't take long for the demons that left the King to alight fast on others with nought better to do, and malice in their hearts to do it with zeal. Tis always for the 'good' of fellow men to rid us all of evil, the better the pay, the greater the good. They London folk bring informations from the East counties of one Master Hopkins that hath declared himself Witch-Finder General for the greater good. Tis five days ride from here to there in summer time, longer in winter. No matter, news of malice travels. They said he found and brought to trial two hundred or more, all said to be witches. Not that they'd done nothing particular to be called for a witch. Folks they'd made as enemies just had to tell as they were seen consorting, or thought to have consorted, with the Devil himself. Or folks could report as they had heard other folks had said as they heard other folk had seen it. Even a Clergyman, tis said, was thus proved with bewitching of children. Master Hopkins died young he did, mebbe from so busy a life he had of it. His fervour found great favour with Lord Justice Hale that prosecuted them that Hopkins hunted out. News of witching always gains open mouths and tuned ears. Much ale be spent for a good tale".

The trials spread quickly from one Assize to the next. Sion listens to the tales, shaking his head.

"True or false, the more fanciful the accounts, the better for re-telling by a warm fire of a cold night. And many folk to tell. Many folk to listen. All happened far off, way north, then over east. None to say if tis true, or just tall tales".

*****

"Time flies they say, more slow-footed than fleet-winged where I sit, faster with good tales to speed the hours. The Statute rules us still ... The law must be enforced with tales of witchcraft now coming close, in Somerset. There be witches everywhere for sure. Bideford Justices can do with the trying of them, but what to do then? Daren't put em in the stocks for fear they should spell those that stand to look. Have to duck 'em in good water, see if they drown or not. If they drown ... If they don't drown ... Gone either way seems to me. Right good trade it be for carpenters. Tis said Richard Hals — they say he's Richard on account of better birth than his other name do show, but how would I know — makes the best ducking stools in these parts. Makes 'em for Fremington, Appledore, Barnstaple and beyond - right up to the Quantocks. Much call for the stool up Somerset way. Constables there be busy with protecting against the danger".

The Bideford Constable is certain of his duty. He tells Sion,

"The law must be enforced. No cause to feel pity for our Justices. They has the tools. Sheriff do say the dead King and the living Church tell of the exact qualities of witches for the hunting of 'em. Tis for the Sheriffs and Constables to find the offenders and the Justices to prosecute said offenders. An honourable new trade the witch-finding be".

"And what other task will pay so well with no cause to waste the time to train in lawyering?"

Sion wonders, "And much saving of moneys for the parishes that rid themselves of the burden of care for all the destitute widows and spinsters, in the best case, riddance to their kin too".

He knows better that to voice his thoughts. Never know who might be sitting quietly in the crowd. And Constable is certain,

"Tis a matter of security, the security of the King, of the nation".

The sign is on the door at Saint Mary's

> "It is clear that all citizens are the target of choice of witches. Their powers are great. Their weapons secret. We must all be vigilant of the threat".

*****

It seems so dark here in the Public Bar when we first come in from the sunlight. Only narrow shafts of bright sunlight, defined by dancing dust particles penetrate the rippled glass of the old windows. The sunlight brings into focus only what it falls on directly, an empty table, three empty pint glasses, two empty chairs, the third chair pulled up to another table. It even seems to light the smell of stale beer. The intensity of the beams leaves the rest of the room in deep shadows. The lamps above the high-backed wooden alcoves around barely pierce the gloom over the tables. A few old men are sitting there. We come to The Arms for the real 'Scrumpie' whenever we get back to Bideford. Real cider is hard to find these days when most places for a quiet drink have been converted into pretentious wine bars or worse.

It's almost fifty years since we first sat here listening to the accents I knew as child, accents that haven't changed much in the five hundred years The Arms has stood here. The men who seemed old when I was eighteen, don't seem any older now, nor any younger for that matter. Sion is there, still wearing that wool coat over a fisherman's jersey, a wool cap. His full sailor's beard is grey like the straggly braid of hair that hangs down his back. His eyes are white, always turned to the ceiling. He leans forward or turns his head to hear more clearly the surroundings he can't see. He's always listening. Doesn't say much. I call him Blind Sion. Everyone does. I tapped his arm and said Good Day to him before we sat down.

My husband sets the halves of scrumpie carefully on the mats that advertize Somerset bottled cider. He looks over to the alcove and says what I've been thinking,

"Look over there by the window. There always seem to be old guys sitting there, always. You could think they're the same men, still having the same conversation with the same old pals. As if we never left".

"Maybe they are the same men. Blind Sion is still here. You remember him. Why not the rest of them?"

He laughs and rolls his eyes. He won't have it. Doesn't make sense to him. Of course he's not from here. He shakes his head.

"Can't be the same man. We saw him here 40 years ago. He was old then. He'd have to be over a hundred now. Can't be him".

No point arguing about it. No point trying to convince him that there's always someone like Sion in pubs like The Arms. The old man who sits listening, not saying much. My Mam used to tell me,

"Nothing happens up Bideford market, down Bideford quay, but old Sion knows it by day's end, Blind Sion sat in his corner".

It isn't rational, but I believe I really have always known Sion. And my Mam knew him. He would have known my Welsh grandmother — I called her Mamgu — and her Mam if she came over from Wales to Bideford too. Who knows. He's here and always will be here. He sits here and the rest of us keep coming back. Some came centuries past, some decades ago, some like us are here now. Life's like that. Nothing new ... Of course, most strangers would only meet Sion and the old men once. The rest of us come to sit a while, leave, and maybe return years later, or not.

Blind Sion doesn't need anyone to understand. He knows I understand. He told me once, "Leave they always do, to live their lives somewhere else, sometime else".

I deliberately walk by his seat and touch Sion's hand as I go up to the bar and order another half of scrumpie. A while back, that would have seemed odd to Sion. Back in the day, his day, not mine, he would have heard my voice through the hatch to the Saloon Bar. Before that, a woman would have been served at the half-door by the carriageway. Or if I'd been rich, the drink would have been delivered to the house from the dark fragrant cellars that still stand on the High Street. Today women can go to the bar and sit with the men. I wonder what Sion thinks of that.

CHAPTER TWO
2007

> *"The home of the three Bideford witches ... burned down in 1894"*
>
> (Old Bideford and District, Muriel Goaman, 1968)

They drove down this morning on the old B road through Crediton from Exeter. She saw a plaque that's now on the wall of Rougmont Castle, a memorial to the "Bideford Witches". It was the first time she'd noticed it. She copied the inscription in her little travel journal.

> *"In Memory of Temperance Lloyd, Susannah Edwards, Mary Trembles of Bideford Died 1682 The last people in England to be executed for Witchcraft tried here & hanged at Heavitree.*
>
> *In the hope of an end to persecution and intolerance".*

"In the hope ... What hope?"

Blind Sion's is leaning towards her, listening and nodding. She's been walking round town with her husband, along Mill Street, up High Street to The Arms. She looked for faces from her past, saying "Hi" to people whose familiar faces are now framed with white hair, who walk with canes, or walkers. Remembering the history of the buildings, the house Richard Granville built that's now offices, the Pill where the fair rides were set up, the old Woolworths that's now a charity shop. And, as always, they'd sidetracked up the High Street to see where the Witches' cottage used to be up by the old Rectory. She can describe what it was like, the way she knew it, the feelings.

"It was wartime, a cold and hungry time in England, little food in the shops, little money in Mam's purse, and ration books so even the rich folk couldn't buy much of what there was. Well, Mam said they could buy on the black market. I looked all over our pannier market, but never found any black wicker stalls. In my mind's eye I can see the child that was me, a skinny girl in a green coat and bonnet, just as I saw myself from outside my body in the ambulance after a head-on car crash.

I can sense Blind Sion listening. "There I am, five years old, standing holding my mother's hand, looking over a broken wooden gate in a low stone wall. We had walked up the High Street from the river. The wall must have been low for me to look over it, to see the moss-covered broken path that leads to the door of the old cottage ... "I wanted to go inside to see it — to see it ... again?"

"Years later, I found a picture of the "witches' cottage" in a book. It was just as I remembered it. I glance over to the alcove. Blind Sion is nodding. He knew I was right. Does he remember me coming in, talking about the cottage? He might have thought it strange, being as the house wasn't there. Still, I was young and he knew how it is with little kids.

Once when I was about 20, home from University, Sion told me he remembered my Mam, her Welsh voice. I loved to listen to his reminiscences. He said my mother used to pop in to The Arms on her way home from market to use the lav some days.

"Back then there was no law against the little uns coming into The Arms. Or if there was nobody bothered, what with the men being off to War and the women alone with the kiddies".

"Not wanting to frighten me by feeling my face, he'd asked Mam what I looked like. She'd told him I was a pretty little thing, thick red-brown hair and big green eyes. She told everyone how we'd met the Queen up in Edinburgh on Princes Street. I was just two then but I'd curtsied nicely when she told me to. Queen Elizabeth had smiled down at me and asked where I'd got my pretty curls from. That was how adults talked to children back then. My mother told me the story often.

"Sion said my Mam was so proud of me. She'd tell everyone that I was the seventh of a seventh. She was glad about that too. He told me again today that I was a good little girl. Loved my Mam, not like the kids nowadays, always screaming to get what they want, he said. He didn't like to hear them yelling blue murder out on the street, making such a noise you can hear even with the door to the snug closed tight.

"I look across at Sion. He's sitting quietly, as usual. Except ... I think he's talking to himself,

"Lovely woman they say her mother was when she came over to live with the grandmother down Union Street, a widow, but still handsome. Now the grandmother, she really would have known the witch house up top of the town, before it burned down. Some fire twas. Could smell the smoke in Th'Arms blowing over right to the market, I could. Smoke would have gone over the Grandmother's house too. When was it? A few years before the Old Queen died... The woman's right about where that cottage was. Right too about me always being here. Maybe she did see that house, whether twas there or no. What she saw was what folk here saw when Temperance and Susannah lived, till they were took up County".

"I can't stop staring at old Sion. Well, its not exactly rude to stare at someone who can't see you, is it? My husband's voice startles me."

"We should think where we're going to stop tonight. Do want to try the hotel where we stayed when the kids were little, or that B & B by the river? Or there's Appledore or Westward Ho! It's a lovely day for a walk on the beach".

They decide to check in at a Guest House on the beach road.

"On our way to pick up the car, we detour through the Rope Walk to see if my old house, the rope-walker's cottage, is still there. I spent what I recall as a mostly cold, hungry childhood on that back alley. No one lives in the house now. It's been empty for years. I've photographed it several times. We took the kids to see it once. At the river end of the lane there's a pottery now that makes reproduction seventeenth century Bideford pottery. Back home I have an ugly glossy ochre and terra-cotta glazed coffee mug from there engraved, "Ropewalk, Bideford".

One day photographs of a derelict house and the mug will be all that's left of her Bideford past except for her memories.

So they make the most of what's left of her Bideford whenever they come over.

"Lundy Island was too clear on the horizon from Westward Ho! yesterday. We could pick out buildings above the rocks. I know it will rain tomorrow. My husband said we should watch the forecast on TV."

The rain came in on the morning tide.

"We parked by Saint Mary's Church, not far from the old bridge, and went inside. The door was open. A couple of women were doing the altar flowers. It's changed quite a bit inside, pews removed from the rear of the nave to make a pleasant area for the Sunday School classes. The stained glass windows still cast coloured light on the stone floors. I have to read again the list of the Rectors from 1261 on. There's Michael Ogilby who led services in Temperance's time, who questioned her, testified against her."

It's a short walk to the Public Library. The new Guide Book says it's "of historic interest" and is "equipped with computers for public use with free Internet service".

"We'll e-mail the family back home. My husband is happy looking at the old local poetry books in the small reference room. There's no one else waiting for the computer I'm using. I google, "Bideford".

According to Wikipedia my home town is now best known for its "Witches". And there it is, the plaque we saw two days ago in Exeter. I search, "Temperance Lloyd, Susannah Edwards, Mary Trembles". A nano-second later there's the memorial plaque again.

"Growing up in Bideford with my somewhat superstitious mother who loved local history, Temperance Lloyd and the others were part of every-day life. They seemed closer than the War we knew only from letters from soldiers at the Front. I lived with them, always had. Now they're on-line exhibits in the cult of the occult. That's not right. Blind Sion knew that.

We stop in at The Arms for lunch before heading over to Dartmoor. I want to see Sion again before we leave. I wonder how many of the old men around him have always been here too. You don't ask older people their age. We eat Scotch eggs and Cornish pasties — no upscale stuffed mush-rooms here. I pay at the bar. On my way out I stop to say goodbye to Sion.

"See you next year".

He nods. She smiles.

CHAPTER THREE
2008

1682: Temperance Lloyd, widow of Bideford

I still believe I saw that house. So what if the books say it burned down in 1894. Mam took me there. It was before the War ended. I remember her lovely Welsh voice as she told me about the women, explaining it so I could understand,

"They said they were witches. You know what that is? It was a long time ago, before you were born, before I was born. Yes, even before your Mamgu was born".

She pronounced it 'Mam-gie', like 'Cymru'.

"Those women lived a long, long time ago — yes, even before your Mamgu's Mamgu was born. They were just women who grew their herbs. They helped the town people, especially the women. They were better than the doctors then. Better than them now, maybe".

Blind Sion reaches for my hand. Takes it in his. Then in his deep Welsh voice he says he believes I saw their cottage. These things happen. Some folk don't understand. They just don't know. He knew because he'd been there and he knew how it was. My husband thinks I'm crazy but he humours me. I tell him,

"As a little kid I knew about herbs. Mam grew them out the back. She picked them to brew hot drinks that cured colds and flu and upset stomachs. I remember the stone walls of the witches' cottage were almost three feet thick, just like the rope-walker's house. Those old houses were always cold and damp in winter, damp in summer, never really warm. Both houses had two steps to the door. Of course, the steps of the deserted house were dusty and faded. Ours were shiny. My Mam cleaned them every day. The broken shutters on the derelict house were stuffed with rags.

"I knew, well I must have imagined, that the witches' house was quite like ours inside too. The chimneys were similar, and the windows. Their roof was thatched, ours was slate by the time I lived there. There were two rooms downstairs, the kitchen and a back kitchen. Our iron fireplace was several hundred years old. On dark winter evenings, before the days of TV, I used to watch pictures in the fire with my mother until we took the candle up the stairs to bed."

Women have watched the pictures in the fire for hundred of years.

"I could imagine Temperance seeing her own stories in the flames of her driftwood fire, all those centuries ago. Perhaps she escaped the difficulties of her life in those flickering pictures, like today's TV sitcoms ...

*****

"There be pictures of flowers in summer fields by the woods down the riverbank flickering in the fading fire tonight. Pray God my man keeps his drinking from the Harbour Master. Pray God ... Be home late again he will, if he come at all. Sleep down yere as like as not. Wake in the morning with a sore head and foul mouth. Still, worth putting up with his oaths to have good wood enough to set the fire in the bed chamber tonight, the wind, so bitter cold it is. Worst of too many bad years — cold enough to freeze the salt sea the sailors say. Have to fight their way in across the bar they do, ice floating on the waves. Embers cool enough now to shovel into the warming pan for the bed".

*****

Blind Sion is leaning forward listening to our conversation.

"I used to wonder if their back kitchen might be like ours too. But — we had a tap in ours. I saw a well in their back garden. And did their stairs wind up to the bedrooms through a door from the kitchen, just like in our house? My Da worked away a lot of the time. Did Temperance's man do that? Was he a sailor or just one of the hundreds that laboured down the quay by the moorages?"

*****

"Better, much better, the warming pan than a drunken man to warm the night".

Her thoughts are interrupted by a loud knock at the door.

"Who's that banging so late at the door? Can't be him. He'd just fall his way in. Alright, alright, coming I am".

The Constable stands on the step. He takes off his hat.

"Mistress Lloyd. Sad news Mistress Lloyd. Your good man be found in the river when the tide left tonight".

"Sad news..."

She holds her shawl across her face to hide her blackened cheek.

"Sad news — for him maybe — for me?"

She stops herself, she should not think such thoughts. Must be the sombre widow.

"Sad news ... News ... How did it happen? Last I saw of him, he was off back to his work down the Harbour Master's shed. Just this afternoon. Had to catch the ebb tide he did, just like always. The rain was ice on the slate slabs on the quay. Would that be it?"

"Or 'em do say maybe he was dragged off the quay when painter released to free the barge for it to go back cross the channel".

"So crushed between the collier and the river wall was he?"

"Terrible way to go Mistress".

"Aye, indeed. A terrible way to go".

Temperance bows her head.

"Don' like to ask 'ee, but Master Browning did offer as crew was drinkin' as boat sailed out".

Temperance shakes her head.

"Well, he wouldn't never go drinking on the collier. Not at noon. Well, indeed, never. And the seamen, they would for sure not be drinking afore casting off".

"Nay. Indeed. 'Arbour master said to ask 'ee about burial. Down Saint Mary's yard, will un be?"

"Yes, that would do. Yes. Yes. He was of the Welsh church, same really".

The Constable nods, puts his hat on and turns to leave. Temperance closes the door and goes back to her fire. She breathes deeply to calm herself.

"Some things the Constable don't need to know. No business of his the herbs I tend so careful for my curatives. Only thinking to help my man stop the drink with herbal brew mixed with honey, wasn't I. Told him twas for his bad head. Well, he wouldn't 'ave took it against the drink. Said to him, 'Yes, dearie, you will get a bit dizzy, but that will pass in the salt river air. You'll see'. Oh well".

23

*****

Sion sits listening thinking of those long dead, mostly forgotten, women. He knew that not much had changed for poor people in Bideford in 300 years. War-time life wasn't much different from life back in the seventeenth century. It was always about making do with whatever you could get free. The old and poor picked sticks down Appledore woods in the War, just like Temperance and Susannah did.

"My Mam probably took me past where their house had been, and talked to me about how they lived to distract me from the cold rough chore of picking sticks. Her stories made it seemed more like acting in a play. On market days when the town was busy, Mam got me up in the dark so nobody would see us. The woods were alive with river rats. Owls shot down to catch them, carrying them off, sometimes dropping them in the river. I would curl my feet to grip the tree roots that criss-crossed the narrow path to stop myself slipping on the black mud. Mam said if I was a good girl and picked lots of sticks we would make pictures in the fire and she would tell me stories about the women".

Sion nods.

"Right she is, they would have burned wood mostly. Folk down here only started getting coal around the time of the Lord Protector, and it was dear then, just like in the War. My but it was colder back then too".

"We'd take the wood home and then go to see my Mamgu. She always gave me sweets".

Sion smiles. All grandparents saved the sherbet powder and liquorice allsorts they got with their coupons, to reward their little grandchildren for being good, or just for being.

"The wood made wonderful pictures in the fire, better than the coal that was rationed in the War. My mother would point to the fire, sometimes holding my head gently on one side so I would see where a piece had burned through and fallen down by the front of the grate. She asked if I could see the lion? Or is it a dog?"

Sion nodded again. Children will see what you say is there.

"Oh yes, I saw it. And the little waterfall, and a bridge, and a cockerel, and, and, and ... I loved those pictures. Gas fires are convenient but where's the magic in artificial logs? When Temperance watched the pictures in her fire, were they the bad dreams of her past, dreams that always returned on a dark winter's night?"

*****

"Bideford folk must never know his shaming up in the Valley. Such a dreadful business. Not that I seen it happen myself, mind. Twas all long before I ever met him. Confessed it to me he did when he was in his confessing days. Told me the whole sad story. Well, twas only later I saw that was just how he got his way with me. I did hate the drink so, the devil's curse so it is".

A piece of wood drops off a glowing log. It becomes a man, her man, flying through the air out of the door of that tall slate-roofed house of worship in Aberdulais. He'd been completely honest with her, in the way only a reformed drunk can be. She could almost have been there when he stumbled into the middle of the service, and stood there in front of the whole village dressed in their Sunday black. He shouted his disagreement with the sermon on the evils of drink, vomited up his fill of ale, then fell in a stupor right in front of the pulpit. It took four strong men, one at each limb, to lay him outside in the rain.

"Held a special meeting of the church elders that same afternoon, they did, Sunday though it was. It had to be decided there and then. Dewi Lloyd was not suited to the post of gravedigger and keeper of the Church proper. Blind eyes they'd kept in hope of change. No longer".

That day the house that went with the job — his job and his father's before him — was gone. He must be gone the next day.

"Well, he walked all the way south to Port Tennant, to the Swansea dockyards. Suddenly sober, well he would be, afraid as he was to lose even the hard job of shovelling coal from the quayside into the holds of the colliers. This new Mr Lloyd did not drink. Stopped it altogether he had. Such a good man he was now. I believed his every word. Well you do don't you".

He told Temperance he'd never been much of a talker, only ranting foul-mouthed when he had his fill of ale. Then once he was sober for good he found the gift of the gab. Temperance watched him saving of the souls of seamen in the hall by the docks, such a lovely speaker. As good as any up the Valley. Soon he was rewarded with a post in the Harbour Master's pay, good work and good money too. Temperance was in love. He was such a good, temperate man, earning a shilling a week.

Her life had been so very hard those first months down in Swansea. Dewi Lloyd was the answer to the prayers she prayed on her knees every night. Here was someone to share her life, to care for her, to give her the children the gospel said was a woman's joy and bliss. She had been known as "Temperance by name, temperance by nature". And Temperance was all he said he wanted. The day he asked her to marry him after Bible reading down Seaman's hall, she knew her life was turning around at last.

At the Seaman's Hall they fought the good fight against the evils of drink, a place alive with talk of the devil's work ale and metheglin, the accidents, the falls, the fights. So many tales of so many deaths. Temperance was careful to say nothing when she heard the tale of three men drowned in the dark dock waters after falling from the porch of the old Ty Morwr Inn, seventeen years past. There wasn't much doubt in her mind.

'My Da ... Must've been him. Must've been. How many men named Howell did come down the docks from up by Castell Nedd round that time? They did ask if I knew Castell Nedd, being as I was from a bit up the same Valley. I said yes, I come through there once. And that was an end to that. They never asked again".

The Constable's footsteps rang out on the frozen roadway, then faded away. She might as well put a couple more bits of driftwood on the fire and sit quiet by the fire, watching the pictures in the grate. She no longer had to fear his mood when he fell through the door. The memories of her life with her man disappeared. She saw herself a child again back up the Valley with her mother.

"Temperance ... My Mam, church bred, had give me that name at birth. Loved that name. Everyone in our village loved it. Mam wanted to let them all know as she would never be one to have to do with the evil drink. She was respectable. Twas her not her fault her drunken man let poor simple Jo-bach die caught twixt the millstones. She never knew how it happened. Gone off down the road Da had before the Constable come looking for him next morning".

Two years went by before they next saw him.

"Mam pretended not to hear the whispers as she walked home from Sunday morning services. She'd no need to hear what men got up to down at those docks. Knew it anyway. He did come home every now and again, always without warning, as if he expected Mam to be up to no good. She never would be up to anything. One man's enough to last a lifetime or an eternity. Better off on our own".

He came home less and less often.

"When he did come Mam tried to keep him from the Inn, more for my sisters' sake than for hers. Often as not, she paid the price with another pregnancy. Mam knew those babies were the gifts of God. She thanked Him when they came. Thanked Him again she did for his mercy in taking half of them back, so she had just three to raise. Moneys came if Mr Howell had not spent it in the ale-house, or the whore house. Mam never used his Christian name, didn't seem proper him never living Christian life. Then I come along, her last born".

She never knew her father, though she was born in wedlock.

"Ieuan the Hay brought Mam the news of Da's end along with cartload of oats for the horses stabled at the Coach House. He was Ieuan the Hay on account that his cart would be lined with empty sacks and piled with hay to go back to Swansea. He didn't say quite how Ap Howell the Mill died from drowning. Well, Mam never said. Didn't matter really. Taken before you was born, she'd say. I never knew him, never missed him".

*****

Sion sips his scrumpie and listens. It's harder to hear now with the tourists all asking for menus, and being told to read what's on the board over the bar.

"I really thought cottage was there when I was little. In an odd way, I still believe I saw it, still see it in my mind. I could feel Temperance there too. The road onward from there to Abbotsham was paved. The Rectory then and in their time was on the other side of the street, and just a bit nearer the Georgian houses built later at the top High Street. The yew trees are tall around it. There would have been yews then too. And Rector Michael Ogilby would have lived in the same Rectory".

Sion had known Ogilby as a Cleric like most in his time, younger son of minor nobility, sent into the church for which he had no special calling, because he had no other special calling.

"I was always asking Mam about the witches. She would tell they were just poor old women, grey hair, ragged clothes. She pointed to the herbs Temperance probably planted around their house — chives, thyme, and sage spread out from the tiny garden into the cracks of the narrow pathway. Back in a sunny patch, the feverfew had spread to cover the whole garden where vegetables would once have grown. The roots of an old elderberry tree were growing up through the earth. My mother would pick a mint leaf and crush it for me to smell".

Sion smiles again. He recalls Wartime when every one planted herbs in their Victory Gardens. If they couldn't grow a potato they could still say they were doing their bit for the Effort.

"I used to pick mint at Mamgu's house. It grew right outside the back kitchen door. Moonless nights came sweet with the fragrance of thyme under bare feet if you had to go out to the lav in the dark. Nestled in the corner of the house and the wall, warmed by the winter sun, there was a rosemary bush. I'd hide behind it when Mamgu wanted to wash my face under the cold water tap before tea. There was bitter-smelling red valerian pushing skyward from the tops of the crumbling brick walls around that garden. Mam said it smelt bad but did good"

Sion remembers it as Capon's Taile in Temperance's day.

"Nothing in Mamgu's little garden went to waste. Down beside the lav, the huge bright green leaves of horseradish would trip you up when you ran to hide from the Rhondda cousins that came to visit. In autumn, she would dig up the roots to make sauce so hot it brought tears to your eyes. The whole house reeked of it".

Temperance's kitchen like her Mamgu's would have been alive with the scents of the herbs steeping in the 'special' pot not used to cook food in.

"I loved Mamgu's kitchen. The sunlight filtered through jam jars of green, brown, pink, and purple liquids, clear as glass on top, opaque with sediment gathering at the bottom. Mamgu would sniff through the pin-prick holes in the lids to tell when the medicine was ripe but not off".

Sion knew the people that went to Temperance's door in the evening, just as he knew those who called on Mamgu.

"My Mamgu listened to them, but said very little. She took their clean jars, asked had they washed them properly and let them dry on a clean cloth? Sure were they? Won't help much if the jar is dirty. I watched her lift one of her many jars carefully from the window sill and tilt it gently to pour the coloured water into clean jars".

She'd put the jar of liquid by the front door, and a piece of paper with her instructions, how much to take, when and for how long, under a small stone on top of the lid.

"Be careful", she'd tell them, "More isn't better. Come Sunday morning tell me how you feel. No. No. Only pay if it works. No charge if it don't. A little pigeon would be alright".

She didn't like duck, not much meat and too greasy.

"My Mam told me Temperance Lloyd was said to be the seventh of a seventh of a seventh. Not that it meant anything. She didn't come by her knowledge of the herbs, the bark, the roots, by nature, any more than she and Mamgu did. 'She wasn't born knowing', she'd say, 'No one is. It wasn't in her family either. No. Temperance came to her skills by learning. They say she could read. Not many women could read back then. Well, the Queen could read, but not ordinary women. Some say Temperance could read the Latin too'. Mam said I would learn Latin too, when I went into The Big School".

Sion knew the time when folk believed a woman who could read was the devil's daughter, unless she helped with the Town business. They said ... everybody said ...

"Mamgu used to tell me you have to watch what you say. She told me we don't call them witches any more. 'That's long past. But we still know the old ways. We don't talk about it, but we know, see', she'd say. And even at four, I knew. People don't understand".

Sion understands. He's smiling at me, well he's smiling in my direction.

"I know little kids aren't supposed to feel empathy, but standing there looking at their cottage, I felt how they lived. I guess hunger and cold feel the same in any century. The War was hungry. I could imagine that watching the pictures in the wood fire helped dull their hunger, as it dulled ours".

*****

A gust of wind sends a small shower of soot down the chimney. Temperance pulls her shawl tighter round her shoulders.

"Can see my whole life coming back this night in the embers. I know not how to think of the Constable's news. God forgive that I should be glad of his death, of any death. Twould be wickedness to think that, I pray God let me not think ... The beating he gave me Saturday past give me such black swelling round my eye. And he so angry after, bidding me stay in the house for fear people might think twas his red finger marks on my face. He did not die in the grace of the Lord, less he repented at the end".

Her whole young life up the Valley was there in the fire that night.

"Patterns of home and Church kept closed my mind, as rough corsets bound my growing body. Mam sewed the neatest stitches even if she couldn't buy soft cloth for the job. Twas not all bad. There was the breathless joy of running to the top of the hills to see the sea of a rare clear day. That sparkling sea fed dreams of escape from a life that crawled by one week after another, after another ... Wrong it was, wicked, to wish my life away. I knew it. Still I wished ... And wished ..."

How she dreamed to leave a life measured out week by week in drudgery.

"Monday washday, wet or fine, had to get up at dawn to help Mam fill the copper boiler out the back by the privy. She lit the fire. I helped carry heavy baskets of dirty washing down the path of cracked slate stones. Mam measured the lye and grated rough soap into the boiler, stirring with the wooden spoon till the bubbles formed. In went the wash. Only then could I wash my face, put on a clean pinny and go across the street to the School".

Temperance swung her slate in its strap joyfully free.

"Free to read, to listen, to sing praises to the Lord God. Later in the morning, I'd slip away from the class to go to help Mam haul the heavy wet hot loads into a tub, splinters from the great wooden tongs piercing into my fingers and palms. Then down to fetch buckets of water from the big pump in the square to rinse out the soap".

She held up the soaking clothes to push them through the mangle, pulled them out the other side, caught the soapy water in one barrel to wash the floors, guided the clothes into the other barrel to haul them to the line.

If it didn't rain — it generally did — she helped to hold a big barrel steady to keep the clothes and bedding out of the mud while her mother struggled to heave them on to the line. On wet days the wash hung on the wooden racks from the ceiling by the iron stove, filling the room with the sharp smell of soap.

"The Valley I collect was always wet, winter drizzle, spring and autumn mists, heavy summer rain. It's the hills see. They break the clouds coming in from the sea. Good for the garden Mam said. Good for nothing, I thought. Mam said it was wicked to be ungrateful to the Heavens above. Where would we be without the leeks and parsnips that battled through the clay? There'd be no good Welsh cawl less there was money to go to market".

There was never much money anyway. Her Mam never said.

"The children at Church School did say. Never stopped saying. Das that worked down the docks put their wages on the barrel not in the mail coach. Never mind, Mam said, God would provide. And provide He did — as long as Mam did the Minister's wash of a Wednesday. He provided better when Mam did for Mrs Evans the Milk who got so sick after her babies she couldn't get out of her bed".

Monday was washday, Tuesday ironing.

Nothing changes. Temperance's palms would have burned through the wet rags they used to wipe the red hot irons straight off the hob — just like mine did when I was twelve.

"Wednesday wash the other folk's clothes, market day, and the house to clean. Thursday taking the bread down the oven to bake, more ironing. Careful not to get black soot marks on the clean clothes, or you have to wash them again and they pays less if they're late back. Friday ... Saturday market day over the town for the leg of mutton — scrag end if we're pinched - onions, flour for pastry. Then it was bath night to be clean for Church on Sunday. I got to wash last after my Mam and my older sisters that come home from service in the big homes down the Valley. The water was scummy and almost cold by the time I slipped into it. Mam said twould be really dirty if there was a working man going in first. I should be glad of that. One thing about having my own place. Always get into the bath first and make the water hot as I like."

Then it was Monday again — washday ... Temperance saw her mother's life draining away week by week with the wash water. The rustle of the water on the cobbles echoed the whispers of the villagers watching the girl with no Da.

"Oh, I can see them now, the shaking heads behind the lace curtains of the windows they paid me a penny or twopence to clean. And now, I stir the fire. Burning bits of wood fall. Be they heads toppling off shoulders?"

*****

Sion whispers a name under his breath,

"Temperance, Temperance Lloyd. How soon people forget. Three hundred years..."

"Mam said that all she really knew about the women they hanged as witches, was their names and maybe Temperance was Welsh. Well, with that name she likely was, Lloyd — not a Bideford name, Welsh from way back. Temperance wasn't a witch name either. I wonder, was that her marriage in the Archives? As a kid, I must have tried my mother's patience, wanting to walk up by the house every week on the way to market. She'd explain over and over that we had to get on or we might not get the best of the bits of scrag end. Only the fatty, bony bits would be left. Cheapest meat you could get but the same price no matter how little real meat there was. I'd beg to go home that way. She'd tell me the bags of tatties and swede were too heavy to carry up that hill".

"Very persistent, that one", Sion smiles to himself.

"I would ask my mother if we would always be poor. She said we would be unless someone died and left us money. But I could be rich one day... If I was a good girl and learned everything I could at school. Then maybe I would become a teacher, or a nurse. 'Earn good money they do', she would say, 'Don't need to scrimp and save. Eat meat on weekdays and live in warm houses with nice things they do'. She'd tell me Temperance likely had it harder as a kid than I did. A bit like telling kids today to eat their food because there are people starving in Africa".

*****

As Temperance watches the world of her childhood in the flames, she recalls it wasn't all endless dark.

"I collect the good things. There was the reading. Oh, I did love reading by the candle of a winter night while Mam sat and sewed, and outside in the back on those long summer evenings. No one to see me there. Eight I was when my schooling stopped. Time for me to start work cleaning the Minister's manse. Didn't matter. Mam said by then I could read my Welsh as good as could the Minister himself. And I had more English than most. Read the Bible first, cover to cover, again and again. Then other books I got them from the Minister, read them I did".

A hill went up from the village, at the top of Gwydr Street.

"See it now where that bit of wood burned out and left the peak there. Could see the sea from there, not Galilee, but beautiful as that must be".

There could be anything across the sea, over the other side of that bright water.

"And then there was the best of all, my Mam's little garden, oh not the parsnips and leeks, had to grow them to eat, didn't we? No, I loved the rosemary bush, and sage, thyme, feverfew, horseradish growing in the earth that was mostly ashes, and the red and white Capon's Taile atop the wall of the privy. Mam showed me how to tend them. Then, one day seemed like a miracle happened. Walking up the hill behind the church, I was. Twas such a windy day, dust getting in my eyes, and dead leaves flying into my face. Then there was larger, white leaves going all over in the wind. Twas pages of a book rustling across Church Street cobbles. I ran after them, jumped on them to trap them. Too many to go in my pinny pocket. Tucked them into my bodice".

She didn't tell her mother and hid the pages in the Bible.

"So strange writing twas. Not prayers or Bible verses. English, like the travelling tinkers talk down the square on market days, them that comes sharpening knives and scissors. I read all the pages and torn scraps that I found, over and over. Learned it all. Twas all about herbs. My Mam used herbs to help the rhume. Not like these papers. Said how to heal boils, cure the palsy ... And pictures there were on some pages so as to know the plants. Some of it real fanciful. Daisies, surely don't have the power 'to mitigate all kinds of pains in the joints and gout'? And the juices from their crushed leaves will soothe eyes that water, and drinking a decoction of the leaves made in water be good against the agues? Well! I hid the pages, read them in private, tried remedies to see they did no harm. The beauty of the shining sea, our herb garden showed and now this knowledge showed me the Lord is good".

She sips rosemary water sweetened with wild honey and puts another piece of wood on the fire.

"Thirteen I was when I went to work making the fires and cleaning the privies down the Coach Inn. And that proud to help Mam more than just with the washing. Had real wages to give her, not the bits the Minister gave me when he thought to pay at all. I walked down the hill to the Cross Road of a dark morning, back in the winter dark nights, singing all the way sometimes. Could have had board down there, but the keeper took that out of your pay. Mam still took in washing on Wednesdays. I lit the boiler fire before I went to work".

She was seventeen when her mother was 'took to a better place'.

"Any place would be better than the dirty washing, wet washing, drying washing-filled house in that always damp, always grey-skied Valley".

Temperance would never forget that day.

"Never forget folk that had no time for my Mam when she lived, standing round the grave with me they were that dark wet Monday morning. Said she was gift from God. Such a good woman she was, worth her weight

Temperance Lloyd: Hanged for Witchcraft in 1682

in gold. Shame they never paid her what she was worth. Would have eaten better and lived longer she would. Three of them asked if I would like come into service. A young girl like me could not live alone, they said, even if I could stay in the house with Mam gone. I thanked them kindly for being so kind. Kindness? They knew I was a good honest worker. Cheap help they wanted just like they'd had from Mam till this Friday past. I said nothing. Just went home".

She spent the day cleaning and clearing out her mother's house.

"Kept her wedding ring and the hard soap. Culled seeds from the dead heads of the herbs out by the privy. Folded up Mam's best apron, almost new it was. It wasn't stealing. She didn't need it now. Tied them in my work pinny. Sewed most of the coin I saved from my pay into my skirt. Just a few pieces I held in my hand as I walked, almost danced, down to the Coach House that one last time".

The Keeper shouted she was late, had taken a long time just for a funeral. Had they buried her with ham? She told him,

"She was my Mam. No. You don't bury a widow washer-woman with ham. Yes, I am wearing my Sunday best. I know it won't do for cleaning out the grate in the Public room. Where do I think I'm going? Not down them cellar stairs again that's sure".

The Coach horn sounded. Temperance paid her farthing and climbed on to the back of the Stage to Swansea. The Innkeeper stood with his mouth wide open watching her leave. She waved farewell. The ride seemed short to a young girl who thought Swansea was a world away. It was indeed another world, so much noise, the folk all rushing about in a great hurry, and coaches and traps flying by so fast.

"Knew to keep my head. Dockside hostelries be always looking for a good cleaner. Servants come and go so fast, don't like hard work".

She had a job, a clean bed and a good supper that same day.

"I was down in Swansea now, but I was still a good girl. The first Sunday I went to Church up Port Tennant Hill. Lovely Welsh service it was. Miss that in Bideford. Didn't have but a half day off and didn't know anyone. Soon met good Christian folk helping serve black bread, nettle cheese and cawl at the Mission house. There was no strong drink there."

The seamen didn't complain. They'd been months away on ships that fished the western Banks.

"Told tales of a New Found Land, fish so thick in the sea you could catch them in barrels. They do use nets. Merchantmen ships brought in all manner of wares from the Eastern lands, and the Indies. You only see them seamen once in many months, no time to make friends. And the scullion at the Ty Morwr said a girl mustn't trust a sailor. Some of them do have a wife in every harbour. I should keep my friendship in the Church or Mission".

So Temperance spent what little time she had after work at the Mission and it was there she met her man.

"Dewi Lloyd walked in from the Valley sober and stayed sober. Told me he had made mistakes, had the weakness for the drink. But now he was a reformed man. Like for all new workers down the docks they held his pay till he proved himself, just gave the landlord money for his bed and board. He was every night for a month at the Mission".

Temperance prayed with him for strength to stay sober. Just three weeks later, they prayed for blessing on their marriage union.

"No one knew us there, me with no Mam or Da, everybody passing through. Didn't have to wait to be respectable. Mr Lloyd soon started getting his wages so we could take rooms right beside the Mission. Saved my money and what was left of his after the rent and we soon moved to a two up two down further up the hill. It was a small house but there was a tiny garden out back. I sowed Mam's seeds".

Temperance was so happy.

"God be praised, and I praised Him with all my heart and soul".

CHAPTER FOUR
1645

Susannah Edwards of Biddiford, aforesaid widow ... Mary Trembles ...

"Ti, Arglwydd, a adwaenost ddirgelion ein calonnau" "Thou knowest, Lord, the secrets of our hearts"(Burial Service - Welsh Book of Common Prayer 1587)

Buried him on the Wednesday I did, me face still covered in the bruises he gave me Saturday night. Mistress Browning give me her black veil to wear when she saw my face down St Mary's Sunday morning. Heard about his death, she had. Well everybody knew, didn't they. Nothing private down the quay and up High Street. Nice thick veil hid the bruises well. Hid the smile on my face too. Seemed my life was taking a turn for the better. Didn't last. Never does".

Temperance stood by the open grave. She felt a hand touch her gently on her arm. It was the Harbour Master.

"Bad news, Mistress Lloyd. Seems no doubt. Smell of spirits hung strong in your man's mouth after body been washed by the tide, and 'eld by the mud half a day. The Masters 'ave thought on the matter. In compassion, us'll let 'ee live on in yer cottage up the top of Town, for as long as 'ee should survive 'im. Give 'ee somewhere to lay yer pretty 'ead. Masters won't be furnishing the widow's purse by the week. Not a penny. Us already paid the grave fee".

Temperance nodded.

"Twas least us can do, seeing as yer man was found in the river. Last seen working the boats. Be all us can do. 'Ee must think on what to do. There be the Poor Relief".

"No. Never. Never would I take that".

" 'Ee could go back to yer Welsh Wales, or maybe stay 'ere in service. Merchant shippers' womenfolk be always wantin' good 'elp".

Temperance shook her head as she walked down the hill from the graveyard. She would never return to the grey skies of Wales, to that muddy moss-green Valley, silent, but for the church dirges.

"Never will I live my Mam's life washing the filthy clothes of them that looked down their noses at them that has do it. And the docks — no better there. Never mind my Da — didn't know about him they didn't. Dewi Lloyd now ... There's another matter. With the boats going back and fro, soon know all about his dying they will".

She walked up the hill over East-the-Water to a clearing where she could see the sands all the way down by the estuary, and sheep in the green fields over Instow way. Why should she leave?

"Tis good over yere. I can take my bread and farm-fresh cheese up the hill to Alverdiscott any time I like, and watch the boats come up river. Dream about all the far places they've been, the stories mariners have to tell. Listen to the seamen talking strange down the quay of a summer night. Just a stroll down the riverbank woods I can walk the sands of the windy Channel shore, breeze in my hair, salt on my lips. And the cottage up Old Town, mine tis now. I'll go into daily service at a big house over Bridge Street, just a hop and a step across the top of the town. Back in my own bed of a night".

Sion remembers.

"When the bruises healed they say she'd be seen down by the bridge picking mussels for her dinner of a night. Well, Billy Hill was the one that said it. Truth to be told Billy Hill took his eye for a lovely woman down there special to watch. Seen her get off the boat from Swansea just a couple of years past. Said at the time a woman like that'd be trouble in the town, mark his words. And her man nothing to look at. Wouldn't notice him in a crowd of one. But that Temperance! Taller than many women, tall as many men Billy said she was. And all that hair! Thick, red-brown, shiny hair, flying behind her as she strode up the High Street, and eyes green as leaves in spring. The men all agreed twas a sight to see, never said nothing when the wives were in hearing, mind you. Men, they talk the hind legs off a donkey, if 'n they say tis the women that gossips".

Sion wouldn't know about that. The women don't come into The Arms. They stop out by the side door with a penny for a jug.

"With her man dead and gone, Billy said she grew beautiful as she'd been when she stepped off that collier from Wales. If only you could see her he said. Billy, if God should be so good ... For just one sight I'd take back my blindness from the Lord for the rest of time. Have to go by what he says. Can hear her voice beautiful of a Sunday. Lovelier than any chorister for all their schooling. Sound straight out of Wales".

Temperance went into service.

"Cooked and cleaned for Mistress Jamieson, I did. Best worker she ever had, she said it oftentimes. And more. When the rhume was come on the Mistress, I helped her with herbal teas. Made horseradish and linden poultices when the young Master's grazed knees took infection".

At first all went well. Temperance worked hard and earned a good wage for a while.

"Not six months did it last. The Mistress died of the pox that come off the boat from Ireland with the pigs. No sooner was she in her grave than there was talk of herbal poisoning, but no proof. Couldn't be. I did no harm. Nobody ever died of a right measure of feverfew. Never mind the truth. Once gossip starts, it don't stop. Heads turned, mouths shut as I passed. Looking for work again I was. Every door shut in my face, though I knew there was need of a good servant behind them".

*****

Sion often wondered,

"Was it her being Welsh made them look to find faults in her? Being as she was a woman alone and proud of it didn't help much either, did it? And the quacks ... The quacks, they were quick to fuel the gossip. Just like they were quick to collect good fees but slow to deliver good cures. Back then, their schools of discourse gave them the Latin. Gave them precious little English wit to back up their grand promises of healing. No matter. For all their fine gowns and high airs, the quacks sharp tongues didn't stop the good towns people from calling on Temperance".

She had more trade than she could deal with. Still hers was a hard life, poverty always at her hearth.

"Folk didn't always pay for her potions, despite the gossip she might bewitch her debtors. Somehow there was never a purse in the house if she should be so bold as to ask payment when she delivered the cures, nor often when she called on them later".

*****

She was always careful to speak English in the town, though Sion sitting in the sun on a bollard down on the quay would hear her speaking Welsh to the mariners she helped with their ills. She didn't want another man, though many offered. She lived on alone in the Harbour Scalesman's old cottage in Old Town, just like any born Bidefordian.

"I was never what you'd call lonely in my cottage the year since my man's death. Alone, not lonely. Alone. No man to take care of me. Only care a man ever took of me was to hit me if another doffed his hat in passing. Wasn't easy mind, being there alone in my cottage of a Saturday night. Too close by half twas to the Bell Inn. Word soon got around the Public room of a woman living alone just a drunken stumble across Top of the Town".

She would bar her door and shutters to keep them out. When they ventured close and banged on the door, she would drown their sotted shouts in a shower from her chamber pot out of her upper window. She knew it was no use to complain to the Constables. Both of them went drinking with the merchants and would never stop the nuisance, even when they were not themselves too drunk to do so.

"Sometimes I prayed to my Welsh God to take away them drunken fools. Or least to help me deal with them. And then ..."

Her prayers were answered.

"Twas very early morning, the first day of May, a good omen Torrington folk would have said. They still dance for May Day over there up river see. Such loud cries outside I heard, fit to raise the dead. Brought me right out of my bed it did. Found a woman lying down there in my front garden. Well, twas hard to tell at first what it was, she was bleeding so from a great wound in her head. Said her name was Susannah Edwards. Come from a farm out Abbotsham way. Been laying as dead there all night, hid from the street crouched down in the comfrey behind the stone wall out front. Screamed with the pain when she come to. I got her into the house. Made her strong mint tea, and washed her wounds, salved and bound her head. She knew of the evils of drink and the brutality of drunken men. I knew what she was on about. Talked and talked to me and to herself she did".

" 'Ad to tell 'er what happened. Knowed 'er keep it safe. Knowed it. Told 'er 'ow me cowherd man found me belly swolled with child be the Young Squire. Beat me senseless 'e did. Beat the babe out of me. Left the dead thing up in the hay loft".

Susannah had sheltered in the chicken shed from his anger and the thunder storm. She knew she had to get away.

"Cowman woulda killed me. An' squire, 'e'd call me for a liar for sure. 'Ad to get to town".

To her Bideford was a big place where she would be safe enough. A drayman had stopped to give her a ride.

"Not for nought. 'ad his way with me afore 'e tossed me off on the street 'ere".

Temperance nursed her back as close to health as she could, healing her outside and in.

"Be no more babes for er. Just as well I daresay. No need to tell her. No more for me neither after the Mr Lloyd knocked 'em out of me with his fist of a Saturday night. Just have to clean her up right now".

Susannah smiled. When her face was washed clean of the caked blood and mud, Temperance saw the deep lines a rich woman would have at 50. Susannah was 25. Her left eye sat still in her head, blind and whitish grey. Her thin straight hair was twisted into an untidy bun held in place by a piece of ribbon that may have been blue once. Temperance was tall for a woman and thin with it, but Susannah – she looked like a waif from the Shebbear Home wearing Temperance's apron till her own frock dried out on the line. Temperance told her,

"Not to offend, dearie, but I can't have that stinking up the house".

Susannah didn't mind.

"Us was in no way to take offence. Never knowed none like this Temperance afore. Never 'eard a name like that neither. Spoke funny 'er did. Said twas Welsh. And 'er bin all lone 'er 'ad, after 'er man was gone. Wouldn't take no 'elp from the Poor Relief. Too proud 'er be for that. Said 'er'd bin honest and worked 'ard all 'er life. Wan't gwain a change now".

Susannah's face was a mess of bloody streaks and bruises. Temperance took the bent copper reflecting piece down from the wall till some of the scars faded. She'd feel so much worse if she saw herself. No need for that.

"First, just a quick comb through my hair. What old face is that looking back at me? Wouldn't know me they wouldn't back at the Mission now, sallow gaunt old face, them green eyes shining out so unearthly. No wonder they calls out Witch as I pass on the street. Hunger and hard work do that to a woman. Scarce food, dawn to dusk work tending or finding my precious herbs, tramping miles in all weathers to attend the sick that want service and won't wait. Take the colour from any cheeks, twill. And my hair, not red like it was - still thick but streaked all through with grey. Oh, it was me alright, that aged woman looking back at me".

She looks at her hands, all rough and covered with black cracks from gathering and shredding the herbs. As a child her hands were always so clean from the washing soap.

"Me feet be as bad, swollen from walking miles in old shoes I got no moneys to repair and the chilblains that itch so from autumn to spring. Still they heal in summer when I walk barefoot down the pathfields".

For all that she could still stride out with a straight back, and look into the eyes of any she met. She stood for no wickedness and hypocrisy when she saw it. On her say so, her customers sent packing the physicians that practiced only quackery. As for Susannah, there was no reason she shouldn't stay, every reason she should. To Temperance she was a gift from God. Hadn't she prayed to God for help.

"He must surely have sent her to me for company. And I got the two rooms upstairs. I take my rest in the smaller one since my man went to his peace under the earth at Saint Mary's".

She didn't believe the chamomile he drank that morning had anything to do with his fall. It was meant to keep him off the drink. According to the Harbour Master it hadn't stopped him from supping too much strong ale that day. That was his choice. She'd meant no harm. Her man would know that.

"Still", she thought, "Never hurt to be careful did it? Alive he never went in the small bed chamber, so dead he wouldn't neither".

In his last months Mr Lloyd never made it up the stairs without falling back down cursing the devil and Temperance for making the stairs uneven. Just to be safe, she burned seven sprigs of sage and rue in the hearth before she pulled the feather marriage bed into the small room. He never knew Susannah. She'd come to no harm sleeping there.

"Besides what you don't know ... And God did bless us with a good sleep pad... "

They found the old horsehair mattress out back by Talbot Inn. Temperance put up branches for them to set it over a bonfire to smeech out the bugs. What a day it was. Susannah laughed for the first time since she'd arrived.

"Clapped us 'ands us did as they insects popped open in the fire. Danced round it for joy us did. Fat with seamen's blood them bugs made flames shot up and singe the ticking. Us 'ad to run an get it off the wood. They bugs stopped droppin'. Us shook the mattress. Last of 'em falled out".

It took both of them to get it through the back door and up the stairs. Breathless, they laughed as they sank in a heap on top of the pad on the bed chamber floor. With two of them it was easier to pick wood for the fire. They didn't have to go every day, but stacked it against the back wall of the house where the street thieves couldn't see it. Temperance taught

Susannah how to see the pictures in the fire with her one good eye. She told her the story of her life before her husband died.

"Put up with a lot 'er did with that man of 'ers. Told 'as 'ow 'er married 'im when 'e was off the ale. Not that 'e was off it for long".

"I was that happy, Susannah, praised the Lord each day. My Mam always said you should count your blessings before they go away. I do believe he tried to be sober. At first he did his drinking just of a Saturday, the boats not being worked on the Sabbath. It got worse. I tried to explain away the mornings he missed on the weigh scales. A bad piece of meat made him sick. It could have been something he caught from the boat in from the Indies. I would never outright lie. The warnings come every week, then most days. He stopped drinking, started again, stopped. Too many Mondays he were "too sick" to show up at his post with the South Dock Harbour Master's. Then it came. One final warning. No drunkard works here. He protested. Well, they always do protest".

The reality of the evil of drink for him seem to register only when he hit his head on the cobblestones one night outside the Brewers Arms. That seemed to bring him right to his senses. Temperance knelt to tend his wounds and to thank the good Lord. She kissed those wet brown cobbles.

"We had the chance to make a new start. I prayed with him, how I prayed. He moved to the new Royal dock where colliers and grain and lumber boats tied up to ply the Bristol Channel. No strong spirits in that cargo. And a fair good step to the closest ale-house, the old Ty Morwr. Another blessing that".

The Channel crewmen told tales of the England to be seen on a clear day from up top the hills over Tawe Bay. Over there was the County of Devon where the air is good, the hills green, the woods lush. Boats come and go daily over to a busy town the men called Bideford. They told of a lovely safe moorage there, round a headland and up a wide river. There were good tides to take the ships in and out in deep water.

They described a pretty town, rich, so much trade, sailings from Bristol bringing goods from the Indies. And fish piled high on the quay when the codmen arrive from the Banks. A hundred or more ships came every day up that river. Great explorers built their grand houses by the Broad Quay. The pannier market sells good fresh meat, vegetables from farms all round, all at a good price. And there were rumours of the smuggling trade. And there was more. They said,

"Seems wealthy merchants can gain handily from the carriage of port, rum and brandy with no duty to the King. Of a dark night, they say rowboats go silent up stream from vessels anchored round the headlands to caves above the long bridge. The Custom House and Harbour Master need men to find the trade that lies outside the law".

With the local men tempted greatly with good payment of spirits for their silence, little finding was ever made. So the crewmen said there was always work for "good sober Welsh men to work in the King's interest".

"Mr Lloyd come home with the good news. Good news, and he was sober. Lifted me up and swung me round till I was dizzy, he did. We would start a new life when he got good work in Bideford".

The first mate of the coal barge let them tie down the seaman's chest holding the featherbed and cooking pots on the deck. The crossing was calm, the sky flushing pink as Temperance stepped on to Bideford quay.

"Red sky at morning ... That was Bideford, the town of white houses, green hills in the year of our Lord, 1643".

Up in The Arms, Sion soon hears the talk tonight of another Welshman off the boat to take work from honest Devon folk and good money to catch those not so honest. Soon enough he'll take the moneys from both kinds. They all do. Soon enough.

"Keep my own Welsh mouth shut for the better hearing the tale. Lloyd his name is, they say, proper Welsh that. Soon smooth-tongued his way into managing the weigh scale down the quay. Big help being able to speak the Welsh and the English with the colliers, isn't it? And there was a lovely wife. Caused a real stir among the men, well more like a stirring if you gets my meaning".

Sue was still afraid to go out in case the Abbotsham farmer might be asking round on market day to find his milk maid.

"Good milk maid us was. 'Ard to come by good uns with the right touch to get the most good milk. If 'e 'ad the choice 'e'd likely want me back iffen 'e'd 'ave to let me drunken cowman go".

A fortnight passed. Nobody came looking. Temperance asked round down the market. No news. Nobody had heard anything.

" 'Er said as Abbotsham farmers don't come this way much, Buckland way bein' closer to the farther holdings".

Temperance let her help in her back garden and had her stir the pots to boil leaves market days. She gave Susannah her hood to cover her face so she could take her turn going for old bread down the town ovens.

"Us looked just like t'other servant women that 'ad jealous men up at th'ouse".

Soon it was safe for Susannah to help Temperance deliver her jars and powders down the town and over East-the-Water. Eager to help, she would say to Temperance,

"Us can help 'ee, Temperance. Us can read some, an' us can count yer mixes for they medicines".

Temperance Lloyd: Hanged for Witchcraft in 1682

Temperance found Susannah was helpful indeed, a ready apprentice. She could name every herb in the garden in no more than a fortnight. A month more and she knew their uses. "Hellebore and castery for apoplexy. Root of comfrey for the bone breaks. Poppy seeds for sleep absence. Feverfew for lightning headaches. Speedwell for the rheumatics. Bird's-foot trefoil for the nervousness".

Temperance couldn't be sure Susannah knew what the sicknesses were, but she took directions well. Always used the right pan for the job — copper pot for infusions, black iron pan for ointments and poultices, yellow Bideford ware jar for soaking. Temperance taught her to paste the penned labels on the jars. It was good to have someone to talk to as she worked in the scullery. She would talk of the happy times she'd had when Mr Lloyd kept sober a while. After their work, they would talk by the fire. Susannah could never get enough of Temperance's life story.

"I was so happy. Prayed to God on my knees every evening to thank Him, I did. I sowed the seeds brought from Swansea out the back, seeds that came from my Mam's seeds from Castell Nedd. My way to say I be home, see. So happy. Bit of Wales over here in Saesneg country. Kept his cottage so clean, our garden tended".

Sometimes Susannah looked puzzled. Saesneg?

"That's what we call the English. An' tis Welsh I pray in the house, the English just of a Sunday. There's things you wouldn't know of out there on the farm, Susannah. Times be uncertain. So much gone on in England, not like Wales at all. Kings changing the religions, the people changing the Kings, And now they say there's no King up London, just Master Cromwell. Funny thing that is indeed, a King they call Master. And wars about it all around. Tis safest to pray down Saint Mary's. Nice enough it is of a Sunday. Now you're all healed, you'll come with me. Listen right at the back we do, being as we're poor".

Temperance missed the fiery preaching of the Welsh ministers. Sometimes of a summer night she went to stand quiet at the back of the crowd when the Welsh reverend passed through town on his way down to Launceston. She always kept her hood over her face, had to be careful. Wouldn't do to be seen by the watching sexton who'd run right back to the Rector to report what he saw.

Sion remembers Temperance always being at Saint Mary's on Sunday, standing straight in the pauper's pews. She had her pride. She listened when the gentlefolk thanked their God, but held her peace when had little thanks for her services. Thou shalt not steal ... Sion heard the sermons too, church attendance being required of those living on the Borough's alms. He wondered if Temperance and Susannah ever thought to ask why it's right to haggle over the pittance to pay for the help you accept from a poor wise woman. For wise woman Temperance was. Made folk fearful that did, no less for there being two of them now.

It was safer for them of a Saturday night when the road from The Arms past the cottage echoed loud with drunken laughter. After Keeper threw them out, many a lost sailor would lay his head down in Temperance's front garden. Temperance didn't ask the Constable to move the drunk, no longer needed to. The two women needed no help. Together they could heave any senseless stranger over the low front wall on to the road. And if the man should fall into the path of a cart ... what did that have to do with two poor women sleeping quiet in their own beds to be ready for church on the Sabbath?

"Our two words 'gainst the Constable's one", Temperance would say to Susannah.

A month later as the Evensong bell rang out, the two women heard that voice calling loudly outside. Temperance looked over the half door into the most frightened eyes she'd ever seen.

"Twas a woman, I think. Hard to tell at first. Stood there in a cloud of sour air. Stench of dung left no doubt what cart she had ridden to town".

She asked for Susannah, said she was a friend of hers.

"What could I say? Susannah was there right behind me. The woman had nowhere to go. Didn't know nobody in Bideford. Poor thing took on so, crying and kneeling down there on the step. Folk out on the road stopped to gawp. Alright ... Alright ..."

Temperance poured more water into the vegetable broth on the stove.

Susannah said the woman was Mary, Mary Trembles. Sue thought she might have a cousin over East-the-Water. Temperance said she could stay, just till she finds her cousin. She had to be firm about that. Just till then ... No longer. They can't feed another mouth. Susannah took Mary out the back and washed her down.

Back indoors, Mary crouched in front of the fire, rubbing her hands. The wailing died down, but her breath came in little snorting sighs. Temperance took Susannah out the back to find out more. How long had Susannah been friend to her?

"Mary Trembles, Mary-Mary".

Susannah said everyone called her Mary-Mary, on account she said the last thing she heard over and over again, and on account she needed to be told everything twice, or more. Susannah thought she must be about nineteen. No one would have thought it. To Temperance she looked twice that, so broken she did appear. One side of her face drooped, Susannah said it always had, as long as she'd known her. She'd been brought to the Squire's house in Littleham late one night from the Home over Shebbear way. She'd have been about six back then. Out of the kindness of the

Mistress's heart, Mary was allowed to clear the ashes, set the fires, tend the fires — as long as there was no company at the house. She stoked the fires for the night in winter, cleared the ashes well before dawn … In summer she could pick root crops, as long as someone showed her and reminded her when she forgot what she was doing. She was given her food, a tiny cot to sleep in by the coal cellar, and two aprons, one for wear, one for wash. She wasn't paid. She wouldn't know what to do with pay, had nothing to do with it anyway. Well, she never left the house, did she. Mary-Mary was simple. Susannah asked round and came back from market with the story.

It seems the Old squire had died and the Young Master was back from Bristol. The Young Squire liked his female workers pretty, even the under-scullery maid. Mary-Mary did not suit at all, with her drooping cheek and eye, crooked mouth that hung open except if she closed it to chew. So Mary was put on to the back of the dung cart to Bideford and dumped off in the back alley behind the Talbot Inn.

"So how did she find ye?" Temperance asked Susannah.

"Well, tis Market Day. 'Er must've gone over market lookin' for food. Seen us and followed us 'ome".

Mary-Mary didn't seem to know, or she didn't remember by the next day when Temperance asked her. She asked Susannah what else she knew about Mary.

"Stable boy out Littleham said groom said cowman said 'er was found new-born up in cattle barn loft, 'er ma layin' dead from the metheglyn on top of 'er. Woulda died of cold else".

"So she be simple Mary-Mary?"

"Simple".

Susannah knew it was best to tell Temperance the truth. She'd soon realize anyway that Mary-Mary wasn't the quickest. She was more than a bit slow-witted.

"But 'er's no 'arm. Knowed 'er since us was in service up in squire's 'ouse over Littleham, me in scullery, 'er down coal 'ouse. Come out poor 'ouse for babes folk don't want. Under footman said as 'er ma tried to get rid of 'er fore 'er was born, with the spirits. 'Er died of the spirits. Mary-Mary was born simple. 'Er's still simple. Don't learn nothin'. Tries 'ard".

Temperance asked if Mary could ever earn her keep. Could they put her out to service in town? Susannah shrugged. She said they could try, but there wasn't much hope of it.

" 'Er's alright down the coal 'ouse. Can't let 'er 'bove stairs".

With all the gossip in the town, Temperance knew they must take care. Folk already thought they were strange.

"One woman alone is odd. Two be afeared. Three…"

She tried hard to place Mary in service, went to all the big houses. She told any who would listen that Mary was a good worker, and honest. She would'nt know how to lie or cheat, can scrub a floor till you could eat off of it. A few head maids took a look at Mary. To put the best face on it, Mary was not presentable. What could Temperance do? She couldn't put her out on the street, not with the nights drawing in cold and wet.

Winter was the hardest time for them. They can't afford dry wood from the yard. The driftwood stays wet. The branches from the woods hold the moss like a coat burning with much smeech, but little heat.

*****

300 years later, Sion has seen so little has changed.

"That's how it's so easy for her to imagine it".

"I remember the rope-walker's house was always cold, bone-chilling cold. Stone walls, almost three feet thick, kept out the sun in summer, but the bitter winter winds would whistle in through the gaps in the cracks in the windows. Mam couldn't get it fixed, all the men being off at the Front, all the glass needed for the War effort. The rain and snow blew in under the front door. In their house it would blow right into the front kitchen. In our house it blew into a little lobby, but we still had a heavy curtain hanging from a rail fixed to the heavy oak door to keep the draft out. They might have had a curtain too. I expect theirs would be blackened by soot. Our was red and Mam washed it in the summer with Rinso to get it bright again. My Mam told me they didn't have Rinso. Temperance would only have had hard soap like clay".

Sion nods.

"Her man there has never been inside that old cottage, just as she was never in the 'witches' house' that was a pile of stones before she was born".

"Our house. Their house. On an iron hob — firebox to the right, oven on left — a dented iron kettle sat murmuring gently all day, or at least it did when we picked enough drift wood from the river bank to keep the fire going. When the wind blew down from the North, even quite dry wood smeeched but gave off no heat. Breezes from the east would fan the flames making the wood burn the wood too quickly to keep the room warm for long".

*****

Susannah had never lived in a place to call home before. She has to know where everything came from, like the coconut hair mat that keeps their feet off the mud floor.

"Came in on a boat from the Indies. I collect how pleased Mr Lloyd was to pick it up on the quay for me. Twas a time he was n't at the ale, that was. A good time".

*****

"We had a coconut mat, blue and orange. Uncle Bert brought it when he came on leave from Singapore. Our floor is smooth cement painted red. I used to wonder if Temperance hung a curtain across the entrance to the scullery, the back kitchen, like in our house. And did they have a wooden pantry cupboard in the corner? Ours held a frypan and two iron saucepans".

*****

Temperance keeps her "special pots" always clean up on the shelf. Susannah and Mary know they must only use them when she's there to watch they do it properly. A fretted vegetable rack often sits empty, and there's two metal meat hooks hanging down from the beams. They can rarely afford meat. Hog's Pudding is cheaper.

*****

Hog's Pudding is still made from the same recipe today. The women's would have tasted just what we did at breakfast today.
"We had a large ewer faintly patterned with roses standing in a dusty washbowl on a washstand. Maybe Temperance had one like it".

*****

Susannah admires the washbowl.
"Yes, it's pretty. Very fancy that is, Susannah. Brought it from the house in Port Tennant all the way on the boat".

*****

To the right of the hob, a small door opens on to a narrow stairway that winds behind the fireplace and chimney up to one small, and one smaller, bedchamber.

*****

Temperance saw soon enough they'd never find a place in service for Mary, so she said she could stay. Mary-Mary was so happy to have a home.

"Well, I had to let her stay, didn't I? What else could we do? Never known such a life afore she hadn't".

Susannah was happy to see how much better Mary-Mary's life was now. No one was shouting at her for forgetting to take away the ashes. No one was pushing her around. No one was blaming her for all the things she did not recall having done, or for things she didn't remember to do at all. Mary worshipped Temperance, adored her.

"It was so ... Well, she didn't mean no harm. She listened to me showing Sue what to do. Likely didn't know what I was saying. Sue said Mary-Mary just liked the sound of my voice, the Welsh. She followed me round the house. She sat so quiet in the corner of the scullery, made me jump betimes. Watched my every move she did. As I sliced, bruised, soaked the herbs for my potions, those eyes followed me. She would follow me, I do believe, into hell-fire. She follows me cross country miles in all weathers if I forget to say to stay in the house. When I teach Sue a recipe Mary-Mary repeats the last word she heard".

Sometimes she would echo the words in a toneless voice hours later.

"Heal the ague. Seal the ague. Heal the ague. Seal the ague".

"That cracked voice "...

Temperance came to hear it in her sleep. She prayed God for patience. Susannah would have to be careful not to let her go out in the town alone. She could go down the river to pick wood, but must remember to come straight back. She must keep her mouth shut. Her nonsense talk could get them all into trouble. Sue told her every day,

"No one needs to know the 'secrets' Temperance know".

Winter comes on them again. Three mouths to feed, only two pairs of hands to do the work.

They don't wash much in winter, themselves nor their clothes. It's too cold to strip off, and there's not enough wood to boil water for washing. Nothing dries in the drizzle on the slimy line out the back. The days are short, cold, sunless. Rain falls every day except when it changes to heavy wet snow. Often the icy drizzle makes the streets so slippery they can't walk for falling. Try as she does, Temperance can't make enough to feed them, let alone get warm clothes. They have only the rags they live and sleep in.

Against the cold, the women sleep as much as they can in winter. Temperance met a crewman from far up the North at the market buying the Hog's Pudding. He said it was just like they made back home.

"Had the English, enough to buy stuff, enough to tell tales of his home land. Said as our winters be bad now as where he come from. Told as how

Temperance Lloyd: Hanged for Witchcraft in 1682

in his country they "sleep out the cold dark times of winter" way up north in the cold dark times. His folk do try to sleep through day and night. Soon as snow comes, families sleep near right through winter to spring. Take to the bed altogether for warmth, stack up wood for fire, bread enough too. Gets up just once a day, eat a bit of bread, go back asleep".

At sunset, Susannah packs the driftwood pieces firmly together on the fire to keep it burning slowly. Temperance shares out small pieces of bread, reminding Mary-Mary to chew it carefully so it will take away the hunger. She hides the rest where Mary won't find it. Then they all huddle as close together as they can on the horsehair pad by the fire, pulling Temperance's feather bed tight around them. They sleep the first dead sleep till around midnight. The first awake will poke the fire and stack on more wood.

A month goes by. Temperance talks them quietly back to sleep each time they are wakened by shouts on the street or a knock on the door. They talk quietly. Susannah sometimes wonders what it would be like to be a mother.

"No Susannah. After that beating by your cowman, there'll be no more children for you. Same for me dear. No more after Mr Lloyd beat me of a Saturday night. Always cried on the Sunday how bad he wanted children. Losing them was all my fault he said. I tried to pray away the troubles. And he prayed with me, betimes, he did. God helps them as helps themselves. My Mam said that".

She sighs.

"I thought to help him stop the drink with herbal teas made sweet with honey. Told him, "for your head, dearie". His head was always so bad after the drink. I warned him he would get a bit dizzy. I told him he must be so careful not to take drink the same time. Well, he's gone on now, and praise the good Lord we can be safe in his house, my house now".

Another bit of bread and they would sink back into sleep till sun up over East-the-Water rises earlier with Spring light for them to begin their work again.

Come summer, they pulled the feather bed back up the stairs. Temperance wrapped it right round herself for a top covering and bottom mattress in the small room. There was no room for a bed in there. They dragged the horsehair pad back up and tied it tight on to Mr Lloyd's iron bed frame that was slowly rusting through. Susannah and Mary share a patchwork quilt sewn of odd pieces of wool cloth scavenged from the lanes at the backs of the King's Head and the Gold Lion on a Sunday morning on their way home way from Matins. They usually found food scraps, buttons, even coins down there too. Temperance sewed that quilt.

"Took me a whole month of long June evenings. Real regimental record tis, cloth torn in brawls from the coats of troops and crews that come and go off boats moored down the Quay. Navy, tan, red..."

Life gets harder and harder by the year. Temperance keeps praying in desperation.

"Three mouths to feed and Mary don't do much. Well, not much she can do, is there. Not her fault but tis hard to collect that at times. Folk pay little for our potions but gets us up from our beds all hours to attend to fevers, the ague, upset stomachs. Always tired we are, often hungry, always cold".

Susannah soon knows enough to be able to work on her own. She rushes to the door to get the best custom, folk who pay the fee they ask right away or at least in time for market day. And Mary...

"Lord give me patience with her slowness, She's getting on my nerves. She's trying me every day. I know she can't help it, but help me Lord. When Mary does round the house it just holds us up. I could do the same in half the time. Susannah too. We go to help her, she starts to cry and snivels on for hours after it's all done. Can't trust her to go to market. Forgets what she was sent for. When a messenger comes to the door she gets muddled. Who was the customer? What the complaint? Which house? Mary never knows".

And then there was the cat.

"We can't feed a cat, can barely feed ourselves. We tells her and tells her again. We don't need a cat. Not like we have rats or mice, nothing for them to feed on. And with all the superstition round the town ... If a cat be seen round the house of three old women living by our physic wisdom we shall surely be called for witches".

That starts Mary-Mary up,

"Witches. Witches. Called for Witches".

Over and over Temperance shoos the cat away, tells Mary to leave the cat be. The black scrawny creature comes down the road into the front garden to nibble at the mint. Cats like mint. Temperance pushes it away. Susannah sends it away. But Mary ... Mary lets it be.

One Saturday Temperance toils, hot and tired, up the hill from the market. Coming round the corner she saw the cat.

"Jumping all round on the path right by our house. Up and over the wall. Round the herbs. Into the grass by the wall. Saw it chasing something, a vole maybe? No. A piece of twine. And what should be at the other end of the string but Mary. Went off picking twine for it down the Rope Walk she did, on her way back from picking sticks. And she dropped the wood to get the twine and left half of it there". Temperance shouted at her,

"How many times do I have to tell thee, Mary. That cat'll be the death of thee. Death of us all twill be".

Susannah tries to say Mary just don't understand why Temperance is so angry. She just loves the cat. Wants it's warm body on her feet at night.

"And right enough, tis the only warm thing in the house in the darkest hours. Mary, Mary, Mary ... Susannah says again how they called her Mary-Mary up at Littleham to save having to tell her twice when she didn't come the first time. Have to tell her everything twice, thrice. And Mary-Mary, she just says it back".

"Death of us all. Death of us all ... "

"Could think 'er knows what 'er's told. 'Er don't", Susannah sighs.

A year later, the Constable came for Temperance. She must be a witch, on account she lived with two other women and they had a cat. There being no other evidence, she was not charged.

CHAPTER FIVE
1670

"Line or Linden Tree: The floures are commended by divers against paine of the head proceeding of a cold cause, against dissiness, the Apoplexie, and also the falling sicknesse, and not onely the floure, but the distilled water thereof".

Herball or General Histories of Plantes, John Gerard, 1597

Several years passed quietly for the three women. They lived on quietly in Temperance's house, barely eaking out a living as healers. Blind Sion is in his seat under the window at The Arms, as he says, "Sitting and listening, listening and sitting".

He has no need to go down the quay or over bridge to know everything that's happening in Bideford, and in most of the rest of the country.

"Hear it all sat here. Much there be to hear, much goings on in the town. Up London the Lord Protector be in his grave, King Charles on his throne. Ten full years of great busyness brings many folk to The Arms, and to all tother ale-houses. And t'aint just Bideford folk. Strangers come from all over these days they be, from away. This day noon didn't I come in to find one of them sitting right in my seat. Near sat on top of him I did. Would have done if twere'nt for old Mr Browning put his arm out. Gent got up when they told him he'd been sat in Blind Sion's place. Filled my ale-pot too, twice over he did. He come off a boat from over Virginia. Lives there now he do. Born over Barnstaple way, said his name was James".

Ships bring cargoes to Bideford from across the ocean almost daily.

"Come and go now far over the sea to that Newfoundland and Boston town, like they was off down to Appledore for a Sunday outing. Well with them colonies all starting up, they do need goods for their houses and there be no potteries and kilns like in Bideford, well, and Barnstaple. Nigh forty works in the town there be. John Manning started up last June past. Folk said he'd never make nought of it. Last week he sent a full hold over to that County of Avalon, down south part of Newfoundland. Greatly profitable trade there be in Bideford Ware. Good sturdy pots and pretty enough too, so the wives like the look of it".

George Darracott had been in the night before. Sion enjoys relaying the news to the Bristol seamen.

"Building a nice little town there now, they be. Big houses for fine gentlemen. Doing it all for the King they say. Well, and for the moneys I daresay, truth be told. Straight run in a good wind south down to Virginia and they brings the tabaci back here".

He nods knowingly.

"Making pipes to smoke it down by the Rope Walk they are now. Who would have thought it when Master Raleigh showed us them leaves round the fire here not a hundred year since? Lovely soft smell left by those crushed soft damp leaves twas, sweet as sugared pig. Master George Darracott takes his "Delight" to fish by Avalon every year. And he do say as they got witches over the sea, just like they say be round here. They say... Best say nought about Temperance and her friends. Not doing no harm are they. Don't stop Old Jack Carracott saying a cat been seen up there. Said it could be a witch. Well, didn't that make the men laugh fit to spill the ale".

Temperance knows it's no laughing matter.

"Mary-Mary she's at it again. Got herself another darned cat friend that's in the door soon as I open it. Rector himself stopped by the gate last night. "Pretty kitty, Pretty kitty", and Mary was so pleased. Had to say as it was her cat, her own cat, her cat. Picked it up and brought it inside she did with Rector watching her. No use trying to get her to see sense. I tell her to mind no one thinks she's a witch — tis all the talk round the town these days — she just keeps saying, "Witch, Witch". Over and over she says it. Sending me mad she is".

Susannah nods. Mary-Mary means no harm, but Temperance is right.

"One of these days she'll be saying it when we'm out to market or down the oven for the bread. She don't see as Rector be no friend to folk like us no matter how much he says the Lord Jesus loves the poor and the meek

Temperance Lloyd: Hanged for Witchcraft in 1682

of a Sunday. Tis all talk with him. No better than he should be neither that man. Saw him staggering in his cups down the Conduit drang thrice last month. Pulled my shawl up over my face not to let him see me looking at him his hands on the wall holding hisself over the drain. The deacon's business that is, not mine, and not for me to say what's there to see, me going along Allhalland to Bridge Street to attend Mistress Johnstone. Turned out it wasn't for her but for the Mistress of a fine gentleman from London way that come on the coach. Shook up she was by the journey. Soon got her head soothed and her stomach calmed down with some fresh leaves of feverfew in a bit of bread".

Blind Sion enjoys the town's good times, knowing trade is never reliable.

"Been some bad times over the years. Seemed like half the men of Bideford went off to find better lives in the colonies. Off to Ireland some of 'em. Right little Bideford tis over there. Boats taking all the butter farms out Abbotsham way can make off to Ireland. So much coming and going with the trade on our river, bring that many mariners with that much coin to spend, ale-houses can scarce keep up with it all. And the tales they spin of a night by the fire. Such goings on over in America. More silliness over there than we got in England. Got it from here they did, not but what that's reason to forgive it".

Sion shakes his head as he thinks of it all.

"There be the coaches up and down from London twice a week this year past. Coach run don't just turn round up Exeter any more, do it. Nay. Comes right on down the Crediton road though it ain't no more than a cart track and rough with it. They gets down all stiff and complaining their bones be shook out their bodies. Complain away in here too. Folks here knows the complaining'll stop if we ask of news of far off places. They do like to tell us ignorant country folk all manner of wonders. Fills our ale-pots for our listening. So much of the politic up there, folk don't know what to think".

The Londoner looks around and lowers his voice,

"Must be careful what ye do say, or say nought, for safety's sake".

Sion knows London politics can be trouble for Bideford too. Soldiers coming and going, for the King, for Lord Cromwell, for the King.

"Pray God twill settle down now they say King Charles is back and safe in charge. Politics be London business. Us down Bideford way, we just want to know what's coming next so as to keep low from it. Tis coming closer. Lord Justice Hale that caught such a passion for witch finding from Master Hopkins over East, he been doing his judging at the Somerset Assize these several years past".

With the boats moored down river in Appledore to clear the Torridge for the dory races, the seamen walk along the pathfields through the woods to see the Show. There are tellers and seers to consult, games of skill on the Pill, dories racing on the river. Talk of the trials spreads fast at Bideford Fair.

"And such tales they tell of the Assizes... All sworn on oath. Must be truth told. That many folk, men and women both, be took up to Somerset Assizes one day, down to the gallows the next. Right there in Wincanton, so close by Bideford a horseman can ride there cross the moor in a long day. Hard to credit it. Such goings on be fitting far off in the wild north. Believe anything them folk do, same as them in the popish regions cross the sea. And now ... Well, Master Browning reads from the Broadsheet that come tonight".

> "The effort will require involvement of the country at every level. Everyone must play a part. We ask the people for their awareness and their resolve. There are some things we can do immediately, and we will. Others will take more time".

The constable's grasp on Temperance's arm was firm, not really rough, as he walked her down the High Street towards the river. It was a short walk downhill from Top of Old Town to the grand Town Hall by the bridge. The Constable was relieved to get inside. So early on a dark morning no one should have been up to see them. But you never know...

"Well, I knew. And what if I were witch for true... My that would be fine thing. God knows there be no witches, nor witching. Men of the Church know only what they been told to know".

The Constable pointed Temperance to a seat at a large rough table. She looked across the table at the Justice.

"Well, he's the Mayor when he's not justicing".

The sun rising across the river throws beams of light through layers of greasy grime on the window.

"You'd think they could clean them windows. Said they had no need of cleaners three years since. Come down here in my Sunday best to ask for work I did. Told me to go for Poor Relief. If I wanted the Poor Relief I'd not be goin' round th'houses and shops asking for honest work, now would I? So why am I fetched down here so early?"

The Justice reads from a paper.

"There been a complaint about thee, Mistress Temperance Lloyd. Tis said ye did treat one William Hebert".

"Indeed, that I did. The elder William Hebert, over East-the-Water, I did give him a feverfew decoction against the violent headaches. Good feverfew twas, grew it myself in my own plot from my own seeds. Same feverfew as my Mam and her Mam before her had used for the head pains. He felt much the better for it, and quickly. Well enough he was I met him walking over the bridge two days later".

"He did walk out?"

"Saw him with my own good eyes. His neighbours saw him too. They could vouch for it. And Master Hebert was in Saint Mary's for Matins and for Evensong".

The Justice nods and the Clerk writes it all down. Temperance watches to see that he gets it down right and his hand starts to shake. He drops his quill under the table. Temperance picks it up and hands it back to him. Then the Justice asks,

"Mistress Lloyd, didst thee utter a spell across William Hebert's bed?"

Temperance frowns, shaking her head,

"What kind of question is that? Why would I do such a thing? I be no witch. No need for spells when I got the good feverfew, is there?"

Then the Justice says,

"A neighbour did tell as a black bird did fly from Master Hebert's window".

Temperance shrugs.

"There may have been one. I could not say. I did not see it as I collect".

The Clerk speaks,

"William Hebert didst name thee a witch on his deathbed. His son swore to it".

"Would that be the older son, he that plays games of chance with the good Doctor? The same Doctor that threw his urine flask at me when Mistress Jane Aiken sent him packing? Mistress Jane did swear my herbs helped her head more than did his leeches, as they would".

Mr Justice, the Mayor, was quiet. He whispered to the Clerk, loud enough for Temperance to hear,

"What should be done with this woman?"

The Clerk considers.

"B'ain't Exeter Quarter Assizes to start soon? Best send 'er up there".

The Mayor nods.

"Our first charge be to our town. Tis a good time for Bideford. The town be coming well set as a Port 'gainst claims of they Barnstaple folk. News of witchcraft'll bedevil us trade".

The Clerk looks up from his writing,

"Ships from foreign parts bring such folk as hold fast to all kinds of superstitions. London coach passing Bideford to Cornwall come by Somerset. Witch Hunters over there do find many by rumours. If this woman later be found a witch, the town will be seen a devilish place. What then of us trade ... And then ..."

"And then..." The Mayor is smiling now,

"Tis not sure we be sending her for to be hanged. She might be found acquitted of the crime. Justice must be done. The Rector tells it so, to deny there be witches be to deny God himself. As for us, we can never be heard to deny ..."

The Clerk looks at the Mayor.

"Then again ... We could think to let us, the town Justices decide by Trial, the Jury being local. Bideford would thus be thought able to rid itself of a witch. A powerful town".

The Mayor would have none of it.

"A trial up the County Assize will show our citizens, and especially the Justices, do know the law in respect of evil. Our town dignitaries shall be seen to have hunted down a witch and sent her to trial, a truly God-fearing town indeed".

Temperance sees there's nothing more she can say. No one can stop her thinking,

"Oh so God fearing this town, with a Rector like ours, a Church full of hypocrites. Not my place to say. I've done nought wrong, nor would I. Got nothing to fear, I haven't".

The Constable kept Temperance overnight in the disused church that served as the town lock-up at the East end of the bridge. It was still silent on the river, seamen sleeping on the boats moored at the quay, when he pushed her into the cart the next day. The carter was well on his way towards Torrington before dawn.

"A full day that ride up to Exeter took, the sun travelling near across the sky. The cart rolled side to side, wheels going from rut to rut, had me sliding from side to side on the straw. Carter slept from Torrington to Meath, reins hanging loose in his hands. I thought a time or two to jump over the side, walk away 'cross the high moor. Could have done it. Then where would I go? Folk die out there in the bogs. And if I did escape, twould be a life of hiding. I did no wrong to William Hebert, may the good Lord bless his soul. Never seen him in a full six weeks before his demise. Well, never save when he was out walking in the town. Said only Good Day and nought else as I passed by on my business. They will not find me guilty, how can they?"

As the cart rolled through the great gates of Exeter City Temperance gazed up at the many big houses, inns, shops. Hawkers and tinkers shouted at every corner. Exeter seemed even bigger and noisier than Swansea town. A huge crowd was gathered in the streets for the Assizes, all crying out in a witch hunt fever. The carter laid sacks over Temperance to try to hide her. It didn't make any difference. The folk had been watching the gate from the Crediton road. Some had waited hours for the cart carrying the Bideford witch to arrive. They chased after it as it rattled its way toward the gaol inside the Castle walls. The Assizes were theatre for village people who came to the County town in hopes of getting in to watch the show. Temperance was afraid.

"I wished the Lord I had run off on the moor. The noisesome drunken merriment of the crowds outside the gaol kept sleep away till past the midnight hour. Back again they were at sun up. Thronging around the courtyard doors they were, all trying to get a look at me, like they hadn't never seen an old woman. Shouted at me that I was dirty. Well, they hadn't give me water to wash the dust from the road off my face, had they".

People crowded into the courtroom until the Sheriff's men decided the room was too full. "Fought each other like drunkards to keep a place to watch. The Justice and the Jury came and sat themselves down. The Jurymen was quiet not seeming too feared of the mob. They listened careful-like to what was told them, looked at me quite kindly".

The Justice asked Temperance what her work was. He was respectful, telling her to take the time she needed. She replied looking him in the eye,

"I minister to the sick".

The Sheriff asked,

"By what means?"

Temperance described her usual remedies...

"Lily of the Valley flowers distilled with wine for to restore the memory and speech of them with dumb palsie, burned willow bark in vinegar for corns and callouses, feverfew for the lightning headache, groundsel boiled in ale to provoke vomiting after a man has eaten bad meat ..."

She looked straight at the Jurymen. One by one she saw them nod. Yes. Yes. Yes.

"They knew these were for sure remedies used to good effect by many healers. The Chartered Physicians — Chartered Quacks I call them — use just such medicines. The Jurymen, maybe the good Justice himself, have partaken of the same curatives to good effect".

The Lord Justice spoke,

"Mistress Lloyd, when didst thou last treat Master Hebert?"

Temperance curtsied,

"Twas a full six weeks before his death, Sir".

The Justice read from the papers the Sheriff handed to him. Then he asked,

"Is it the truth that in the time between Master Hebert had been seen walking in the town?" Temperance nodded.

59

"I say truly I did see good Master Hebert with my own eyes. Saw him in church. Many, even the good Rector himself, had seen him there".

She could see the Jurymen and the Judge believed her.

"And why not? I told only the truth. I looked direct at the Jury. I saw them nodding and I smiled at them. They could see that I meant no one harm. I be not an evil creature just a woman with greying hair, wrinkled face, dusty from my journey. I kept myself upright. My clothes be well mended, cleaner than many that come from the cells".

The Sheriff told her she could sit down. He called for William Hebert the Younger, William Hebert the Elder's son.

William Hebert the Younger swore that he heard his father in his dying words accuse Mistress Temperance Lloyd of bewitching him to death. The Justice asked who else had heard the man's dying words. Master Hebert the younger replied,

"No one. No one else heard it, the servants all being out at the time".

The Justice read again from the papers. He asked,

"Was it not just afore the time for the supper the manservant brought each day to thy father's chamber?"

Master Hebert could not recall what happened to the supper. The Judge asked if there was anything else Master Hebert wanted to tell the court. Master Hebert looked down, breaking into a sweat, his hands shaking. Then speaking very loudly he said,

"I myself had no part in my poor father's sad death. I was not even there when he breathed his last".

The Justice then asked,

"How could ye have heard thy father's dying words, ye being absent from the room at the time?"

Master Hebert wiped his brow and muttered,

"That is of no matter. I know my father's death was all due to bewitching".

Then he screamed loudly at the court,

"My father was bewitched, I tell you".

One Juryman started to laugh. Then they were all laughing. The Sheriff called them to be silent. The Judge smiled. He told Master Hebert he could stand down and be thankful the enquiry was done.

Temperance was free to go home. Before dusk, they set her back on a cart for the rough ride home to Bideford with three groats in her pocket for her trouble.

"More'n I gets for a quart of good potion".

Blind Sion had barely taken his seat at The Arms, when Master Peter Akin came flying through the door. It was all over town. The men hauling their nets in the Bridge pool had seen the cart come down the track from

Temperance Lloyd: Hanged for Witchcraft in 1682

Torrington with Temperance Lloyd sitting on a sack of grain, her head held high for all the world like a queen going to be crowned.

"Temperance be come back, acquitted. Justices say she be not a witch. Borough Justices have her still lodged in Church of All Hallows over East-the-Water. Carter brought the papers to them, but they be keeping her safe till William Hebert the Younger come to give his account".

It was another three days before Temperance was allowed to walk free to her own home. Susannah was one of the last to hear the news. She believed that once Temperance was taken off to Exeter she'd likely be gone for good. Temperance had been warning for months that with all the talk in town of bewitching they had best be careful in their work. Susannah and Temperance went out alone, each visiting on her own, returning home separately by night to eat together. Poor Mary still wanted to follow Temperance everywhere. They would send her back home, but she would hide round a corner and run to catch up to them once they were far from the house. With Temperance gone up to Exeter, Mary-Mary kept trailing along beside Susannah, taking side trips down every drang to chase cats. She could see no reason why she shouldn't let a cat into their cottage. How could a cat be any danger to them? She would say over and over,

"Cat's a cat. Woman's a woman".

Temperance often said that for a simple soul Mary knew more truth than those credited with more sense. Susannah was down by the bread oven when she heard that Temperance was back. She knew it was best not to show any interest by asking any questions. They'd wait till Temperance came home to hear what had passed up Exeter. She told Mary to stay in too. Told her,

"Don' 'ee do nought or e'll be sent up Exeter too".

It was no good. Mary didn't know what going to Exeter meant. No sooner was Susannah busy in the back kitchen than Mary-Mary was off down to the Market. Temperance was there. Mary ran home fast eager to tell Susannah.

" 'Er said twas warm in there. Warmest 'er's bin in a long time. Gived 'er good food, too. Bread, an' carrot stew. Bits o' meat in it an' all".

Susannah looked doubtful.

"Mary, Mary, when will 'ee learn? Temperance — 'er's got 'er pride. Make best of anything 'er would. And 'e... wouldn't know truth if un up and bit yer on yer backside".

Mary-Mary stuck her chin out.

"Us bain't deaf, Sue. Us 'eard what 'er said down market. Stood right by 'er, by Jimmy 'Earne's stall waitin' for sprout leaves from bottom of pannier afore 'e closed up".

Susannah wished Mary had the sense to wait for Temperance to tell all inside their cottage. Still. What's done is done. So where had Temperance been held since her return?

"Twas over East-the-Water lock-up. Left 'er a good sack to sleep on. An' a candle to pray by. 'Er went up t'Exeter in a covered cart. Come back in 'un too. After Justice said 'er didn't do nought wrong. 'Earne gived 'er a bit o' 'Og's Pudding for 'er tale".

Susannah shakes her head.

"More like for want of 'er tail when Mistress 'Earne be gwain out packin' cart".

Mary just looks blank, her mouth open so wide she could catch flies. Then she said,

" 'Earne says 'er's a witch just the same. Says 'er told 'e 'er flied off with the Devil be nights".

"Us collect 'er did say same to us. Past winter twas. Drunk 'er Capon's Taile broth afore bed. So sleepy 'er was 'er fell straight asleep. All winter us all bin slep' with 'er feather bed atop of us gainst the cold when fire be dead. There betwixt us 'er was when us went asleep. An' 'er was there when Rectory cock crowed dawn and woke us up. Iffen 'er'd bin gone off anywheres 'er'd woke us up. Capon's Taile brew makes dreams come real".

"Or real come dreams".

"'Ow many times do us 'ave to tell 'ee. Cease yer foolish talk, Mary-Mary. Yer tongue'll be the death of us all".

Susannah tried to be patient, telling herself that Mary-Mary was "soft in th'ead from birth".

She tells Mary the talk of witches is getting louder in the town. Acquitted or not, Temperance being taken by the Constables would mean trouble and more trouble for them all. They had to be careful for their lives.

"Folk'll think we'm friends of a witch and no good ever come from that. Stay alone. Leave cat alone. For to be safe".

Susannah has been alone with Mary long enough. Mary won't stop arguing. She sounds deceptively cogent on one of her better days.

"Did good down market, us did. Got they sprouts, us did. Good boil-up 'em made too. Didn't see Sue Edwards turn 'er nose up at 'em. If 'e be so fussed, go 'eself Saturday".

"Aye, us'll go ... So soon as 'ee comes up from Appledore and bring us firewood dry enough to burn without smeechin' us out th'ouse".

"Us near slipped down wet mud into the river. Twas 'e let a great mess of river mud in us boots. Take days to dry 'em out, an' us gwain barefoot till then".

Susannah prays God for patience.

Temperance Lloyd: Hanged for Witchcraft in 1682

"Tis a short walk down market, an' folk gives us more for bein' barefoot. An' Temperance, 'er'll 'ave warm toes, warm all over 'er'll be when 'er's standin' on the dry wood up County, less they 'angs 'er first. An' us'll be 'anged with 'er if us bain't more careful being seen with 'er. An' with that cat".

After days of early Autumn mists, beams of bright sunlight reflect from the ale-pots on the stained tables at The Arms. Though he doesn't see the reflections, Sion feels the changed mood of the folk around him, the talk, the whispering, as if folk were afraid, uncertain what to think of the acquittal at the Assizes.

"Rector, he'll be preaching the evil of witchcraft once a month after Trinity. Temperance'll be back listening to him come Sunday. See what he says to that. Praise be. Susannah'll be glad to have her back to help look after tother one".

The Fair brings many more strangers to Bideford, carters fighting each other to make good speed on the track from Crediton.

"Much merriment around yere today. Pushed benches all back into the far corner for the floor to be clear for the tumblers to turn and fly. Players they be down from London town, speech so pretty they could be in the royal court, not like the pageant players from Crediton. Great shire horses pulled the long cart that stands out Th'Arms yard, be stabled now out back so they be. Since the new King come back, bands of players come to gift us with their acts. Full garbed as men of old Scotland George says they be, save one that's in a woman's apron squeaking his part, as they prance and prattle on the cart become a stage. They say their play tells of a murderous Scottish king, and there be three witches. Master Browning makes a laugh of that, tells them we got our own three witches just a step away up Top of Old Town, and a law to murder them if it comes to that. They would have none of it. These be Scottish witches from days of yore, not real witches alive today. I tell them ours be just poor women, one of them accused but acquitted by the Lord Justice up County the year past. This ain't the wilds of Scotland, not now, not then. Pray God never".

"Amen to that", George mutters.

Sion can still see trouble coming,

"Temperance be back home acquitted, though folk don't put much stock by what they Justices up county said. The witch-hunts wax stronger over in Somerset, so short a journey across the moor. The fervour for the hunt be getting closer by the week".

The seamen on the quay had other fears, worse things to worry over. Empressment to service in the navy was starting again, despite the law against it. Young Peter from East-the-Water burst through The Arms door with bad news. While clearing the bottles from the Captain's table aboard the Charity, he'd found the letter with an official seal. Master Jeffries read it off to the assembled crowd,

> "We have formed our orders for impressing mariners under the old Act and will put them into execution on the north side of Devonshire, about Bideford, Appledore and Combe, where he assures us there are many mariners".

"Oh right that be. There be many, many mariners. Well, Bideford be that busy with all the trade. Master Browning, not wanting to lose his crew setting for the Banks the morrow, ran out soon as he heard it. Him and Master James was off to every ale-house, Master Browning running all over town, Master James over the bridge to East-the-Water. Gave out word of the press gangs. Sent the crews scattering off down the woods that fast, didn't it just. Join the boat off Appledore at dawn they will. Do as they been told. Paid as they been promised. Nice bit of extra that".

CHAPTER SIX
1670-1680

"...there still contiues such a drought as has hardly ever been known in England" (Evelyn, 1677)

The Constable turned the rusty key to open the lock-up early that morning. The river sparkled like polished silver in the brilliant sunshine from the bridge down to Appledore woods. Temperance walked back on the bridge from the lock-up, stopped by the quay, looked down river, then set off up the High Street to the market.

"Such a good day twas when I climbed back up High Street. Well, any day would seem good to me, being free and alive, wouldn't it though. My how folk stared to see me. Folk that always crossed over the road lest their skirts should touch mine, men that held their hats over their faces lest I look into their eyes, now raised them to me. Oh, they all wanted to speak to me that day. Come right up to me.

"'Ow be doin Mistress Lloyd?"

"So ye be back 'ome, us see?"

"As if they cared. Hearne left Mistress Hunt to find her own tatties, so as to ask me what happened up county. Give me a nice piece of Hog's Pudding just to keep me there. Mistress Hearne come back. Told him to send me on my way. Looked at me jealous-like, she did. As if ... As if ... Mary-Mary was by the pannier looking to get left over greens".

Temperance went to walk home with her, but Mary was off up the hill running like a hare in a storm.

"Never mind. Twas a day to go down the woods to sit in the path-fields, eat some of me pudding, maybe watch the boats come in on the evening tide".

Temperance savoured the warm sun on her face, the sight of the sparkling river, the smell of fish by the quay. Mary-Mary would let Sue know she was back.

"Pity to waste the day. Got groats for my trouble in my pocket. Can buy a bap and have coin left".

She walked down the quay through the dark woods to the sunny path-fields. She sat down in the grass, smelling the golden rod, the wet driftwood and seaweed on the rocks below. She fell asleep in the warmth of the sun, to the sound of the breeze in the grass. She slept peacefully till the chill of the shadows awakened her as the sun set behind her. Time to go home.

It was dusk when Temperance strolled up Coldharbour to the house. Susannah was standing at the door.

"She couldn't wait to ask why they'd let me free. I told her I was found innocent, not but what twould have done me much good less the Judge had his wits about him. Will the Younger showed himself a liar. Confused he was. And confusing. Said he were there by the bed when the old man died. Then said he was not there when the old man died. And for sure he got the old man's heritance. When she did hear that, Mistress told Constables she was mistook about the magpie. And that cat, it was seen to come from neighbour, Johns the Saddler. Got a cat against rats in the saddle soap, he do. Nothing to do with me, nor with any".

Susannah looked at Temperance with disbelief in her eyes, her head on one side. Temperance told her again,

"We know we do nought wrong. We still got to watch Mary-Mary's tongue though. So much talk up the County about witches. Even rich folk with schooling in the City come to believe it. They do so. We must go about our work careful like".

She was back home again. Temperance knew she should be happy. She had her freedom.

"I'm said innocent by a Lord Justice himself and those Jurymen honest and true. Makes no difference back here in Bideford. If the Lord Himself and a jury of angels said me not guilty, once the tongues start to wag, they just keeps goin'. Have to be careful. Susannah knows it too. She's happy to work without me. Mary-Mary, she's another matter. Too simple to see we must take care. Don't see she must leave the cats be. And her tongue, too simple she be to keep that still. Can't let her go down market, have to get her right home after church. Poor Mary-Mary. I pray the good Lord for patience and kindness, but tis hard".

Temperance Lloyd: Hanged for Witchcraft in 1682

They were soon back to their work, picking the leaves, drying the flowers, keeping the seeds. September came and went with the weather still warm into October.

"We were wakened just as we settled down the night. Mistress Jannings started her pains. Her first it is. Wanted for me to come. I sent Susannah. No need for me to go. Sue knows what to do".

Temperance didn't want to be seen in the town that day. She'd seen the "Phillip" sail in on the evening tide from Virginia and tying up across the river at East-the-Water.

"Edmund Prickard, her master, was friend to my Mr Lloyd, here and over in Port Tennant. Drinking together they were many nights. No need to stir old tales. He don't need to know I'm still here and living in the same house. Might give him cause to gossip. Best to let the dead sleep. Heard tell he thought to get himself one of them grand new houses down Bridgeland Street. Praise the good Lord, he changed his mind. Down market I heard Beatrice from The Arms talking to her cousin, Gilly, that's parlour maid down the Granville House. Gilly's sister be wed to Master Prickard's brother. Gilly heard tell that Master Prickard be indeed building a fine new house for hisself. He be not building in Bideford nor in Bristol where he has two other boats. Oh no. Master Prickard's house, well they call it Rooms, be over in the Newfoundland. Fine harbour and many Devon men there. No word if his Mistress in Bideford knows of his doings over in St John's town. St John's, such a godly name for men to live in such iniquity as we do hear of. Still, if tis true he'll not be tied up so much over East-the-Water. None of my business what Master Prickard be up to, but further away he be, the better for me. Dreamed of my man I did again last night. Saw him rising from the river, dripping with the stinking black mud".

The week of fine warm days at the start of that October was too good to last.

"All good things lead us back to despair. Keeps us humble for the good Lord. All of a sudden it seemed, winter was on us".

It was such a bitter cold season, that hung on till April. The swedes the women left to keep in the wood ash soil out the back garden didn't keep. They froze into tasteless striped flesh, hard to cut, slow to boil, and no good to eat.

"The garden herbs, rue and sage – even the rosemary bush growing against the privy wall that's lived through every winter I've been yere – they all started to die off".

The wild herbs down the riverbank were white with hoar frost even under the noon sun, limp and dead when the frost was off. The women were left with nothing to pick for decoctions to help the townspeople and merchant seamen against the winter ills.

67

Soon it was hard to get water. They had to break thick ice to pull water from the shallow well even at full noon. The ferns that shade the holes left in the bricks of the well wall for butter and cream – not that the three women ever had butter or cream those days – froze to black limp strands. By February they could draw no water from their well and had to go down to fetch town water. The Well-Master often turned them away from the square fearing the water would be bewitched and turn bitter. Temperance being found innocent didn't stop the rumours of witchcraft flying round the town. The Well-Master said it was within his right to keep the women away from the well "lest the waters be soured if their faces be reflected in it". His smile belied his fear.

There was no point in arguing with him. If they protested and he fell ill, that would show them to be witches. He told them they could draw their water from the river, an open sewer, thick with excrement that flowed in daily from the drangs. There was nothing for it.

Across the broad street that narrows down to the cart track to Abbotsham, the Rectory stood hidden from townsfolk's prying eyes behind a row of tall Holme Oaks and Yews. If not for the trees, the women could have thrown a stone down into the Rectory well from their top window. It was a well so deep it never froze, with a fine strong pump. It was good water, sweet water. The Rector surely would give the women leave to take a little water. Susannah and Mary went to ask at the back door as befits their station. The manservant told them to get their water from the town well, and if not, from the river. Susannah curtsied, thanked him and went home.

On Market Days, the Rector and his wife always rode off in the trap to Saint Mary's. The country folk on their way to market stopped by the Church to make their confessions to the Rector, leaving some produce for his trouble. At the same time the Rectory servants went off with their baskets to get meat at market. The women took their chance to fetch water from the Rectory well.

Temperance stood by the bend in the road. If the servants came into sight she would wave to Susannah who was keeping watch by the street while Mary-Mary crept down the back lane, with a bucket hidden under her cloak, to draw water. They knew that Rectory water was only for the Rector and the Constable could take them in for theft. But with their well frozen, and Well Master on watch, what can they do. Mary-Mary doesn't see why she has to be so careful.

"Rector, 'e won't 'ave us charged. 'E be a Christian gentleman bain't 'e? Tis on'y water".

Such innocence. Temperance shakes her head and looks at Susannah.

Temperance Lloyd: Hanged for Witchcraft in 1682

"Mary, Mary-Mary. When will you learn girl? Rector is a man. Tis his work to be Rector of a Sunday. Well, and on funerals and festivals. He's not one of those Popish saints. He be not truly Church good neither. Be careful what you says for pity's sake. Careful mind".

Susannah nods.

"'Er be right Mary. 'Er knows. 'Er knows lots. 'Er's canny".

"Rector be a good man, bain't 'e? 'E won't do nought to us".

Temperance rolls her eyes,

"Have to watch Mary-Mary don't get too bold, Sue. Just ye collect, keep careful watch on her".

She tells Mary again,

"Even if Rector be good... Can be all sorts of bad things in them Yew trees. Devilish plants them yew. Stay behind 'em, Mary-Mary. Devil might be up Parsonage Close of a dark night. Day time too. Don't ye be going over there for water less we be with thee. Right?"

*****

Sion listens to the woman drinking scrumpie.

"Mam said it was really cold those last years the women some said were witches lived in Bideford. We had it cold too while Da was away doing the War work. I remember our well froze up and the sprouts went black in the garden. Didn't matter about the well. Our house had a tap in the back kitchen. Still one cold year, the pipes froze. A man from the Council had to come and help us get them melted. Mam wrapped rags round the pipe to keep them warm after that. They sent a water cart down the quay for people to take buckets for water. The rich people in the big house on Bridgeland Street said it wasn't good enough. They didn't get enough water for their hot baths. My Mam said they were lucky to have hot water taps and baths every day. We only had the one tap and the kettle on the hob to boil the water. I used to think about those poor women some nights when it was too cold in bed to get to sleep. And then, of course, I would dream about them in their little house up Top of the Town".

*****

Temperance is working in her back kitchen putting dried feverfew into a jar of the icy Rectory water. She hears Mary-Mary talking to Susannah, asking the questions she'll forget the answers to, and will ask again next day. She'll be pointing towards the scullery. Out of sight out of mind, Mary thinks Temperance can't hear her.

"Sue, be it true 'er can talk to spirits?"

"What be sayin'?"

"Down quay of a night. Us 'eard 'er talk to them seamen, they from away. 'Er talks funny. Says 'er prayers funny too".

"That be Welsh, you daft binny. 'Er comed from Wales fore 'er lived 'ere".

"Be that in the sky then? Like preacher say?"

"Just crost the water. Over Wales".

" 'Ave 'ee bin over there?"

"Nay. 'Er comed on a boat, married 'er was then".

"Where'd 'er man go?"

"Down Saint Mary's graveyard. Died drunk in the river. 'Er got th'ouse though".

"Oh".

It was a lot for poor Mary's brain to take in. By time Temperance was done with her herbs, Mary had fallen asleep. Later in bed beside Susannah she woke up. Temperance heard her whispering,

" 'Arry down market said as 'er witched 'er man in't river. 'Er did'n, did 'er?"

"Nay. 'E felled in drunk all of 'is own. 'Er b'ain't no witch. An' you be careful what you listen to. An' what you'm saying. They'm out there looking for witches. Pedro as come down on London Coach, 'e says there be trials all over. No way to get off. If 'ee be called for a witch, 'ee be done for. Don't 'ave to be with a man when 'e dies to 'ave killed un. Don't ave to do nought. Iffen Constable come for 'ee, you'm gwain to 'ang".

"Constables took 'er in afore "...

"A year past. 'Ee collect "...

Mary-Mary had a hard time recollecting what happened last week, let alone a year back.

" 'Er was let go without charge. 'Er was lucky. Justice 'ad 'is wits 'bout 'im. They said 'er turned 'erself into a cat".

"Like my black cat 'ere?"

Temperance heard Susannah sigh.

"Mary, Mary, yer tongue'll be death of us all. B'ain't yer cat. Us don' 'ave no cat. Us don' never 'ave no cats. Cats be bad to 'ave round th'ouse. Temperance be right, Mary-Mary".

"Mary-Mary starts to snivel, then goes into howling. What will become of us if she won't stop her foolish talk".

Sion sits closer to the fire up at The Arms. He pulls his cloak tighter around him.

"Seems like the world be going to freeze us all to death. Four year now winter come early, stayed late. Such cold. Janna that works up Rectory say the privies the poor folk use up the Rectory when they come to see Mr

Temperance Lloyd: Hanged for Witchcraft in 1682

Ogilby, they be all froze up from Christmastide to nearly Easter. Told her sister, Beatrice who be serving maid here. So much cracking and booming of the beams at night, some folk say tis omens from the Devil — bad things to come. Frost breaking right to the cellars in the big houses souring the wine. Never felt nothing like in all the years I been sat yere. More than a century, and such cold as this I never seen. Just hope twill change before my time is up. Oh, tis alright for me. Always a fire in the grate in The Arms. Landlord he knows how to bring folk out of the cold and in to the snug, don't he just. Always warm over the almshouse of a night too".

Sion has a kind heart.

"Feels for them three poor women up Top of the Town, I do, living on less than nothing. Farmers got nothing to spare for them come market day. Nothing for 'em to boil up to make the cures. Wood froze fast to the ground down Appledore way. Find 'em froze in their beds they will — if ever any take it in mind to go look".

One cold year followed another, too cold for the women to sleep upstairs, too cold to lie alone. Another October came in cold and snow is on the ground before Christmas. They had to keep warm as best they can. They dragged the horsehair pad and Temperance's married featherbed down the narrow staircase straight after the September neap tides. They stacked what wood they have tight in the grate so it'll burn slow and long and put a bit more wood on the hob to dry for later.

"The nights draw in so fast come Michaelmas, fast as them grow long come April. We got no moneys for candle tallow. Soon as dark falls we lie to sleep head to feet by the fire, all under the featherbed. Nothing we do can warm us against cold so deep".

The fire fades, then dies, in the night. The wind blows in under the door driving rain, or snow, into the room. The curtain behind the door soaks up some of the wet in October, till November frosts make it too stiff to keep out the draft. The dark hours pass.

"We hunch our bodies tighter and tighter against the cold, pulling the feather bed around us. Mary-Mary pulls it all round her tiny body. We pull it back to share it".

Temperance tucks Mary's share round her. Hour by hour, their muscles stiffen and grow sore. They take turns to try to keep the fire going. It never lasts till dawn. They can scarcely move for the pain by sunrise. Temperance brews the herbs to bring sleep against the cold. She tastes the brew as it steeped.

"Have to be sure tis good. Makes me that sleepy my legs scarce bear me to my place on the floor between Mary and Sue. Tis so cold for us lying together. Apart we'd have frozen. Colder to get out from under the cover at our midnight waking. Have to try to sleep till winter dawn no matter how late she come".

*****

Sion sometimes wonders why God had not taken the three women peacefully of a night in that cold decade as He took so many later in the Second War. Poor folk in Bideford in that War lived not much differently from Temperance. Maybe that's why he listens intently to the woman who seems to remember them too. He thinks perhaps she really does, though that's a foolish notion. All the old cottages were cold and damp, but in the War at least there was running water and the schools were warm.

"I used to run off to get to school before the other girls to sit on the radiators in the cloakroom, warmest place in the world in the War. Those poor women ... I was so much better off than them. Food every day, hot tea for breakfast. Mam sent me to bed every night with a potato hot off the ashes to warm my hands and send me to sleep".

Sion smiles as she talks about the potatoes. He's back in 1675.

*****

"Winter passes. Another seems to start, too soon, each colder than the one before. Hard to collect the summers much. The year past, snow fell in January, stayed on the ground in shaded places till the end of March, Eastertide. Bart says the tide down Westward Ho! leaves ribbons of salt ice high on the shore sparkling in the noonday sun. That would be a sight to see. Well for me anything would be a sight to see, would n't it just. Then at low tide there's barely any cockles on the Appledore sands. Ice clings to the piers of the bridge for months on end. It freezes the mussels in their shells and kills off the seaweed that's good Welsh food".

"Oh, I do still love laver. Grows as good down the bottom of the Bideford slipways it do as ever it did on the seawall of the Swansea Mission. Sue and Mary-Mary wouldn't eat it when I cooked it first time. Said twas grass, for cows not people. Funny how starvation bends the mind. They soon got to like the taste. Brought the colour to their cheeks it did. No use now. These winters the icy river tides turn the laver from green to slimy brown. It stills boils black. Looks right, but eating of it brings on the vile sickness".

Summers came cold and damp. Then there was drought. Sion hears the dismal news.

"Crops failing all up and down the countryside. Crops fail. Cattle die. Nothing much up the market. Only them with good moneys can pay the prices. What reason? We do nought to offend the good Lord. Can't say about them folk up London way".

For a whole decade unseasonable weather caused the crops to fail.

"Failing for years now they been, bad year after bad year. Folk be asking what's to blame. Say their prayers. Don't do no good. Don't dare blame God. Be blasphemy to do that. Some turn to pray to the Old Gods. Best the Rector don't hear of it. Folks ask what is it makes the weather so bad, the crops to fail? Must be witchcraft. Look for the witch. Round here they thinks they don't have far to look, just up Top of the Town. Talking about poor Temperance and her friends they are".

Anyone can be accused.

"Up Barnstaple way just a month past, a man refused alms to an old woman on the road. He was took that night with the palsie. Can't speak nor walk for all he tries. Old woman must've been a witch. Folk say she overlooked him, she did, wished him evil. Getting the same everywhere it is".

Superstition flourishes with great encouragement from the doctors.

"A new one of them is come to town they tell me, Chartered Physician he be just like Dr Beare. Not that they knows much, truth to tell. If they cures, or if they don't cure, tis much by chance. When folk die with the treatment, tis by chance. When folk live by the cure, tis honour to the Doctor. And they do need good custom to live in the big houses down Bridgeland Street and buy fancy gowns for their good wives for the Harvest Ball. Can't afford to have their cures be seen to fail. And death comes to all betimes and whose to say the good soul gone to rest had not been bewitched? Better still if he been bewitched by that same old woman whose herbs had done more good than the physician's leeches. Pass on the blame and rid the town of a better healer. Save the doctor's good name, make the doctor good money. Come to pass these days that any man that wants can blame any misfortune he cause himself on bewitching. Name the witch and have the Constable make arrest. Asking round the square will bring forth rumours, gossip, tales of such nonsense as make the minstrels' tales seem commonplace. A little say so will put another poor soul on the list sent up to County Sheriffs for trial next Quarter Assizes. So easy tis, and so good for the towns. Another old pauper taken off the rolls by the Court with no burial cost to the Parish for graves beside the County gallows".

Despite the cold and drought, Bideford Town was too busy with so much shipping, too rich with all the trade, to be overly concerned about witches. Temperance had been acquitted and the women went about their work. The danger though was coming closer. Justice Hale with his determination to rid the country of witchcraft was just over the moor in Somerset. Temperance and Susannah were too busy surviving to listen to rumours. Winter always has to end some time and April should bring spring rains. It doesn't. Drought goes on to summer. There's nothing to eat in the women's garden. The woods are too dry for Temperance even to find mushrooms.

"Who knows what the cause be of it all. So much talk round town of weather witching. What must the Good Lord that sends the rain and sun make of that? And the wells so low the water sours and makes folk sick. Doctors don't learn that in their schools. Nothing for it in their quackery. They gives the sour water to the sick to cure them of the sickness they do. And the new doctor be worse than Dr Beare for blaming lives lost on magic and charms".

Temperance and Susannah keep on working as best they can, trying to avoid customers who use the physicians. People still need help with births and with laying out the dead. Susannah serves Mistress Coleman. She gets paid when the Master's ship is in port if they can catch him. They take turns sitting down the quay to watch for his boat coming in. He has ten or more ships to his name now, six in Bideford and more down Plymouth.

"Hard to know which boat he sails himself unless we see him in the town, or hear he be in the ale-house. He'll try to set sail again before he pays, sneaking across the river in a dory to board his ship so we don't waylay him on the bridge. Other folk be waiting to be paid too. Folk like John Coleman get rich that way".

Weeks go by with little for the women to eat.

"Nothing to pick and sell. Not too many asking our services. Have to scavenge the alleys, crawl through the filthy waste water in the drangs, for bits. Only difference twixt winter and summer be tis not so cold in June. Still damp though".

Sometimes they get lucky, like the day Temperance walked up Upcott Lane, thinking to find wild strawberries up at back of the farm.

"Found apples, many as I could carry by the old orchard wall. Fell right off the tree they had and ripe enough to eat. Took 'em home. Saved some for us and said to Sue and Mary as we can sell the rest in town".

Mary-Mary was so happy.

"If us goes stand with 'ee, us can 'elp 'ee".

Susannah knows they shouldn't be seen together in public with all the talk of witchcraft in the town. Mary-Mary doesn't see it. She wanted to go so badly, she started to snivel and moan. Sue gave in.

"Long as ye'm careful Mary. Watch who 'ee sells to. Do what Temperance tells 'ee".

Mary trots along happily by Temperance's side to find shade to sit by the Harbour Master's shed. Temperance had polished the apples and set them in the old trug they used for collecting wild herbs and carrying goods from market.

"Laid them apples careful-like on a piece of blue silk we found behind the Talbot. Covered over the missing and splintered slats nice it did. Red apples looked so pretty with the blue".

Temperance holds out an apple to those who walk by.

"Apples to buy. Pretty apples. Want one, dearie?"

They sold two for a groat each. Then a boy came skipping along with his mother.

"Just up and took one he did".

Temperance was up and after him. She called out to him,

"Boy! Put that back till tis paid for. Boy, get back yere",

He started to run. Temperance caught the woman's skirt. The woman took the apple from the boy, tugged her skirt free, and started walking away, shouting at Temperance,

"Ye stole them first. Ye should give them away".

"Don't ye tell me how to be. They're mine to sell. Thine to buy. Give me a groat".

The woman throws a penny.

"Here".

She starts to walk on, shouting at Temperance

"Old witch".

Mary-Mary repeats,

"Old witch, old witch, old witch".

Temperance jabs her elbow into Mary's ribs. Mary rubs her side and starts to cry. The boy puts his tongue out at them. Temperance lets them go, calling out,

"Little devil".

No sooner was Temperance seated again, than the Harbour Master came out and moved them on. He didn't recognize Temperance.

"Don't know me no more, though I be widow of his dead Scalesman and living free in a harbour cottage".

They cross over the road to the quayside, dodging between the carriages that fly up to the bridge from the Pill. They can try to sell to the seamen.

Temperance looks to see Mary-Mary is still with her with her mouth even further open than usual. She's gazing up at a man on the lower deck.

"Temperance, what that?"

"Tis a man. Just a man".

"Nay, can' be. 'E'm brown, near black. Be'm dirty?"

"Nay. He's from away over sea. Like all the people in the Indies. Used to see a lot of them back in Wales, come over all the time they did".

" 'E be a man? A man, not the black devil?"

"Nay, Mary. The Devil ain't black. They do say as he wears black".

"Like they up there?"

Mary-Mary is pointing a skinny finger at the ship's Master standing on the upper deck. Temperance pulls Mary's arm back. She doesn't want to give cause for offense, or worse, to start rumours. The black crewman buys an apple. He makes a face as he bites into it.

Temperance smiles.

"Tis sweet, but not so sweet as the fruit from the Indies. Oh, that be sweet. I collect when my man come home with some back in the good days".

Mary-Mary laughs at the crewman. In the twilight Temperance sees a boat coming up river. It looks like the "Phillip" again. She pulls Mary-Mary away. Time to be off back home. They went back to Upcott for apples in the good years.

"Not much good any year for us, winters getting worse and worse, year by year."

"They had slept a lot in the winter till then but 1679 was the worst winter yet. Their swedes froze into the ground again. They tried to dig them out but there was only mush on the shovel. They picked some early to store in the back kitchen, but rats got right into the boxes.

"Rats got fat on our crop while we starved. This bitter winter followed hard on so many we could not collect any better".

Temperance and Sue decided once more to keep the Norse custom of sleeping through the winter again. For two months they slept night and day.

"Calmed our bodies with sweet brews to send away the melancholy. Better than freezing to death. Made bread go further too it did. Got up in March. Winds was still bitter cold off the river when we went down to beg on Allhalland St".

It was a terrible time. Between them Susannah and Temperance managed to eak out a living. Mary-Mary was always hungry. There wasn't much she could do to help. When summer did come, they picked what herbs and seeds and roots they could find to see them through. Many sick people still sent for them.

"Trusted us they did, as well they should. Mistress Wakeley could scarce leave her bed after her sixth was born. Too melancholy to move. Just wanted the dark to take her up. Wouldn't have the curtains open. Didn't want to see the child. Such a bonnie little scrap he was too. Kept him alive with a wet nurse from Appledore till the herbs took their effect. Brought her back to her right mind. So grateful she was. Kept sending good food over to us for a full year. Didn't have no idea how bad she'd been. Well, she wouldn't would she. When you'm out of your mind, tis hard to collect what happened"

With good food in their bellies they set out to clothe themselves. They scavenged clothes thrown out at the back of the big houses on Bridgeland Street and searched the Rectory bins.

"Lovely petticoats Rector's wife do throw out. Never think it to see the plain frocks she wears on top. Found good aprons back there after Ginnie the scullery maid got fat with child and was sent away. Got to have a clean-ish apron to wear on our calls. And calls we still had betimes".

Mary-Mary wanted to wear the good apron all the time. Temperance told her,

"Got to keep the one for best. Gentlefolk are none too fond of dust falling off us on their fine floors. Learned all about that when I was chambermaid over the Coach Inn. Keep the best for Sundays and visiting the grand houses up Bridge Street and down Bridgeland Street. Like you better for that they will. Pay us better too".

Temperance had her pride. She went to Saint Mary's church twice on Sundays and Feast Days, listened to the Rector, often wishing other folk would do the same. She curtsied to folk that thought themselves her betters. She sang sweetly to her Good Lord and prayed the weather would change.

In 1680 they thanked the Lord when the decade of cold ended.

CHAPTER SEVEN
1680

"Dorcas Colemen, his wife, has been a long time sick... And he ...sought far and near for remedy, (whilst he [John Coleman] was at sea)...(Deposition of John Coleman, July 1682) The said Doctor Beare did repair unto [Dorcas Coleman] and upon view of her Body he did say that it was past his skill to ease her of her Pains ... that she was Bewitch'd".

As the skies darken, Temperance runs up the High Street to get home before the rain that would soon start to fall.

"Tonight will see the storm come in over the bar on the new moon tide. Clouds so dark and flying wild cross the sky. Wild, wild wind blowing black air from the sea that's grey beneath but foamy with the white horses that leap so high one over the other fit to ride right round by Appledore and up river. Saw it this noon picking the cockles and driftwood down Westward Ho!"

Huge pieces of driftwood rode in on the high waves. She dragged three weathered branches back through the pathfields on a sheet of sailcloth tossed up on the pebbles.

"Some days a storm be a bit of good luck. Keep us warm for a while that will".

She had just thrown off her shawl when they heard loud banging on the door that sounded fit to break it open. Abigail, Mistress Coleman's maid, stood out there, her skirts flying up in the wind that drowned out the sound of her voice. It didn't matter. They knew what she was after. She wanted Susannah to come quick to her Mistress. Susannah took her cloak and would have been out the door, but Temperance said they should go together.

"Night like this, a woman alone could blow right off the bridge into the river, and Abigail be going only the one way".

Susannah was glad enough to have Temperance go with her. For many months past, she had been lying awake at night worrying about Mistress Dorcas Coleman, trying to think about what more she could do for her. She had been attending on Dorcas for several years by now. Temperance knew the score.

"Don't take no learning to see what's wrong and what can make her well again. Poor Dorcas be so taken in her mind with fear for her man when he's at sea, she makes herself sick. Longer he's gone, sicker she gets. Colour comes back in her cheeks with his boat coming back up river. And Master Coleman ain't like to help by staying longer in port. He don't want to stay his voyages even to help his wife. Would rather keep sending for Doctor Beare that do more harm and hurt than healing".

Against the fierce storm, the women had to hold together to stay on their feet once they were down the High Street and on Allhalland Street. It was worse on the bridge. Susannah held to the side rail. Temperance held on to her and Abigail held tight to Temperance. Their skirts and shawls billowed round them like sails flying over the Bar. Temperance prayed God that saved His disciples on the Sea of Galilee to save them from the Torridge.

On the East-the-Water side of the river, Mistress Dorcas Coleman lives mostly alone, just the maid, Abigail, for company.

"Slow-witted too is poor Abigail. Not simple like Mary-Mary, just slow".

Susannah has told Temperance about Dorcas Coleman's life. From her window of her chamber in the big white house so high on the East-the-Water hill, Dorcas can see the whole town, the Quay, the Bridge, the Town Hall and Saint Mary's Church. Bideford with its houses scattered on the western hill makes a pretty picture, but Mistress Coleman looks only northward down to the estuary where the Torridge meets the Taw and the sea past Appledore. Last night she watched the boat carrying her husband, John, off to sea on the ebb tide. All the while her John is away, Dorcas sits watching, worrying, waiting, all day, every day. When she can't sleep at night she gets up to sit and watch. She doesn't go to bed at all when his ship's due back on a dawn tide lest she miss the first sight of it through the morning mists.

"Reads the signs of the weather hour by hour, poor Dorcas does. When the lighthouse stands out clear on the headland, the rains will fly in on high winds with the turning tide. A mackerel evening sky foresees a stormy night. A red sunrise foretells a stormy day. Over and over she whispers to her self, 'Red sky at morning...' A red sky at night ... Her eyes don't see that".

Dorcas notices nothing that would calm her worry about her beloved John ... Slowly she lapses into sickness and sends often for Susannah to ease the pain. As they take off their capes, Susannah points out the picture on the back wall of the chamber. It shows Master Coleman so handsome in his Naval dress at his marriage twenty years back. He had money enough to pay a painter even then. Dorcas stands beside him, such a lovely girl, seventeen, slender, eyes bright with hope. He still cuts a fine figure as he walks down the hill to his waiting Merchant Ship, his calves so strong in his white hose, his good belly held firm by the brass buttons on his white waistcoat. Temperance remembers when she had first seen Dorcas walking the High Street.

"Mr Lloyd pointed her out. Said she was wife to the Master Mariner. Had an eye for a lovely woman had Mr Lloyd."

Susannah had warned her how Dorcas would be now, fat from constant sitting on her self-enforced watch over the river traffic, her face ashen pale from staying inside, her eyes peering out from the deep black circles that cradle them.

So many boats sailed out every day, armed merchant ships for the Newfoundland trade, the "Pearl", the "Crown", the "Pelican", pinnaces, barks, even caravels, colliers, sand barges.

"I knew them from Mr Lloyd's reports, see them as I go about my business. But Dorcas ... She knows every detail of their outlines. Through the densest mist over the bar she can tell the type of vessel when tis barely come into view".

Master Coleman's been gone down the river just one day. Tonight Dorcas sits looking for his return. She will sit waiting through his two month voyage. Her shoulders are hard and tensed, her jaw clenched, her cheeks drawn tight up around her eyes as she strains to see better. For a moment, her shoulders drop down a little. Then she puts a name to the returning ship that rides the heavy swell round the bend to safe harbour from the storm. In Dorcas's own private world every seaman that has not drowned, will one day drown at sea.

Susannah tells Temperance she has tried to reassure her of the normal ebb and flow of shipping. Temperance, widow of the Scalesman, knows the patterns well,

"Bideford be a sailing town, a merchant town, where men are become as at home in Virginia or on the Banks as they be down Appledore. Boats come and go, and come again. Most that call Bideford home port come back when the Harbour Master awaits them. Others leave with intent to anchor safe in another port".

Every month or so, more often in the winter months of bad weather over the Atlantic and the North Sea, the Harbour Master posts a notice of late return.

"Mr Lloyd nailed that sign some days. No need to go read it. Can tell by the wives with children clinging to their skirts down the quay leaning on the bollards. They watch the bend in the river as if their gaze would haul the vessel into sight. Betimes I wished my man would go to sea. Well, he did in the end didn't he".

Nothing will convince Dorcas of a reality different from the one in her head. Sitting at her window she can see further and know sooner what boats will arrive. Master Mariner John had thought to build the house on the hill with such a fine view as a comfort to his wife. She would see him soon as he was back home safe, and could entertain herself in his absence watching what went on in the town. Instead she watches her life away.

As soon as her man's ship disappears from her sight round the headland, she can think of nothing but his return. He tells her he'll be gone for several days to Bristol, sometimes a month or more to the Indies or the Banks. No matter. She starts to watch when he has barely time to board his ship. Temperance notices small notches in the wood that frames the rippled glass window. Susannah had told her Dorcas cuts a notch for every ship lost at sea. And what of them that return safely to the port? Dorcas neither notices nor remembers them.

From the Harbour scales, Temperance used to watch the boats sail out on the tides. She'd see the wives go home to clean house, wash clothes, store up food for winter, cook for the children. They spent their days happily enough, women's gossip, women's wisdom.

"Shame Mr Lloyd never left for the Banks".

These days, Dorcas never goes over the bridge, never wishes him farewell lest her word curse his voyage. She won't talk to the other wives in case she should hear bad news. She hardly sees her neighbours except for the few that have nothing to do with ships or cargo. She sits alone in her chair by the window.

Abigail tends the fire that burns day and night in the small fireplace. Nothing can warm away the sea-damp air that seeps steadily in through the window. Poor Dorcas grows stiff with the pain of rheumatism from sitting so tensely at her window. Her jaws clench into toothache. Her head aches from the strain of squinting at the horizon. She feeds herself on feverfew leaves poked into small chunks of bread. After a while that has no effect.

"Susannah says she needs stronger medicines, the kind we can make for her. Abigail is so often sent to find Susannah she can find her way to us at dark of midnight if need be. More and more it need be. Doctor Beare charges thrice to take the trap out after dark and Dorcas don't want his hurting cups and weakening leeches".

All seasons, Abigail walks down the hill to the path by the warehouses, across the bridge, along Allhalland Street and up the High Street. She's learned to skirt around the dozen or so ale-houses that lie between the Salterns and the women's house. A Spanish seaman's rough embraces pulled her wits together and taught her caution. She always knocks on the door of Temperance's cottage and says her message in a voice flat from repeating it all the way.

"Mistress needs a broth for to sleep". "Mistress wants a cordial for her stomach". "Mistress has the ague". "Mistress says come right away to her".

"So often, too many times to count, I helped Susannah put up a cold decoction of valerian root — Capon's Taile, as Master Gerard calls it — to help poor Dorcas sleep through the pain of her stiff joints. Or Sue would prepare a warm elder-flower broth. In early summer, she picked fresh linden flowers that hung over the Rectory garden wall and simmered them for just three minutes over the fire in the Coleman's bedchamber. Three minutes, no less, no more, for perfect taste. I'd taught Susannah to count it tapping her fingers".

Mistress Coleman had her husband pay Susannah well for the services, when she could catch him at home, enough that they could get bread and strong beer and mutton those weeks Temperance wasn't paid. Temperance had taught Susannah how to make the herbs into physics for Dorcas. The night she first went with her to attend at the Coleman house she saw Susannah's real healing skills.

"She had other powers she must've been born knowing, or learned in her life afore I met her. I saw the patience, her gentleness. I knew nothing of that till this night. Oh, she'd said Mistress Coleman was difficult. She knew how she suffered from missing her man so much. If he would only leave his ships to go to sea without him, Dorcas would grow well. Sue did never say how hard she had to work to try to help her. Me, I should have found reason not to go. Or I'd have told that Master Mariner it was he that made his poor wife sick of the worry. Told him, I would have, he should count the cost of his poor wife's sickness against the coin got from riches of the Indies. That night I watched Susannah in wonder ... Her speech still rough from the farms that bred her, yet her ways — gentle as the spring sun. That face disformed by the beating a dozen years past hid a gentle soul. Her attendance healed the Mistress's melancholy as the potions healed her ague and rheumatics. She kept her too from greater worries".

The daily routine of Sion's life, the short walk from the Almshouses up Higher Honestone to The Arms in winter, or down to the quayside of a summer afternoon to smell the cargoes being carried off the boats, was always sweetened with the seadog's tales.

"Me oh my, the tongues wag this night, they do. Making a proper feast of news off the boat tied up this dawn. Master Browning come back from fishin' the Banks with much to tell. Fish so thick he fished with just a pail. Told tall tales of fish and yet taller tales of men".

As soon as they come in, the men haul benches from the walls to join the crowd gathered round Master Browning. He holds his ale-pot out for the refill to pay for his yarns of the distant land.

"Over Avalon, Devon men become Avalon men. Good winds take us new fast ships 'alf the time to sail the seas as most do think it. Thrice so fast as what they tell the wives that wait down Bideford. T'aint the crossing keeps they women 'lone at 'ome. Tis Devon men stoppin' down Cornwall way, takin' on new cargo. An' tis women, not nets, be took aboard for sailin' straight to Newfoundland. An' mark me words, there be Bideford seamen as 'as whole families over in that Pool Plantation — same time as 'em 'as families up Buttgarden Street. Well ... there be fish aplenty for two families".

Sion hears George Darracott sit himself down by the fire and order his ale. The new man had to ask what pot was his. George tells him to look for the initials scratched on the base. Master Browning called out to him to say as what he told be true.

"By me good ship "Resolution", Master Browning be right. Seen three of 'em this year past. Ties up me old "Delight" in the Pool there. Devon men they be for sure, fishin' off the Banks. This last month past, us seed one woman with child, tother at the breast. 'Er man be from Barnstaple, 'er from Plymouth. Standin' right there on the road by Calvert's Mansion House 'er were. Kirke and his lady lives there now".

"And do they wives over Avalon know of tother wives back 'ome?'"

"Nay, don't know nought. Thinks they'm honest wed. Not as 'em could do ought 'bout it. Nor want to. Why would 'em? Need their man, bein' so far from 'ome".

"Cousin Christopher now, 'e takes a score dozen pots from the pottery up Old Town, year in year out. 'E seed same over St John's town. Devon Planters 'ave rooms down by th'arbour all set up with wives and babes. Plenty of sea trade to keep two wives in petticoats. Believe me".

Sion does believe it.

"Oh aye, Bideford and Barnstaple men been always to and fro from the Newfoundland. Master Christopher had me sail there with him the once. Twas after an argument one summer night over the goings on.

Temperance Lloyd: Hanged for Witchcraft in 1682

Browning said if I'd a mind to sail again, there was a hammock on board Philip Greenslade's "Loyalty" lading up Barnstaple. Missed the sea I did, and well..."

The next day Sion had climbed down into a dory to be rowed out and up the Taw. Master Greenslade remembered Sion sailing with his father.

"Before the fall that took me sight, that was. Still the lad was kindly to me. My how good it felt, wind on me face, rough rope dragging through me hands gone soft from so long stroking me ale-pot. Brisk winds on summer calm seas had us past the Lizard before dawn. Aye, Master Browning told it true. Twas an easy crossing. Bare six weeks gone by when Newfoundland come into view of them with sight".

The "Loyalty" sailed past the St John's light, south to the Avalon on a July morning. Sion heard the anchor drop, folk talking on the harbour, seamen jumping down.

*****

A woman's voice breaks into Sion's reminiscences.

"Remember Avalon?"

"She's talking to her husband again. Well, not really. She's probably talking to herself. Women do. He's just sat there".

"That cold day, not like June, well it was June in Newfoundland. We knew it would be cold and wet".

The heavy rain had eased as they set off along the shoreline, heads down against the wind off the Atlantic. A light drizzle obscured the view of the Museum from where they stood out on the Pool. It was all there, though in 2009, "it" was mostly piles of gray stones linked by the old cobblestone road a foot or so below the level of the sandy path the visitors were standing on.

There was the "Mansion House", here the smithy, and the row of workmen's cottages standing back from the road. The excavated buildings were all hemmed in by lengths of string held taut by pegs. Archaeologists' tools lay around, trowels, sieves, hammers, blue tarpaulin sheets. Pieces of North Devon-Ware, bearing the typical Bideford designs, flowers, anchors, waves, jutted out of the earth around one of the cottages. .

"When I closed my eyes, felt the drizzle on my face, heard the waves hitting the old harbour wall, smelt the seaweed and the fishing nets hung to dry by the path, it was like I was back there, back then. With my eyes closed, I could hear the shouts and laughter of men carrying the barrels of fish from the boat to the village, the Colony, of Avalon".

"I just remember the rain, and hoping the coffee counter would be open".

"I saw the Mansion House as it was, such a grand place. I could walk in through the heavy oak door, smell whale oil from the lamps that hung from the low ceiling of the kitchen. I watched the cook, a solidly built woman wearing the apron frock of 1676, pull the long handled wooden paddle from the oven. A pretty red-haired young woman, she must be about sixteen, takes the loaves carefully from the paddle, a large rough woven cloth protects her hands. Faint steam rises from the round loaves. The smell of new-baked bread fills the room. The cook bends towards the iron kettle that hangs over the blazing wood in the fireplace that fills most of the east wall. She stirs the pot and steam rises from it carrying the smell of mutton and turnips. I hear sheep grazing up the slope. The door opens. Another serving maid comes in carrying a basket of eggs".

Then she heard the carriage wheels rattle along the cobble road from the causeway inland, the horses neighing as the driver pulls at the reins to stop by the door.

"Master be back from St John's". The voice is unmistakably Bideford.

"Aye. 'Ome again. And glad of it".

The man in the black woolen cloak speaks in a Scots brogue. Sion nods.

"Yes, I heard the Scottish Lord, back then".

The drizzle started working its way through the zip fastener of her jacket. Cold water dripping down her T-Shirt brought her back to the present. Then they heard another voice,

"Bring 'em back to the kitchen, Pat. Die of cold and wet out there 'em will. Us got the tea ready an' brade's comin' out th'oven".

This local woman of the twenty first century was dressed for 1676. The reconstruction kitchen was lit by electric light bulbs in lanterns. The bread smelled good.

"Made be th'old recipe", she told them.

They ran through the rain into the Museum.

"That was the best part. Seeing it all there, pottery from Bideford, all manner of supplies for the colony. And those drawers full of fragments of plates, bowls, serving dishes, mugs, all with nautical and floral designs, flowers that never grew over in Newfoundland, but lined the pathfields through Appledore Woods. Temperance's herbs and flowers".

There were binders listing the names of those Bideford Sea Captains, the boats they sailed, the manifests of the cargoes they carried. These were the men that came and stayed, those that sailed back and forth over the Atlantic, their ships and the cargoes they carried. Darracott, Browning, Smith, Gifford... "The Pearl", the "Pelican"... And they had families, New World families, and other families, perhaps, back in Bideford?

*****

"So men sat here in The Arms, got wrote down over Avalon in some Museum".

*****

Darracott is pleased to have such an audience. The number of families springing up on foreign shores grows larger and larger as he's plied with more ale and scrumpie,

"Tis not just fishermen with two hearths to warm their feet at. The new trade in port wine's more regular now, twixt Portugal and the Newfoundland. Pushthrough Island they goes to".

"Pushthrough ... tis a right name indeed for a man looking for a place to take a new young wench to a new warm bed in the New World".

Their work done that night, the women pull on their cloaks. Abigail brings them fruit cake for the dark walk home.

A month after her man has sailed, Dorcas barely sleeps an hour even with the potions. Susannah sits many nights holding her hand, stroking her brow. Back home after dawn she tells Temperance,

"Tis a false sleep poor dear be in, full o' dreams of storms, sinking ships, seamen drowning. 'Er 'ears voices of towns-folk tellin' over and over o' shipwrecks on the Banks. Tis 'ard listenin' to 'er screamin' at 'em to leave 'er be".

Dorcas can't drown them out. She wakes with her hands over her ears. Susannah gently takes the hands away from her ears, tells her the storm has passed over, gone up river from the sea.

Susannah knows their healing herbs will not work when given too long without a break. The nights she must refuse the potions Dorcas lies stiff on her bed, listening for the faintest sound of a ship grazing the side of the Quay after it rides a night tide silently up river. When a sea mist rolls in over the bar. She will catch the faint, gentle moan of the fog siren of a departing vessel far out the Channel. Her whole body has become a net of listening.

The pain that begins in her daily watch increases minute by minute through the hours of darkness. Lying still and straight hurts her back. When she turns on to her side, the pain shoots up between her shoulders. Susannah feels Dorcas's back. It is stiff and hard as iron. The more the poor woman attends to the pain, the worse it becomes, keeping sleep away. She wants so badly to sleep. If she does not sleep, she thinks to herself, she may nod off in the day. She might miss her man's vessel when it returns again from the Indies, if it should return... The more she fears losing sleep, the longer she lies awake.

Master Coleman comes home, only to leave again too soon for Dorcas. He takes his last drink at The Arms before he sails again to Avalon.

"Ebb tide the morrow shall take him off again. Tonight Master Coleman is whispering to Master Browning who's going on again about wives in other ports. Think I don't hear? Can't keep nought from old Blind Sion. Master Coleman is offering Master Browning two golden guineas to keep his tales unto hisself".

"My Dorcas, she's sick enough fretting o'er the tides. She don't need no fanciful tattle to trouble her".

"My, but for one so clever makin' money, Master Coleman b'aint too wise on other matters. No coin'll slow the travel of so good a tale in Bideford. Master Coleman should as well keep his purse sealed as place his guineas on Master Browning's tongue that sails on the dawn tide. Now Beatrice that serves us ale hears all the talk. She be sister to Abigail, maid to Mistress Dorcas. Tis Beatrice will be over the bridge afore Torrington farmers get to market, telling Abigail tis secret with her voice so loud the mistress can't help but hear it".

Whenever a storm blows in of a dark night, Dorcas will call out for Abigail. It's always the same. Poor Abigail, half asleep, will stumble into the room, hoping for once she will not be sent out into the darkness to fetch Susannah. Mistress Coleman knows better than to anger her man by sending for the Doctor who charges double fees at night. Abigail is slow, but even she knows that nothing but the Master's return will help her Mistress.

Susannah tries to get Dorcas to see she need not be sitting all alone so much. Despite her complaining she still has some friends and neighbours that do their best to comfort her as is their Christian duty — as Rector Ogilby preaches on a Sunday. It takes a great deal of Christian duty to listen to Dorcas's litany of her ailments. Her fears and troubles would try the patience of a saint.

Still, year by year, winter by winter, some wives of other merchants offer comfort. They repeat tales of miraculous survival in storms their husbands hear from the crewmen in the ale-houses. They tell her,

"Collect that wild stormy night when the Lord Protector died — God save the new King, may he live forever — no seamen drowned. And the year that followed, ships from the coast that washed on waves ten feet high into London itself were found safely anchored at dawn right by the Palace of Westminster. And collect when lightning struck three London steeples but missed the masts of the Fleet in the thunder storms back in '64".

They recall the panic when the "Elwood" had been declared lost with its hold of hops, the bells ringing out in the ports to call the citizens to

Church. The wives had prayed all week in Church till the ship arrived back safe with a grand tale of being trapped by ice in Hamburg port. Ships often survive furious storms that blows down houses.

"God, 'e watch over they ships as 'e do over all down 'ere",

Susannah tells Dorcas their words could do more good than potions if only Dorcas would listen. Dorcas just says,

"Sometimes. Maybe...", and turns back to her window to watch.

In the cold dark days of winter, a few townswomen will while away a dull afternoon in Dorcas Coleman's firelit chamber trying to make her see reason. They see it's pointless, but there is always good strong ale and cake filled with fruit and spices from foreign parts at the Coleman house.

In summer, the women can stroll the boardwalk showing off dresses of the finest silks and laces their husbands can find in far off lands. They have neither time nor inclination then to sit listening to the dark imaginations of the Master Mariner's wife. Only Susannah visits often, called on as much for her time and her listening as for her potions.

Temperance knows that however much Midshipman John Coleman pays, when they can waylay him to pay, their potions can do little to relieve the pain of the Mistress's self-enforced watch at her window. Nothing will calm her worry that her man will one day sail down river forever. Her life will be over when that happens. Her melancholy will not respond to infusions of black hellebore.

"Master Gerard wrote as summer blooms of meadow-sweet in wine shall make her heart more merry. All the meadow-sweet the Good Lord makes to grow down the pathfields cannot raise Mistress Coleman's spirits".

No matter how much Susannah ministers to Dorcas, the sharp pains all over Dorcas's body worsen as his ship sails out to sea. When she was younger, she recovered when with his return to port. No longer. As the years pass she just becomes less sick at his homecoming. Susannah's soul of patience takes her back over the bridge whenever Abigail calls for her. Temperance reminds her,

"Tis not right to use our potions to still the pain and sorrows when the causes be known to all that listen".

She tells Susannah they must try to speak more firmly to Master Coleman. Susannah says it will do no good. Mistress Coleman herself has asked him often,

"How can you leave when I am so sickly?".

As he takes his leave of Sion and the seamen up The Arms, Master Coleman mutters into his ale-pot,

"How can I stay with her when she is so melancholy?".

Master Coleman sits hunched over the fire. His poor Dorcas sits alone at home wishing him there. He spends more precious shore time in The Arms as time passes. Master Coleman grows more successful with each year, and richer with each cargo.

"Does well by the pottery trade. Can't get enough of Bideford Ware over there in Avalon, Cupids, St John's. Standing on the harbour they be just awaiting for his boats. Has his choice to take shorter voyages now. Some say he need not sail at all, with so many good men vying to guide his ships."

Still the Master Mariner chooses longer times at sea with cargoes that pay more and offer more respect. It cannot be denied his sailings to the Banks or the Indies offer release from the troubles of the fat, complaining woman he no longer recognizes as his lovely bride of twenty years ago.

"Darracott do say Master Coleman be smiling at the tales of men who take young wenches and leave them well-housed over Virginia or Avalon. Not that he would do it himself. Still..."

Susannah wonders too if Master Coleman stays at sea just to be away from Dorcas. She's heard the Mistress beg him over and over not to go. And Susannah says it's not as if they need the pay. Master Coleman has ships that sail for him under other masters. He could have a life at leisure, live with honour in a big house up Bridge Street. He could be Alderman, or Mayor. He could take over half the potteries in town. He could ...

"But 'e won't", Susannah says, "Don't want Bideford life. Loves the sea, 'e do".

Temperance laughs.

"Is it the sea he loves so much. Or be it the life in that other land over the sea with its pretty young wenches tending the men in fine new houses?"

Susannah tells her to cease such wicked thinking. Tells her not even to think it in the presence of Mistress Coleman.

"Poor Dorcas 'er 'ave plenty to worry on. Send 'er right out of 'er mind such thinking would".

In The Arms, Sion sits by window open to the evening breeze. Master Jeffreys is in tonight. He lives over East-the-Water down the hill from Master Coleman and Mistress Dorcas. It seems that on a hot summer days Mistress Jeffreys and her lady friends like to sit at the window sipping tea and watching the boats on the river. They enjoy even more watching Doctor Beare sweat his way up to the Coleman house. The tapping of the urine flask that hangs from his belt against his hip sounds his arrival and brings the ladies to their windows to stare as he struggles up the hill. His bone-tipped cane steadies him on the cobble walk by the wharves. The long gown that tells his rank and qualifications to practice physic weighs him down on a summer day.

"They do make sport of him, so 'ot he be. Minds 'is pennies do good Doctor Beare. Loath to pay the services of a driver in summer time".

Sion knows all about the good Doctor.

"Likes to keep his whole fee of one angel a visit, well, save when he be called out to Weare Gifford or Appledore. They say he do be known to refuse calls out there less family don't send the trap for him. Master Coleman moans to all that will listen about the cost of the doctor. And now Doctor Beare now wants him to hire a night nurse."

"Might be of more help than Abigail", he declares to Sion.

"Not to say, as some folk do, a nurse would help keep Mistress Coleman under the doctor's sole care".

Master Coleman pays the good doctor well. The more he pays, the more the doctor visits and the more he gets paid for his trouble. Dorcas would as soon not see him.

"Susannah Edwards does me better. She comes when I need her", she moans.

John loses patience,

"That witch woman from top of the town?"

Dorcas will have none of that.

"She be a good woman. Does me good".

"Not making 'er any better than the doctor for what I can see", Master Coleman tells Sion,

"Both of 'em just curing my purse of money".

Finally it seems the Doctor's patience gives out, or perhaps he too sees her intransigent fears for her husband's safety at sea are the real cause of her ailments. He tells Master Coleman, there's no more he can do.

"Says me wife be bewitched".

Sion almost chokes on his ale.

"Well, that'll start the tattle. And didn't it just. Mistress Coleman's maid, Abigail, be slow, but she knows a story that'll have all the townswomen listening to her up the market. When asked how her Mistress fared she knew that "Up and down. Most down" was of no interest. Bewitched — well that got quite a crowd round Abigail up market, didn't it just".

"Doctor say Mistress Coleman 'er's witched. Tis that Susannah Edwards. 'Er comes and gives Mistress magic. Last night cat come twice. Mistress be worse today. 'Er's so bad er can't move. Can't speak when Susannah's in 'er chamber. Mr Bremincom seed it. Us all seed it".

Rumour travels fast at the Tuesday and Saturday markets, faster at Matins in Saint Mary's Church where Temperance, Susannah and Mary stand with other paupers behind the carved and cushioned pews paid for by the town merchants and shopkeepers.

"Doctor Beare say Susannah Edwards be a witch. Don' 'ee look at 'er, case 'er witch 'ee".

Temperance knows they're in real trouble. The servants in the pews in front of the pauper seats kept their distance and more at the services on the first Sunday after Epiphany.

After matins the three women sit to eat their Welsh mutton stew, cawl as Temperance calls it. Susannah is worried about Mistress Coleman. Dorcas is getting more poorly after Doctor Beare cupped her and had the leeches on her.

"All makes 'er worse 'stead o' better, but 'e won't stop".

Cupping often produces bruises as painful as the stiffness it's supposed to cure. Dorcas has grown too weak to stand with all the blood lost from the leeches on her ankles. All those years she'd refused to leave her chair by the window. Now she's so weak she calls on Abigail to get her to her bed. Susannah is sorry for Dorcas, but knows what the talk is all over the town. Temperance tells her she must be very careful. Mary-Mary echoes,

"Careful. Very Careful".

Susannah insists she cannot abandon Dorcas.

"Mistress Coleman needs 'er potions. 'Er pays well. Where'd 'ee think us mutton come from? Us needs 'er pay".

Mary-Mary was slow, but not so slow she didn't see the malice in the faces of those who glared at them down the town these days. She has one of her rare moments of sense.

"So let 'er pay Temperance. Let 'em all pay 'er. 'Er'll share with us. 'Er's got off at th'Assizes. 'Er knows 'ow".

Temperance knows Mary could be right. But despite her occasional flashes of good sense, Mary-Mary still tries to follow Temperance or Susannah everywhere. Susannah has Temperance distract Mary so that she can get out alone to attend at the Coleman house. Temperance tries to persuade Susannah to stop seeing Dorcas, especially as Master Colemen becomes enraged when she asks for payment. He owes her for a whole month of her care, and potions, and tries to avoid paying Susannah and other town merchants by boarding his ship just before it weighs anchor. Sometimes he has young Will take the dory across the river to pick him up to avoid creditors that might waylay him on the bridge.

Temperance has had enough. She waits in the shade of the chestnut tree near his boat to catch Master Coleman climbing the rope to the deck. She won't let him away so easily. She laughs as she tells Susannah and Mary about it.

Temperance Lloyd: Hanged for Witchcraft in 1682

"Marched right on to the boat I did. Crewmen so scared — woman on board brings bad luck. Such foolish thought. The Lord forgive them that they trust not their souls to Him. Said as I'd leave when Master paid his debt. Threw me off the boat he did, threw a purse after me. Full of coin twas. More than payment".

Later Temperance overhears Susannah is talking to Mary-Mary.

"Temperance 'er should'n 'ave made 'e pay like that. 'E's right angered over 'avin to lay down 'is coin".

Temperance tells them they need Master Coleman's coin. They have to eat. Susannah knows that. She's so kind hearted, keeps saying how much Mistress Coleman needs her. She must go to her, pay or no pay.

"That be easy for ye to say. Got to be careful of that old Doctor Beare, he's that angered with us. Better we do, worse he likes it. And now Abigail be saying to any that listen as he be calling us for witches".

Another voyage, another safe return for the Captain to his bench in The Arms. He's still complaining about his wife's ailments.

"Complaining more of the fees for the cures, he is. She sends for old woman Susannah from Top of the Town. Neighbours say a man of his stature should be sending for a proper physician. When he's home, Master Coleman do send again and again for Dr George Beare. He'll attend in his own good time as befits someone of his stature in the community. Comes not all of a dark night, knowing Mistress Dorcas won't wish to die afore her husband's ship comes in. Makes sure he goes when the Master be due home so as to claim for her better health that comes in on the tide that carries his boat up river. Just afore he sailed this last month past he had to pay the women too. Master Coleman begrudges paying Susannah and the Doctor. Good Doctor, he wants all the pay to hisself. Seems there be trouble all round for Temperance and her friends, though what folk have agin that Mary the good Lord only knows. She be too simple to hardly care for herself, none left for witching other bodies. Only lived through ten cold years, and two winters since, by the Christian duty of tother two".

August came in as cool as most of the summer of 1681, the fire burning many days at The Arms. A late spring and a summer of rain delayed the harvest and green vegetable picking.

"Don't stop Bideford being merry in August with such celebrations of all them old traditions of Weodmonath down on the Strand. Folk most don't rightly know where it all come from, why tis done, mind ye. Them as do don't say in hearing of Rector and his church. Not safe to speak of the old magic. Safe enough it seems to accuse others of bewitching in the name of the Church as now authorises the accusing".

He smiles wryly to himself.

"Funny old century this one been. Politic and religion going this way and that. Kings, Commonwealth, Kings... Mother Church be Popish, not Popish, Puritan, Protestant, Establishment. So much fuss up country. Devon Folk be a canny lot. Keep their notions close, follows in public places whatever they be told, when they be told anything. Safest to keep their land and freedom by the King or the Lord Protector's favour, all with great show and pomp, or with solemnity, as required. Down by the river, and up Torrington Common, they keep the merry customs — Yuletide, Imbolc, Beltane, Lammastide — like their fathers afore them did. Tis no business of the lords and churchmen that never went to fairs and travelling shows. Merriment will always win, merriment and superstition come to harvest in Autumn".

Talk up The Arms is all about the merriment and the trade it brings.

"So much buying and selling. Farmers coming early to market, staying late. Some setting up stalls down by the Rose, buying and selling of spices from the Maine and the Indies. Tinkers coming in from up country, sharpening scythes and bringing tell of more witch trials over Somerset way".

On the bridge, the tinkers coming into town greet the hawkers heading to Somerset. All spring and summer, the hawkers have sold their wares to the boat crews on the Quay. Now their barrows are piled high with goods to sell at Wincanton Saint Bartholomew's Fair.

"Such a good Saint Bartholomew. Nought saintly with the goings-on at the fairs in his name, they say. Not much Christian neither in the talk of witching round the town, up the new market, down the bread oven, round the well".

Temperance and Susannah go in and out of town as quickly as they can for what little they can afford. Folk stare at them coming, look away, talk behind their hands with much nodding of their heads.

Temperance tells Susannah and Mary-Mary they must be more careful. Susannah sees Dorcas, now her only patient, on her own. She is becoming more fearful. In the cool August the leaves fell early down in Appledore woods, bringing in another winter.

1681 was not a severe winter. The first snows fell after Christmas, and melted by Epiphany. Then there was just one light snowfall. It wasn't so bad a time of it for the women. Their swedes kept well in the ground. Temperance's herbs stayed green. Her feverfew flowers came into second blooming. Even better, the townspeople seemed to have lost interest in them.

The Doctor was now the subject of gossip up in The Arms.

"Folk say he be too far in his cups to attend the sick. Say he be letting folk die. What does he say? Swears twas death by bewitching. Talk needs no cause for its believing. Word is the Doctor's talk be making Temperance fearful to go to out to calls. Whether they'm there, whether they'm not there, makes no odds".

Soon hunger becomes stronger than fear.
"We have to work to live ... Or we must beg. Our cures be good. No reason for folk that get well to tell false of us".
Many come to Temperance's door after dark when the moon is new or old.
"Afraid to be seen asking our help, with all the talk of bewitching. Silly talk that it is. Sue came home very fearful from the new market yesterday. Just went for some soup bones up the Row, doing no harm to any. Children ran round calling out 'Witch, Witch, 'er be witch'. Don't shout out so at me. I look right back at them, hold my head high and walk straight past them. If I had the evil eye ..."
The physicians charge high fees at any time. They ask double or more to go out after sunset, to compensate for the risk of having their purses stolen as they walk by the boats and the ale-houses by the river in their fine robes. Fear of bewitching gives way to the wish to get cheaper treatment.
Susannah and Temperance walk the town alone. They work alone, not wanting to be seen together as there's now talk of covens. Mary-Mary still tries to follow either of them everywhere. She's afraid to stay home by herself.
"No moon to see with the clouds tonight, not many stars neither."
It was a crisp Candlemas evening, some snow lying in the woods, when Janet came knocking at the women's door. The congregation of Saint Mary's were all in church for the lighting of candles. Many would light the white candles in church, but later light dark candles to mark the old Fire Festival, the Yule log still burning in the grand houses.
"Janet was come to bid Susannah to tend Grace Thomas who was sick at her sister, Elizabeth Eastchurch's, house. Most particular she was her Mistress wanted Susannah Edwards. None else would do".
Susannah had come home from seeing Dorcas Coleman that afternoon telling of more threats from Doctor Beare. Temperance told her not to go to Mistress Thomas in case the Doctor also happened to be attending at the Eastchurch house.
"Better to go myself. Nobody save the drunken Doctor accusing me since Christmastide a full year past. The Lord be praised for that".

CHAPTER EIGHT
1681-1682

> "And that on the 29th of June last past [Anne Wakeley] did see something in the shape of a Magpie to come at the Chamber window where the said Grace Thomas did lodge".
> (Relation of the Informations against Temperance Lloyd - 1682)

Janet knocks again on the door. Temperance pushes Mary-Mary to open it. She gives Mary the candle to take to the door, which leaves the room behind her lit only by the low glow from the grate.

"Don't let them see Susannah", she whispers.

Janet's voice is muffled at first by the shawl she holds up so no passers by will see who is going the door of the witches' house. Temperance smiles,

"Not that the curious would want to be in our gaze for fear of evil from our eyes".

Janet thinks because Mary is simple she must also be deaf. She speaks loudly to Mary-Mary.

"Mistress Thomas do need 'eal of 'er prickings. 'Er wants Susannah to come".

"Susannah be off t'Abbotsham", Mary-Mary says.

Temperance pulls the heavy door curtain behind Mary. She calls out,

"I can go if it please her. Tell her I be there when I'm finished my food. Still in the big house on Bridge Hill is she?"

Janet nods. She looks both ways to check no one is on the road, pulls the shawl right up to hide her face and slips away quickly into the shadows of the pines. Temperance finishes her piece of bread.

"Me crust won't be here when I gets home if I leaves it. Be in Mary-Mary's mouth afore I shut the gate".

She pulls on her cloak and walks out into the night. A collier crewman nods to her as she passes the Ring 'o' Bells, bids Good Night in Welsh,

"Nos da,"

Temperance responds,

"Nos da".

As she passes the ale-house, the Rector staggers out and lurches across the street.

"He should be doing his drinking in his Rectory. Be the ruin of him if Deacon be out of a night".

She hurries on her way, but walks carefully. It's easy to slip on the icy flagstones on Bridge Street that slopes steeply down to the river. There's an imposing brass knocker in the shape of a bull's head on the grand front door of Master Thomas Eastchurch's house. Since she became sick, Mistress Grace Thomas has been staying with her sister Mistress Elizabeth Eastchurch. The lamp by the front door lights Temperance's way down the stairs to the servants' quarters. The maid lets her in. The servants are still sitting in the kitchen.

"Good food here. Smell of it enough to make me empty stomach cry out".

They are expecting a healer, the under maid, Janet, having been sent for her. Janet looks away as Temperance follows the parlour maid past the table and up the back stairs. The rest of the servants wouldn't know Temperance from Susannah, the woman she was supposed to have summoned. Janet didn't want any trouble.

Mistress Thomas lies on her bed, propped up on pillows, moaning loudly about her aches and pains. Temperance asks her,

"Where does it hurt most?"

"All over. All over. Me knee, me back, me 'ead. They Doctors won't credit 'ow it pains".

"There, there. Don't exert thyself. Be peaceable".

Temperance asks some more questions. Grace tells her the pain started Sunday after Matins, came on with the rain. Temperance nods sympathetically. Yes, it usually does. She asks if the damp makes it worse. Grace nods. She sees that Temperance understands how she feels and believes she can help. She leans back, closes her eyes and breathes easier.

Temperance tells her she has to go home to make a salve for her, says she'll be back after first light with it. She tells the maidservant,

"Bring a brew for her head as well I will. The Mistress must try to get up and walk a little round the chamber. She has to loose it up a bit see".

The maid takes her back downstairs and shows her out by the servants' door. Temperance hurries back up the hill. She must start work right away to allow the physics to mellow overnight. There's still a candle stub left burning. She will need it to see out the back kitchen. Susannah and Mary must sit by the light of the fire.

Temperance goes to the side cupboard that would be a pantry if they had any food to keep in it. She takes several dusty jars from the shelf. One contains a gnarled root of Solomon's Seal, another holds a smelly piece of the strong-tasting swallow-wort root preserved in wine to maintain its power.

"Dug it up in the woods this Autumn past and washed it till twas clean and white. Nice cloudy red colour tis grown now, ready to use. Now ... where is it? Yes, there it is".

She takes down a jar of brownish oil, honeysuckle salve.

"Sue must've put it up there. Have to keep telling her to keep them tidy".

Temperance slices off a small piece of the Solomon Seal root, she has to make it last. She bruises it gently with her pestle against the stone mortar. Then she wraps it carefully in a red kerchief. She pours a small amount of the swallow wort decoction into a vial, then drips some honeysuckle salve into another.

"Mustn't waste it, won't be able to make more till Spring".

She corks the vial with pieces of peeled willow stems. Her work done for Mistress Thomas, she warms a night-time potion to drink with Susannah and Mary beside the dying fire. Outside, the night is noisy. There are boats in from all over, and sailors thrown out of the ale-house fighting fit to kill, shouting all languages. Mary-Mary gets frightened by the noise. Sleeping downstairs, they are ready to go out to chase any intruders off the few herbs left out front.

Temperance tells Susannah and Mary about Mistress Thomas's ailments. Susannah has worked with the herbs long enough that she knows the remedies. Mary listens but has no idea what they're talking about. The fire in the hearth is dying down. They sit closer and drink the dried lindenflower brew. It warms their hands and dulls their senses. Soon they are all sound asleep together under the feather bed warmed by the embers. The shouts outside fade away as they fly into their separate dreams, the recurrent dreams that visit them every night.

Susannah wanders the streets of Bideford while the murmurs of summer insects become whispers from behind human hands ...

"Witches they be ..."

"Doctor say ..."

"Don' let 'em look at 'ee".
"Never knows what ..."
"That Temperance Lloyd ..."
"That Susannah Edwards ... 'er be as bad".
"All same, they be".
"Black birds ..."
"Braget cats ..."
"Don' 'ee look. Get inside".
Susannah wakes, rolls over, falls asleep.

Mary-Mary's dreams are simple. The warmth on her feet takes her into pathfields where she rests before picking up her shawlful of firewood and heading home. Cooler air stiffens her muscles back to the floor of the coal cellar. She will jerk awake, afraid. Has she missed the call to get up and clean the grates? Will they ...? Will they...? Her dreams take her back to a world that she cannot recall when she's awake.

Temperance dreams of flying. Susannah tells her she talks of it in her sleep.

"Fly, Fly, Fly", she calls out.

Mary-Mary wakes, mutters, "Husht", and hooks a bony toe into Temperance's back to wake her up. Mary fades back into sound sleep. As her legs get stiff, Temperance rolls over to face Mary. She mutters again,

"Nay Master, I won't. So ..... Still .... Canst do that..."

They all slip back to sleep. The fire dies. The room cools. They try to find warmth by turning over, turning again, and again, and again ... Temperance spreads her arms, flying ... Susannah shouts out to her to stop.

"Must've hit her in the face. She grunts and pushes my arm away. Cold. I curl into a ball. Got to keep the heat in. Dawn wakes us".

Temperance tells Susannah how that she went out the window down to the river, with the man in black,

"Just like it happened other nights. Again, I did".

Susannah rolls her eyes. She looks at Temperance, her expression showing she thinks her mad. She tells her she dreamed it, that she was between them the whole night.

"Talkin' in yer sleep 'ee was. 'Orrid noise 'ee did make with it. Kep' us all awake. Waked us up twice or thrice with yer wingein' an' rabbitin'. Takin' too much brew makes 'ee like that".

Temperance insists it's the truth.

"I flew way o'er the pathfields, down by the woods. River black and shiny as coal. Grass sweet in the night dew. Met the man in black I did. Indeed, so I did. Twas real as I stand yere now. Real as ye be. See now. Not mad I am. Didn't dream it, neither".

Temperance Lloyd: Hanged for Witchcraft in 1682

Mary's mouth opens even wider than usual. Susannah puts a hand on her shoulder.

"Tis no good tellin' 'er. 'Er's fast in 'er 'appenin'. Save yer breath Mary".

Temperance kept on ministering to Mistress Grace Thomas. It didn't do much good. The potions soothed the pain just enough to keep her wanting to go on seeing Temperance. Then the driest Spring in years came in. Grace recovered.

"The Lord's dry Spring likely did Grace as much good as my herbals".

June rains broke the drought and brought weeks of warm humid air that hung over the town holding the foul smell of the river. Grace's pains came back, and got worse and worse. Not many herbs grew in the dry Spring. Those out the back of the cottage that did start to grow were washed out by the summer storms.

"So wet tis, strange things grow down the woods".

Temperance brewed potions from whatever grew out of the wet earth. Nothing seemed to help Mistress Thomas who was still in great pain in August. Then she recovered as if by magic.

"Must've been something I done".

As soon as Temperance heard the news of Grace's good health from all the talk about it around the market stalls, she went to Mistress Thomas's door. She was paid very handsomely and shed tears of joy to see Grace well again, even more joy to see the coin. Mistress Thomas cried with her. Grace walked slowly up the steep Bridge Street hill to the new meat market. Goaman, the butcher, was glad to pull a greasy stool out from the cutting room for Mistress Thomas to sit in front of his stall. She told of the miracle cure Temperance had done her. Folk stopped to hear the story. She told more and more wonders with each telling, the morning passing to noon. Goaman sold his meat and Hog's Pudding while Mistress Thomas kept telling her tale. By noon she was telling how Temperance worked all manner of miracles. Gill, Pollard and Cox at stalls further into the Row saw no customers until Goaman was sold out and Mistress Thomas was all talked out.

The miracle doesn't temper the talk of bewitching nightly in The Arms.

"They say as tis women that gossip. Them as say it bain't sat here in The Arms listening year on year. Master Coleman be still on about his Dorcas. Says she gets sick more these days. Well, tis common knowledge she comes over sick with the sailing of his ship. Stays sick the more he takes his shore time in here, no doubt. He says he must keep sailing to pay the Doctor, and to pay Susannah Edwards. Dorcas don't want to see the doctor. John don't want to pay the woman. Dorcas says Susannah do her good. Doctor says Mistress Edwards be no more than a witch spelling folk sick so as to be paid for her cures. Master Isaac Browning says Coleman's money be better spent on Susannah. Did his wife, Bess, a power of good this March past when she were took that poorly with the rhume".

Master Coleman doesn't know what to think — caught between the Doctor and his wife.

"Master Jude Couch, him with the pottery works up by Fremington, says he'd put his life in Temperance's hands. She helped his Janey deliver three babes safe into his hands just the past twenty six months. Job says tis a wonder young Jude had time to give her the babes, all the time he spends talking about it in here".

Though he laughs at Jude, Job believes Temperance is a good woman. She went all the way out Alverdiscott in a snowstorm to salve the chilblains he got fetching the cattle in February past.

"James Cullacott vowed as his good lady, Lizzie, would have died of the rotten meat she ate down the church dinner if Susannah hadn't come so quick with the physic. Nought said about Mary Trembles, the one they say be simple".

Temperance tells Sue and Mary-Mary,

"Tis hard to know which way the wind is blowing. Some folk be saying we work for the Devil. Doctor Beare and the new doctor like that tale, better for the quacks to be rid of us. Same time, word of our good powers be spoken in the ale-houses. Even folk in their Sunday best at Matins down Saint Mary's don't pretend now they don't see the three of us standing to worship behind them. And that Mistress Puddicombe, she told some boys that ran behind us calling out, "Witch, Witch," to cease their wicked talk. There's a fine thing".

It couldn't last, good luck rarely does, though one more winter did pass uneventfully for the women. In the middle of May there was a heavy rainstorm. Mistress Grace Thomas was walking home from market when the heavens opened on her, soaked her right through to the skin. By evening, she'd come down with a fever, terrible head, limbs aching fit to break. Her maid was at Temperance's door before the sun set wanting her to come right away.

"I took her a brew of dried feverfew with honey, thinking to help her head first. Had little effect. In the morning Mistress Thomas was still in a fever, moaning with the pain in her shoulders and her knee".

Temperance took her a decoction of poppy head syrup which helped her a little by dulling her senses and the pain. The fever broke after another day. Then on the first day of June the maid was at Temperance's door again.

"Said her mistress was poorly again. Said as she had nine pricks in her knee, though I cannot say how she counted them".

As soon as she went into the bed chamber Temperance could see how stiff Grace was.

"Taken with the cramps that come from stopping the humour in the body. Twill happen like that when folk take to their beds too long. The doctors do like folk to be in their beds, get paid the better and the longer for it".

Temperance had told her to get out of bed and keep trying to walk round her room. She asked Grace if she had been trying to walk.

"Nay. Pains us too much".

Grace Thomas's sister Elizabeth, Master Eastchurch's wife, was by the bed. She shouted at Temperance,

"Walk? As if 'er could".

Temperance replied that she could, and to get better she must. Elizabeth stood red-faced and angry by the bed, glaring at Temperance. She had her hands on Grace's leg, rubbing the knee gently jerking her hands. It wasn't helping, was probably making it worse. Temperance asked Elizabeth to go down to the kitchen to fetch some warm water. As soon as she was gone from the room, Temperance began to massage Grace's knee firmly and then her lower legs. As the feeling in her legs started to return, Grace squealed loudly with the sudden sharp pain and tingling sensations. Temperance told her this was a sign her legs were getting better. Grace breathed hard, nodded, and gave Temperance a smile.

Down in the kitchen, Elizabeth heard the squeals coming from the bed chamber. She rushed upstairs shrieking loudly that Temperance was hurting Grace. She wouldn't believe that Grace would be walking within the hour. She drove Temperance out of the house, yelling loudly for the whole street to hear that the witch had caused the pricking pains by image magic.

Temperance knew what such an idea would do if it got around town. She stood her ground and told Elizabeth that was nonsense.

"The only pricking I do with my needle is to mend my old leather pumps".

That didn't stop Mistress Eastchurch. She shouted louder and louder, running up and down the street. Elizabeth's husband, Thomas Eastchurch, heard the fuss from his shop and came running to the house to see what was up. Temperance stood in the street listening in horror.

"Proper rough 'er was. Made us poor Grace shriek out in 'er agony. Near sick with pain 'er was. Near swooned, that white 'er went. Us swear, if 'er hadn't been lying down, 'er'd 'ave fall down. Din't scream that loud when us rubbed 'er. That Temperance 'er sent us down kitchen for water. Gettin us out the way 'er was",

With Elizabeth shouting, Temperance trying to calm her and Thomas Eastchurch running from his store, the neighbours started hanging out their chamber windows. Then many came out on to their front steps. Master Eastchurch knew his wife tended to believe what she wanted to believe. He asked,

"And did 'er do any good?"

"Good? Evil more like. Twas terrible what 'er did. An' 'er said 'er made the prickin'."

" 'Er did. Be sure? 'ow so?"

"Us said to 'er as 'us knowed 'er'd made Grace's pain come by image magic".

"An' 'er confessed it?"

"As good as ... 'Er said 'er did indeed prick, put the needle in 'er leather shoe".

"As do many folk when they slippers need mendin'. So what be sayin', wife?"

"Temperance be usin' 'er slipper for puttin' the curse on folk 'er be".

Master Eastchurch looks from Elizabeth to Temperance.

"If'n er can do that, we best all be careful. 'Er could hurt us all if 'er so choose. Maybe 'er didn't mean 'er did it".

Temperance looks at him and shakes her head. Elizabeth shouts even louder,

"Don't tell us what us 'eard. Us was there, not 'ee".

"So that Temperance causes the sickness by witchcraft, the pain flying from 'er leather slippers to thy poor sister Grace's legs, givin' 'er pains. Then 'er come in to our house offering more herbs and rubbin' to make 'em better. Good business that be. Us should do as good in me shop".

Temperance told Susannah of the fracas.

"My, Mistress Eastchurch was that angry. No matter what, she'll not be shown wrong. Janet says she sent for a doctor, he that does little good except to his own purse. He was so happy to tell as I did more harm than good".

In a few days Grace recovered. She got up from her bed and sent for Temperance to pay for her services. A month or so went by. Just past the Summer Solstice, Grace Thomas became ill again and sent Janet to fetch Temperance. Mary-Mary answered the door.

The maid opened her mouth to speak but instead broke into a scream. Temperance saw Elizabeth Eastchurch dragging Janet back to the road by her hair. Janet was shouting that Mistress Grace did need of the healing. Elizabeth would have none of it. Temperance told Mary to close the door. There was nothing they could do to help.

Sion hears the door open, feels the breeze on his face. He hears Thomas Eastchurch's voice.

"Thomas be in again tonight. Comes straight from his shop he do most nights now. Well, can't blame him, can ye? Any man would want to get out of the house when there's two women sitting by his fire going on about this and that".

"Just one quick drink to get us through supper", Thomas says.

"Quick one, then two, then … Seems as his good lady Elizabeth be at odds with her sister as lives with them. Hard enough for poor Thomas when they'm getting along, drives him half crazed when they take to arguing. The wife's sister, Grace Thomas, she been that sick these past years with the rheumatics – so bad she can't walk when it comes in wet. She sends for Mistress Lloyd to give her the curatives. Grace do swear by Temperance and her salves and potions and her rubbing of the legs, she do. Thomas has to admit as Mistress Grace gets well. Half the town knows that. Grace was up market again telling all that listened how Temperance cured her ills".

Still Elizabeth was getting more and more unhappy with the state of affairs. She still insists Temperance is hurting her sister.

"Thomas says Elizabeth don't like that Temperance be telling Grace she'll soon be well enough to go back living back in her own house".

"Be that the house over Buttgarden Street that Elizabeth has a mind to sell, Thomas?" Daracott asks with a sly smile,

Thomas nods. Elizabeth be changin' 'er tale some days. She don't deny Grace be gettin' better. Can't argue with that. Oh no. Now 'er says as Grace gets well on account that Temperance does her trade by witchcraft. The good Doctor Beare had said twas so with Mistress Coleman. Mebbe 'e'd say the same about Mistress Thomas.

"Master Eastchurch don't know what to think. If the Doctor say it … It must be so. And yet … And yet..."

Sitting himself down beside Sion, Thomas sounds more and more miserable. He thought perhaps if he were to have another drink that would give Elizabeth time to think it over. He had told her that if she was so certain they must report it to the Constable. And right then, the Constable walks into The Arms, looking very self-important.

"So full of himself this night our Constable be. He been sent for to go up Barnstaple to a gathering of Constables from all round about, last Friday past. First chance he had to come in tonight, being that he stayed over Barnstaple Saturday and Sunday with his brother. All most secret informations he said meeting was for. Well, twas secret, still it wouldn't do no harm to tell just his good friends up The Arms what the Sheriff did say, would it? Very careful with his words seems the Sheriff was".

Sion tapped his stick for quiet, and folk gathered round to hear what the Constable had to report. The Constable stood up, cleared his throat and took a breath. His expression was serious. He frowned with the effort of recalling each word, spoke slowly, nodded as he thought he got it right.

"Sheriff said as,

> 'All should continue to be vigilant, take notice of their surroundings and report suspicious items or activity to local authorities immediately. Tis our duty to make our homes safer by defeating these witches one by one'.

The Constable tells everyone the Sheriff said just that up Barnstaple. Thomas Eastchurch asked him,

"Be there witches in Bideford".

The Constable nods slowly, "Tis so".

"Master Eastchurch left half his drink on the table, told Jem to finish it. He had to go right home to his good wife".

Elizabeth was sure she was right. Never more sure. She reminded Thomas that there been other talk about Temperance.

"Old Master Browning did say 'er met with Black Devil 'imself up Higher Gunstone. 'E 'eard it from Master Prickard. 'E 'eard it from Master Mariner Couch, 'e seed it for 'isself. Well, twas too dark to see clear. Then, twould be dark when Devil be abroad. 'An Temperance be already suspect. An' magpie flew in us window".

Elizabeth had seen the magpie for herself. Thomas picked up his hat and ran out. It wasn't far to the Town Hall. By the time Master Eastchurch was at the door, he was determined to make his report. The Constable arrived from The Arms. Thomas Eastchurch was a man of some substance in Bideford. They had to take him seriously, no point arguing with him. Master Eastchurch told the Constable to listen carefully. Both the Doctor and his own good wife, Elizabeth, were certain that his wife's dear sister had been bewitched by Temperance Lloyd.

The next day, the first of July, the Constable knocked on the women's door to take Temperance off once more to the little Church lock-up on the east side of the bridge.

CHAPTER NINE
JULY 1, 1682

> *"The Attributes of Witches ... they cause any maleficia not attributable to natural causes or ascribed to God... have the magical power to fly out of windows to remote places... can transform themselves into cats, hares and other creatures... raise tempests by muttering some nonsensical words or performing impertinent and ridiculous ceremonies".* (Joseph Glanville, Philosophical Considerations Touching Witches and Witchcraft (1666))

Sleep. Lord, send me sleep. Sleep. No. No. No".

Pieces of straw slide inside her bodice, silky at first, then breaking into pieces, piercing her skin.

"Sleep ... No sweet linden flowers, no sweet linden dreams, just bright blinding violent visions. Flying down over the riverbank wood, feels myself falling, falling, falling. Put my arms out to stop the fall, hit the mud floor. Wakes me right up, and calling out for aid".

Two rats squeal loudly. They turn and race out through the cracks in the rotting plank walls.

"Must've have been lying in watch beside me. Oh Lord help me. They do go for the eyes first".

She buries her face in the straw. The guard heard her cries. The door opens, and he strides in, swearing. He kicks Temperance, rolls her over.

"Muttering to himself he is, minds me of Mary-Mary that muttering. Just doing his job he is".

"Keep 'er wakin'. 'Elp 'er collect 'er crimes. Constable says as us 'ave to. Pays us to do it proper".

He awakened Temperance every hour and told Young Peter to do the same when he came to take over at sunrise.

"Don't 'ee feed 'er. Not much water neither, mind, lest us feed the devil that's in 'er".

Susannah and Mary are now on their own in the cottage.

"Mary-Mary was in such a tizzy when Temperance was took off. 'Er was that set on Temperance, thought 'er be miracle maker. Kep' on at me".

"Us ought go see 'er, Susannah".

Susannah tells her,

"Nay. Us din't oughta. 'Er can get off like 'er did afore. Us b'ain't so lucky".

Mary-Mary stamps her foot and waves her arms about,

"Us be gwain any 'ow".

Susannah knows nothing will stop Mary-Mary when she's really determined. She still tries to restrain her,

"Nay, nay, Mary. Bide 'ere. Be safe".

But when Mary-Mary goes straight out of the door, Susannah has to follow her. You never know what Mary will get up to.

"'Er don' know 'erself what 'er'll do. Get 'erself in the lock-up. So I 'ad to follow 'er, gotta keep 'er out o' trouble".

They hurried out into the dusk. The sun had set and the moon hadn't risen. They walked quickly down the back alleys and drangs, then took the path beside the quay up to the bridge to avoid being seen by too many people. They waited in the shadows of the wharf across from the lock-up till a cloud drifted over the moon around midnight. They watched the two guards come out of the lock-up, put the bar on the door and stroll over to the Ship on Launch where they know the landlord will let them in at the side door. The women then creep over, slide the bar off the door and slip inside.

"Twill be dawn afore guards come back, too drunk to be much use like as not".

Temperance is not best pleased to see them She speaks angrily,

"What in the name of the good Lord dost think ye be doing 'ere? Canst not see danger when it come, Susannah? If the guards find ye with me, we'll ride the same cart to Exeter".

Susannah just laughs.

"Constables be off to th'Inn. Be back drunk as toads. Us'll be long gone".

Mary-Mary sits on the floor looking up at Temperance, "Will 'ee get off again?"

Temperance shrugs and says she did nothing wrong. "Twas the devil in black, he made me".

Susannah rolls her eyes. Mary looks at Temperance, "Devil? When'd that?"

"With Mistress Thomas, so he did".

Susannah responds,

" 'Ee be speaking' nonsense. Devil were a dream. 'Ee was 'ome in bed dreamin' with us. Us collect 'ee sleep talkin' ".

They don't know that Thomas Eastchurch is hiding outside in the shadows, as Susannah said later,

" 'E musta been. Said so to the Justices over Town Hall, an' up t'Exeter after, 'e did. 'E musta crept so soft out in shadows by the lock-up to 'ear us. Cracks aplenty in they walls there be".

Temperance feels she has to describe what happened to her. She tells them,

"I know what I know. Whatever I did, for good or evil, twas by the man in black. Hit me, he did. Hit me over and over he did. I told Mistress Thomas I could help her no more. That's when he made me go back".

Susannah argues with her,

" 'Ee did 'eal 'er, 'ee did. Devil done none of it".

Mary takes a breath. Susannah puts a hand on her arm,

" 'Er won' listen to reason. Us knows what 'appened. Say nought more, Mary. Tis no good".

Temperance tells them to go now. She can watch herself. They must look to themselves. They went. She hears the bar come back down on the door and peers out through a crack in the wall to watch them go. Then she sees a man, tall and broad, wearing a long coat and big hat, slip away into the shadow of the near wharf. She realizes he must have stood there watching Mary and Susannah cross the bridge.

"May the Good Lord help us".

She watches the man walk towards the bridge after Susannah and Mary.

The Constables at the Town Hall were more than a little annoyed to have to break from dealing their card game to attend to Thomas Eastchurch again. He'd come to seek private words with them, said it was truly a serious matter. He told them that he overheard Temperance Lloyd confess to her companions who visited her in the lock-up last night. He'd heard her say to them it was under the influence of the Black Devil she had tormented poor Grace Thomas, all the while pretending to help her. Master Eastchurch had heard every word of it.

The Constable knew the old church was locked with guards there sworn to keep watch on Temperance all night. He wondered how the women could have got in. Master Eastchurch sat thinking about that a while. He didn't want to blame the guards who were good customers in his shop. Well, if the door was barred ...

"They women did get in, must've slipped through the wall, lots of holes in that old place".

If they were witches they could take on the shape of small cats and get in unseen by the guards...

"Yes, that's what passed".

The more he thought about it, the more sure he became of it – no need to put blame on the guards.

"After all, did us not also see a braget cat go into me own shop? Mistress Eastchurch 'ad seed it too. Maybe twas the devil 'isself, Yes. Yes. That'd be it".

That was even more proof.

"And the wife's sister, Grace, 'er'd been seen by they good doctors to no benefit. Unable to help for all their fine learnin'. They did tell 'er truly twas witchcraft that ailed 'er".

Thomas nods and smiles with satisfaction at the increasing strength of his argument.

"Then neighbour, Mistress Anne Wakeley, 'er seed the magpie fly to Mistress Grace's chamber window so as to see evil bein' done. Magpie. A black feathered bird. No doubt twas the Devil 'isself. Neighbour woman, Anne Wakeley, 'er seed it. Swear to it, 'er will".

His duty done, Master Eastchurch went up to The Arms to report it.

"My, what a tale Thomas Eastchurch told. Could have been a bard if he been a Welshman".

In the lock-up, Temperance lies slipping between troubled sleep and confused wakefulness. The day goes by in a streak of sunlight moving like a sundial shadow across the floor. Peter opens the door to another guard, Edmund. The July evening is stifling in the lock-up that's been closed all day in the July sun. Edmund opens the door to get the breeze. People come and go outside. "Lovely night for a stroll". They tell each other.

"Funny place to stroll, through the refuse back of the fish-smelly wharves", Temperance thinks.

"No. They'm come to gawp through the door at the witch woman tied hands and feet against the wall. There be some as come to bring food or water for me. Proper Christians they be, doing their Christian duty. Some offer me blessings".

Edmund takes the food. He sends the people on their way, then he sits to eat it just out of Temperance's reach. He holds out a piece of cold Hog's Pudding for her to smell, then snatches it away and puts it in his mouth. He wipes the savoury grease off his mouth with the back of his hand, then throws the last bit of the sausage into the open mouth of a rat that sits half in and half out of a hole in the wall. Temperance asks him how he can carry his good saint's name and be so cruel, to steal the Christian help from her. He laughs.

Temperance slips between sleep and wakefulness. Weak and sick from hunger and thirst, she begs for water. The day guard tilts a cup towards her just enough for her to get a few sips, never enough to moisten her dry throat. Temperance prays,

"Iesu fy crymorth, Fy Duw, Fy Duw".

The guard is frightened,

"Stop with that Devil talk. 'Ee can' call on un 'ere".

"My prayers be to my God, to my Lord Jesus to help me".

The guard shakes his head. Late in the afternoon, the Constable arrives. The guard tells him Temperance has been talking evil to the Devil, making strange incantations. The Constable sends the guard outside. He questions her,

"Tell how you meet with the Devil. Tell where you meet him. How? How?"

Temperance is so tired. The guard seems a long way away, standing in a mist. She faints, or sleeps. The Constable kicks her gently. She wakes.

"Tell how you meet with the Devil. Tell where you meet him. How? How?"

She stares at him,

"What Devil?"

He repeats his questions. She stares blankly at him. He goes out leaving her alone, barring the door behind him. She sleeps again. Peter comes back a while later, the night watch. Another man arrives as the sun sets. They play with dice, yelling so loudly Temperance cannot rest. One man leaves and Temperance dreams a woman comes and pulls off her apron leaving her naked.

"Or is this real? I hear, or do I dream, a name... Anne Wakeley. I feel soft hands moving over my body, lifting my skinny breasts, pushing my legs apart, looking, feeling. I wake and try to push her away. Her finger tips move back and forth over the sores and warts that cover my stomach. Then she is gone. Such a dream".

She falls back into sleep. Hunger, thirst, sleeplessness dull Temperance's senses. She can't be sure if she's dreaming or awake. All the pain comes back. All is clear, clear pain, clear sight. The sweet rosemary, feverfew, linden have all gone from her body leaving nothing to dull the pain of hunger, to chase away life's cruelties. The lock-up is hot. She can scarcely draw breath. She feels so cold that she cannot stopped her jaw trembling as she shivers.

Two or three rats play by her feet. Then she sees more and more of them. They become an army. The whole floor is a seething mass of pulsating sleek furry bodies, a grey-brown, rippling, velvet cloth. She closes her eyes, slips into sleep. When she awakes the rats are gone. She itches all over.

"I have to rid me of the insects crawling all over me".

She begs the guard for water to wash them away. He sees no insects. She scratches her arms till the dry, brittle skin tears off in strips. She sucks at the blood and skin under her finger nails.

Sion mops the sweat off his brow. It was a warm walk over to The Arms today.

"Had poor Temperance over the lock-up three days now they have. Folk all want to talk to Constable, buying him more ale than he can drink, sitting all round him asking about all them doings down the Town Hall. Constable's real pleased with hisself. More used to the folk staying out of his way lest they be arrested for crimes only they know they've done. Now they'm all after him. Spins his tale out he does. First he tells how he walked over the bridge as the Clerk had sent him. Saw the fishermen get a good haul of salmon from the Bridge Pool. Best he's seen in a while," he says.

"Yes. Yes. But what of the witch?"

"Told the guard to hand 'er over for 'er to go with us over to the Justices. Said 'er'd be a while. Guard could go get 'isself food. 'E 'ad to put the rope round 'er ankles though 'er was too weak to go far".

The Constable had to drag her to her feet. Then he almost had to carry her. She kept her eyes closed against the sun.

"So bright the sun flashing off the river, pierces right into my eyes. My head hurts so with the hunger. I need for my herbs. I feel so sick I retch. I can hardly stand, would fall right over if Constable don't be holding me".

There was a small crowd standing by the Town Hall doors, all waving kerchiefs and shouting as if it was a Fair. As soon as they saw Temperance they called out louder,

"Witch woman. Devil lover"

"Don' 'ee overlook us".

They make the sign of the cross. A woman comes out of the Town Hall door and hurries off across the bridge.

"Found the signs, 'er did"

"Good Mistress Wakeley. Brave to touch a witch".

Temperance Lloyd: Hanged for Witchcraft in 1682

Temperance can scarcely hear them over the buzzing in her ears. Inside the Town Hall it seems dark after the sun. For a while she can see nothing. The Constable tells them she's too weak to stand. He pushes her down on a chair. As her eyes accustom to the gloom she looks up to see the Mayor, Thomas Gist and Alderman John Davie, sitting at a big oak table. She recognizes them from Church where they sit up front in the high seats on Sundays. John Hill, Town Clerk, sits beside John Davie, waiting to take notes, a satisfied grin on his face.

"That thin and pale 'er was, face like a deadman's bones", Constable reports.

"And then?"

The Constable didn't know about that. Mayor Gist had told him he could leave.

"All that ale for nothing. Serves them right I'd say. Taking their pleasure from a poor woman's pain and travail. Serves them right, it do".

The Constable gone, Temperance waits for the Mayor to start the proceedings,

"Thy name be Temperance Lloyd, Widow?"

Temperance looks up at them, thinking to herself,

"Good Lord give me patience. Did they think they had taken someone else to the lock-up?" She nods. Mayor Gist continues,

"Some ten year past, ye did treat William Hebert. And he did die soon thereafter. And he did tell his son on his deathbed that he did die of thy bewitching ... ".

"Yea indeed, I did treat William Hebert. But he died a natural death. A full six weeks later twas. And well he was, well enough to be walking the town. Did him no harm at all. The magistrates up in Exeter did have me freed of that. Can they try me again when I was said innocent?"

"If ye be witch, a man can die because ye think it. Ye did think it".

Temperance asks herself,

"And these be our high and great men of the town?"

Then she asks,

"Ye do truly believe that?"

Thomas Gist leans towards the Clerk.

"She owns to it".

"Did no such thing. I own to nought. No use saying, is it?"

Then John Davie asks,

"We heard witness of teats for suckling the Devil himself on thy body in private parts. What say you?"

"There be warts on me. As on many old and poor".

"She owns to it".

Mayor Gist asks her,

"What dost say of this, that on witness ye hath confessed ye fly with the Devil by the moon?"

"Maybe tis true. Perchance I did say so".

Hunger and sleeplessness have left her no longer knowing what's true, what's false.

"Through many a hungry summer, hungrier winters, I drank my potions to bring me to sleep against the hunger. Then through the night I felt myself fly out through the window up from the garden, across the river and down to the sea. I felt me to be with the Devil. He said to do evil things. He swore he would be with me against those who would harm me. Said he could do me more good than all my prayers to my God did do".

"And did he do good by ye?"

"Seems nay. I wished he would cease the tongues that kept folk from buying my herbs and healing. Without the selling, the hunger gets so much worse. Had to make the potions stronger to dull it in sleep, too strong for this shrinking body".

The Mayor's voice booms out at her,

"We did hear witness that ye did consort with the Devil "...

Temperance no longer knows what she's saying, too tired to think, too hungry to care,

"I did meet a tiny man in black on Higher Gunstone on my way to town. Cloak just so long as my arm, with big eyes. Whether twas the Devil or one of them from the Fair..."

She can recall nothing clearly. She begins to ask herself what they can do to her against the protection of the Black Devil himself. Did she not fly with him in safety? These Devon men can never hurt her. But then, she dreamed that dream last night and for sure that must have been a dream. The Alderman breaks into her reverie,

"And be it not true that Mistress Lydia Burman witnessed against ye up Exeter twelve year back. And Anne Fellow. They did swear ye blinded Jane Dallyn in one eye, killing her, she the wife of Symon Dallyn, Mariner".

Temperance feels the room spinning around her. How much longer can she stand this? How bad can it get? If what they say is true the Black Man will protect her. The Black Man ... What is she thinking?

"Alright. Lydia Burman and Anne Fellow did witness that Jane Dallyn did die when I did think it. And was it that I blinded Jane Dallyn in one eye? Not that I collect. But who knows?"

"She owns it to be true".

"I pray the Lord to let me rest a while".

And then ... The Constable comes back into the room to speak with the Justices. They are nodding. The Clerk says Thomas Eastchurch is come to swear his statement. The Constable pulls Temperance up and pushes her into another room, telling her to wait. What else would she do? She is too weak to walk away. She sleeps a while until the Constable comes to take her back to the Justices. Thomas Gist tells her,

"Constable shall take ye back to lock-up. The morrow Rector Ogilby shall examine ye".

"Surely I'll talk to Rector Ogilby. He talks well from the Holy Writ, though he keep his well to himself. Keep his drinking now to himself as well".

Temperance doesn't remember going back over the bridge. She knows she must have done to get back to the lock-up. The guard gives her a small piece of bread and a whole cup of water. He doesn't let her sleep through the night. Guard Peter kicks her every hour when he walks round the room to keep himself awake. Edmund comes at change of watch with the morning sun.

The Constable tells Sion the messenger was sent up to the Parsonage to ask the Rector to speak with Witch Temperance. The Mayor will deliver Mistress Lloyd to Saint Mary's when Mr Ogilby is finished his daily prayers.

"Need his prayers he will".

The next day is Market day. Peter Darracott runs into The Arms to report he saw Rector Ogilby take his walk down the High Street and along Allhalland street to Saint Mary's. He didn't need the trap on such a fine day.

"Master Darracott says as the Rector was so deep in his own thoughts he walked right past his parishioners that touched their forelocks or curt-seyed as he passed. If they collect the good Rector's drunken behaviour at the King's Arms, and how he did hit the Mayor into a faint just a few years past, they keep their thinking to themselves. Ogilby don't drink much now in the ale-houses. He used to be in one or more most nights — till he been found asleep on Silver Street just before he was due to celebrate Friday Matins. He wouldn't want word of that to get round – and seems the Lord Bishop heard nothing of his mistakes".

The Rector drinks at home now, has the manservant take the dog-cart down the short stretch of Upper High Street to the cellars at the corner of Grenville Street. He always sends the man on a Wednesday just before the shops close at noon, a quiet time in Bideford. The man loads the barrels of sack, porter and ale quickly into the cart, covering them with clean burlap sacks. He anchors the burlap hiding the Rector's household supplies with a bag of flour he's picked up from the mill down Cold Harbour.

"Rector do think no one knows. Don't matter if he's seen or not seen. Nought goes on in Bideford but what Beatrice here in Th'Arms knows it. She got sisters in service to half the big houses about, up Rectory too. Beatrice says Rector has Mistress Ogilby send the servants to their homes soon as evening meal be done. Sends the housemaid to her room up the attic, tells her take the rest of the day to herself. Mistress Ogilby sits embroidering vestments in her drawing room. Rector goes off, he says to read the Holy Writ and prepare his talk. Brandy wine helps the words to come clearer. Mistress Ogilby will be sound asleep when he staggers up the stairs into his bedchamber. Maid hears it all with there being no door to the upper back stairs".

Rector Ogilby is waiting at the Church when Mayor Gist and the Constable bring Temperance to the back row of the servants' pews. Mayor Gist closes the heavy oak door and walks off back to the Town Hall. The Rector tells Constable to stay outside the door. He beckons Temperance to a seat near the front of the church where she's never been before. The Rector looks at her, thinking to himself,

"So ... This is Temperance Lloyd. Don't look much of a threat to any man. So thin, comes like a dusty moth fluttering down the aisle. This whole witchcraft business never meant much to me till now. On the one hand, witches could not possibly do what they were said to do. On the other hand, if this woman was a witch, the maid says my own well may be spelled. On the other hand, this is my opportunity to defend the community, to work as part of the public safety effort. This is my chance to defy and defeat the witches, the forces of evil. Yet in all honesty tis hard to believe the fantastic and strange claims about witchcraft".

Ogilby had to confess, for God would know it, that for many years Joseph Glanvill's treatise, "Philosophical Considerations Touching Witches and Witchcraft", the 1666 edition, had sat unread on a high shelf in the Rectory library. What good fortune the Canon had left him the more recent version, "Saducium Triumphatus". He had read it late into last evening to prepare as best he could to question Temperance. He recalled meeting Reverend Glanvill once in Plymouth. What a life the man had made from his beginnings in Devon, Fellow of the Royal Society, Chaplain-in-Ordinary to Charles II, Rector of Bath Abbey. Such defenders of the faith, they were, Glanvill and Henry More, up there in Cambridge. They saw so clearly the terrible threat that the new sciences coming into favour now might be used to deny religious beliefs. Such a great man, and yet ... Michael Ogilby saw his own limitations,

Temperance Lloyd: Hanged for Witchcraft in 1682

"A poor mind like mine has trouble with the sense of it. Joseph Glanvill did reason that belief in God and Goodliness requires us to believe also in Evil and Satanic forces. Witchcraft shows us the reality of Satan, giving us the only true and tangible evidence of God's supernatural power. Disbelief in witchcraft argues against supernatural powers for good as for evil. Thus, tis said by Glanvill, to deny witches is to deny religion. To deny witchcraft, when others see it, is a great sin. Glanvill wrote very clear about this,

> "Those that dare not bluntly say, There is no God, content themselves to deny that there are spirits and witches".

"I read it over and over last night. Ah well ... so much greater men than I ... It must be so. Who am I, Michael Ogilby, that has never before this examined a witch, to question those greater than me. It must be so. Best I stick closely to text".

Temperance watches him looking at the great book. She waits. He knows she lives just up the road from the Rectory. He knows gossip is evil, unchristian, ungodly, still he cannot help but hear what the flock whispers as it leaves the Church.

"They say she knows many things. They say she came from Welsh Wales. The Established Church is well established there, though their Bible is in the Welsh, a pagan language tis said, a bad sign. Comes every Sunday to service, sings a lovely tune in the back corner where the indigent stand. Could evil come from one with such a sweet voice?"

Temperance is staring at him now, waiting. He clears his throat.

"Dost know who I am?"

"Aye, Rector. I do know thee to be a man of God, and a neighbour to me and my friends Mary and Susannah".

Their neighbour ...

"Ye know them not? That's strange. We sit in the Church Sabbath and Feast Days regular like. Always at the back with the poor as we must".

"Well, yes, I have seen ye in my flock. I hear ye singing too. Dost understand why ye be here?"

"Indeed. Tis an honour to be speaking with such an important person, a man of the Cloth no less. Ye will surely be able to see that I have done no wrong. Only helping people I am. Using the herbs I do. Learnt it from my Mam, may God bless her soul and let her rest in peace".

Rector Ogilby feels confused. She sounds intelligent, educated even...

"Ye be hungry?"

"Yes, sir, very hungry. No food much in the lock-up".

> "If a brother or sister be destitute of daily food ...and ye give them not those things that are needful to the body ...

117

He calls the Constable in,
"Get some bread and ale for her".
Ogilby watches as she dips the bread into the ale. It is gone in an instant. She smiles up at him. He opens his book at a page marked with a silk ribbon,

> "Witches can annoint themselves to gain the power to fly out of windows to remote places".

"Mistress Lloyd, is it true that ye be seen to fly from your house at night to meet with the Devil himself?"

"Sir, betimes I did think that. But my sisters say I did dream it, being beside them all the night in our bed. And Jesus did say it, 'Get thee hence Satan' ".

The Rector nods and smiles. Indeed, she listens well to what he says. He reads on,

> "Witches can transform themselves into cats, hares and other creatures..."

"And what say ye of the charge that ye did appear as a cat jumping into Mistress Coleman's window?"

Temperance rolls her eyes.

"Well, I did see no cat at Mistress Coleman's house. There was a cat that come to our house for food. Poor Mary-Mary, she's a bit simple from birth see, she do love all animals. She feeds it. Cat is not our cat though. But turning into a cat, you ask? Well there'd be a fine thing indeed. To be fed, and to sit on the lap of a gentleman or even a fine man of the church. A fine thing indeed".

"Exactly".

The Rector is thinking that too. What could be more fanciful...

"It is witnessed that ye did cause sickness and death by means of Magic, naming figures carved of wood and piercing them with thorns till those they are named for fall in agony. Be this so?"

"Image Magic? No. No. I be Welsh see. A Christian woman. I did put the doll beside Mistress Thomas in her bed. Well, wouldn't you too, her being sick from so wanting of a child, though she's a spinster and her age far past the bearing of one. A Christian kindness it was. Twas hardly thievery neither, the puppit was thrown out for the ragman. Mistress Jones had no need of it, her children being grown and gone these past five years".

The Rector feels unsure of himself.

"How can I possibly declare her a witch? She seems more God-fearing than most of those gossiping 'gentle' persons sitting up front in the high pews of a Sunday. Yet I have it on the best of authority that the crime of Witchcraft threatens England more than did the Armada – not that the Armada did much harm once it met the good men of Bideford. As the face of Christianity in the Parish, I know what is expected of me. I must show patience, awareness and resolve. I feel myself called on to be of service, something I could accustom myself to and grow to love. Something too that could lead to preferment in the Church".

He picks up the heavy book and opens it. There it is again, the "Attributes "... "When the sick that ye treat feel pain, dost feel with them".

Temperance is really confused now.

"How could I feel pain in the body of another? Never give nothing to my sick friends I wouldn't take into myself. Is that what ye mean? And I stand before ye in health save for the hunger"

Ogilvy nods and reads on. Nought been said about raising storms. He can omit that question. And the good women had witnessed the warts on the woman's body though she had already denied ownership of a cat. He cannot believe Temperance to be a witch. He sees no evil in the eyes of the starving woman who sits with him She spoke no evil. He turns again to the book on his lap,

> "Atheism is begun in Saducism: and those that dare not bluntly say, There is no God, content themselves (for a fair step and introduction) to deny that there are spirits and witches"

How can he oppose that argument? The Church leaders are clear. And the good townspeople who pay his stipend, and had overlooked his over-indulgences, they think for sure Temperance Lloyd is a witch. Mayor Gist might not want to make the judgment himself, but when he delivered her to Rector Ogilby it was for him to declare her a witch. "Judge not that ye be not judged..."

Ogilby feels trapped. It is his duty to write a learned judgment. He will stay firmly with the writings of Glanvill and the late King James's Treatise on Daemonologie. Not the greater of King James's works... He calls the Constable to take Temperance back to the lock-up.

Temperance spent three more days tucked as close as she could in a corner of the old Church, her arms folded round her knees. She tried to keep awake to stare down the two rats that were becoming bolder by the hour. The Rector had said they were to feed her twice a day. The Constable told the guards and they did bring her food, bread, ale and sometimes some meat. Still, she knew what would happen. It was no surprise when they came at first light and put her on the wagon. After the dark, dank days in the lock-up with the rats, it felt good to be in the sun and air on the Coach Road to Exeter.

CHAPTER TEN
JULY 2, 1682

> "The information of William Edwards, Black-smith ... That on the 17th day of July [he] did hear Susanna Edwards to confess that ... she and one Mary Trembles ... did appear hand in hand invisible in John Barnes's house ... also ... that [they] were at that time come to make an end of the said Grace Barnes". (Relations of the Informations against Three Witches - 1682)

That night Temperance's departure was all the talk in The Arms.

"So she be gone now. Sad really. Never did nobody no harm that one, she didn't. Other two of 'em did no harm neither. Some say that Susannah be a saint, have the patience of a saint. Takes so much time to listen to the folk she serves. Gives the same potions as the quacks at half the price, they say, and none of that cuppin' and leachin' that do no good. And that Mary Trembles. Simple that one be. Scarce says ought. Just says over and over last thing she hears. Folk that should know better believes she's spelling them".

Seamus tells Sion he saw Susannah with Mary in tow, sitting over Buttgarden Street. He reports they were sitting there all morning.

"Nought for 'em to do now is there but beg. Dursen't try to sell the healin' now Temperance be sent up county for bewitching", Seamus says, "The two of 'em was sitting there on the mud gainst the wall by the horse and dog troughs, sun beatin' down that hot on them. Looked a proper sight".

He couldn't see if they were live or half dead, just their hands held up to folk, sunken eyes staring up, peering out of filthy brown faces. It was hard to distinguish their dusty ragged aprons and shawls from the dust they were sitting on. The heels of the folk that pass by throw lumps of dirt up into their mouths.

"Only thing they had to eat all day, all yesterday too likely. Terrible time tis for the old women. Still, Seamus says, tis worse over Ireland way. He was there on the butter boat a year past".

Susannah tells Mary the only thing for it is to go begging. Mary-Mary doesn't understand why they can't keep selling their cures.

"Temperance left all 'er stuff on scullery shelf".

It's simple to simple Mary. She keeps saying,

"Us be starvin'. Us must 'ave food".

Susannah tells her.

" 'Earne'll want money for that. Don' give nought for nought, 'e don'. Us don' 'ave none, Mary. Temperance be gone up t'Exeter. No more pay for 'er".

"Folk get stuff up market. Us can beg better up there".

Susannah tells her that's against law.

"Put us away 'em will if us be caught".

She never knows what Mary-Mary will say next. Never very bright, Mary's mind gets worse when she's hungry. Susannah tells her to watch for the Constable, while she does the asking. She pushes Mary towards the corner where she'll be able to see up Honestone Street and watch for people going home from Market, with their trugs full of meat and vegetables. The smell of baking bread wafting at them through the open door of bake oven shed makes Mary's mouth water. She drools. Susannah pokes at her,

"Shut yer mouth and wipe yer face. Folk'll cross street for sight of 'ee".

"Tis me face".

"And tis 'orrible".

Mary starts sulking again. They're selling stale bread for animals cheap across the street by the bake shed. Mary asks,

"Can' us get some o' that stale?"

"Nay Mary-Mary, us can't. 'Ow many times… Us don' 'ave moneys".

"Us could snick up an' get some".

"An' us could snick into lock-up. That what ye want? Shut yer gob an' 'ope yer eyes".

Mary sits back against the wall, puts her head down between her knees, hands behind her neck. Susannah prays for patience. A woman approaches with her maid.

"Alms for us poor. Kindness if ye please. Alms for us poor. Alms for us poor".

The pickings are scant. The woman throws a crust to Mary who catches it and slides along the ground holding it. Susannah makes a grab for it and they both tear at it between them Mary is snarling at Susannah.

"Like a cur 'er be, fightin' for it".

Mary wins and swallows the crust. They keep on begging, and another crust lands beside them.

"Mary-Mary, 'er bain't such a bad soul. Bends over th'orse an' dog trough, soaks one end o' crust in the water, dusty tis but... 'Er pulls off the soft bit an' give it me, then 'er dips t'other piece in the water".

Water runs down their chins from chewing the wet bread.

"No teeth left, jes gums. Comin' old".

Mary goes back to her corner. A horse trots by, its feet sending more dust and droppings into their faces. Mary starts coughing and can't stop till she gags and retches. A young boy stops to watch her. His mother pulls him away and they hurry on. As the women watch the sun fly across sky, the are getting desperate. The market will be closing at noon, another day gone by with nothing for them.

Just then they see Mistress Grace Barnes and her maid servant coming from market. Mary-Mary holds up her hands to them. The maid goes to take a parsnip out the basket, one that's too thin to peel for stew. Mistress Barnes stays the maid's hand and puts the root back. Dried mud falls between the slats of the basket right on Mary's face. She tries to pick the bits of mud from her eye. She doesn't say anything, just looks as if she's going to cry. Mistress Barnes shouts at the maid,

"Nay. Nay. Them as wants food must work for it".

The maid bends down as if to fix her slipper. She whispers to Susannah,

"Come up th'ouse after supper. Find 'ee somep'n then us will".

Seamus saw them sitting there on his way to the bake-oven. He tells Sion they must have sat there all morning, sun rising high in the sky till every piece of shade on the street was gone. They were still there after the market closed, just crouched there on the street begging for whatever they could get, croaking away at all that passed by,

"Bit o' bread, Mistress".

"Bit o' somethin', Master".

They keep on trying, but get precious little.

"And Seamus? No. He didn't give them nought. Well, he wouldn't, would he? Folk do forget what Rector said on Sunday of alms for the poor be time Market Tuesday come round".

The old women eat any scraps as they catch them to keep them from the stray dogs at the trough. Some folk throw food to the dogs, but offer none to the women. They watch the farmers' carts leave the market, and wait a while before giving up. Then they take the back alleys, even the drangs, to scavenge for any bits of food left in the piles of waste at the back of ale-houses.

"Nought to be in 'urry to get 'ome for".

Master Barnes walks into The Arms, greets Sion and calls for Beatrice to bring him ale.

"Always here up Th'Arms when his good lady takes sick to her bed. Did today she did. Such a strange tale he has to tell. Seems the Mistress come from market quite out of sorts.

Just a short walk down from market twas. Took it right out of her, he says".

"Lay herself down to rest soon as she got home. Would have the maid draw the curtains fast and the windows shut tight".

It would be mighty warm and airless in there with the heat today.

"No surprise", Master Barnes said, "She woke with a terrible headache".

Mistress Barnes had walked so slowly to the main chamber when the manservant sounded gong for supper. She knew Master John was there and he was not a man to be kept waiting.

"The Mistress though, she gets sick regular don't she?"

"She do, but this day twas something odd, a strange to do of it. Won't never forget it, Mistress being in such a fair state. 'Er kept saying how 'er din't do right by the poor, how 'er did deserve to be punished. Such nonsense", Master Barnes said.

Still there was no doubt about what she told him and her maid.

"Feelin' that sick, I be. 'Ad a good sleep, but woke with such 'ead pain. Dreamt a bad 'ead, woke with it worse".

Master Barnes told her she had to eat, though she said her stomach was turning fit to vomit. The smell of the food made her feel worse. Then the manservant put that tureen of meat stew with parsnips on the mahogany table at the window. The Mistress put her hand over her dish to stop him, but he ladled the stew anyway. John blessed the meal. Grace closed her eyes, bowed her head. He handed her a piece of bread. She dropped it. She told him she felt so faint just looking at the parsnip in the bowl. The long thin strip of parsnip floating in the thick brown gravy looked much like the bony finger on a hand outstretched for that same parsnip. John was becoming angry. He can't abide waiting.

"Can't abide wastin' food neither".

He told her,

"Eat up, Wife. The stew is a good dish indeed".

Grace shook her head,

"I can't eat, John. My stomach is out of sorts. I see not the food but the 'ands and faces of they poor women that 'ad not bread to put in their mouths".

"What women?"

"Why, that Mary Trembles and Susannah Edwards from Top of the Town".

"Be they not be-devilled. Surely, they have thee bewitched off thy victuals. Eat what the good Lord hath provided and be thankful for it".

Grace Barnes saw the bowl in front of her spinning round. The meat and vegetables become a blur. Only the piece of parsnip keeps its finger shape. She retches and puts her hand over her mouth, and runs towards the door. John shouts at her to stay,

"The meal is not done", says he.

Mistress Grace Barnes has to take to her bed. The pains get more violent. She feels so sick for days.

"Twas Mary Trembles, simple Mary they call 'er. Twas her eyes the mud from the parsnips fell in. Susannah, tother one, she'd been sitting further along".

Grace closes her eyes, trying to sleep the sight away, but she can't. She still sees Mary Tremble's weeping eyes.

"They'm borin' their way into my waking dreams while I lie in bed. Mary's eyes haunt me sleep. 'Er mouth's open, but 'er don't say nought. Tis Rector Ogilby us 'ear".

His words thunder into her dreams from a horse trough pulpit outside a cottage up Top of the Town. He keeps asking her,

"How hast thou helped him that is without power?"

Suddenly in her dream, the Rector's robes become the women's dust-stiffened aprons. The

Rector's eyes piercing into her very soul are an old woman's. The Rector's voice comes out a hoarse whisper,

"Bit o' bread, Mistress".

The voice changes,

"How hast thou helped him that is without power? Bit o' bread, Mistress. Bit o' bread, Mistress. Bit o'..."

Grace awakes calling out,

"No. No. No. I... I..."

The maid hears her cry and comes running into the chamber. Mistress Barnes waves her away.

"Leave me be to sleep".

She falls back to sleep, rolls over. The dream returns. She sees the horse trough erupt again into a pulpit. Mary Trembles stands up there, pointing a bony finger at her. She feels herself suddenly lifted off the ground. Mary's lips don't move. Her mouth hangs open. Through the drool, she spits out the words of the Gospel reading,

> "A new commandment I give unto you, That ye love one another".

Grace turns over in her sleep. She murmurs,

"Love one another ... Love one another ... Love one ..."

The sickness passes. The maid helps Mistress Barnes out of the bedchamber. She sits at the window still feeling weak. The maid covers her knees with a blanket and brings her weak ale and fruit cake. When John returns home he sits to talk with her. She tells him her dreams,

"Can't get 'er out of mind. Poor woman. Us should 'elp her. Rector said so Sunday past". She kept repeating the reading,

"Love one another ...".

John tells her,

"Ye was here in your bed Sunday past. Not in church".

"Heard the Rector say it, clear as day".

"What'd he say?"

"Twas from Job. 'How hast thou helped him that is without power?' And Gospel of John. Asked how us helped the poor. Said us was to love one another ... And truly the old women are them".

John Barnes was startled. He went running up to The Arms for a drink to settle himself.

"Master Barnes couldn't fathom it. None here could neither. Truly he had sat alone at Matins. And again at Evensong, his good wife lying home sick in her bed, slipping betwixt between sleep and wakefulness, twixt calm and fevered nonsense talk. True John Barnes had read the daily readings in the wife's bedchamber this week, being as she did not come to the breakfast table. But he had read her nought on Sunday, nought of Job, nor of John, about powerlessness, about the poor. Too sick to listen she was then... How could she know the Rector's chosen text?"

Master Barnes questioned the maid. Emma was sure that Grace had seen no visitors. She was too sick. The maid had left the house only to get fish down the quay and fresh bread. The little cat had come in during the

Temperance Lloyd: Hanged for Witchcraft in 1682

day. Emma had found her when she returned with the fish. Little cat had been a comfort to the mistress lying on the sick bed and purring.

"Then in come Harry Gifford. He asked after Mistress Barnes".

"Better she be. Still weak. 'Ad terrible bad dreams 'er did. Thought 'em to be real. Kept on and on about that Mary Trembles beggin', last Market Day. Susannah Edwards was sat with 'er. And Mistress Barnes been so sad for givin' 'em nought. And that not the whole matter. My good Wife, she knowed Rector Ogilby's texts, wi'out 'er been in church. Most odd tis. Can't fathom it".

"Harry Gifford, now, he knows something about all things. Always has an opinion he do. He can fathom it all easy. Told Master Barnes so".

"Tis terrible odd. Terrible odd. Only one way t'account for it. Sounds to me like 'er's been witched. And all knows 'ow it 'appen".

A week later, Master Barnes was in The Arms again. Grace Barnes was suffering another stomach upset.

"Nothing for it. Harry Gifford be right, though he wouldn't be hearin' us say it to his face". John Barnes finished his drink in one swallow. His spirits fortified, he walked over to the Constable's house to report to him that Mary Trembles had bewitched his wife because Mistress Grace had refused her a parsnip. The Constable knew just what to do. He sent Master Barnes off to see Mayor Gist right away. Such happenings must be reported for the good of the whole town.

So it was, the next morning, July 10, in the year of our Lord 1682, the Constable went to the door of the cottage at the Top of the Town to arrest Mary Trembles. He marched her down to the Town Hall.

"Right tale the Constable had to tell us of the doings when he got poor Mary there".

She had never seen inside the Town Hall before, with its high ceilings and dark-panelled walls. Mary put her hands up to her eyes to keep out the sunlight from the east windows. The bright July sun piercing the gloom is enough to hurt any eyes. Mayor Gist and Alderman Davie were seated at a table up on a platform ready to begin the questionning. John Hill, clerk, had his pen and inkwell on the table in front of him. They all looked quite menacing to poor, simple Mary. She was very afraid. She realized something was going on, but didn't understand what. Standing in front of these men in black robes, in this big, strange place, she was terrified. Mary usually kept quiet, listened to other folk gossip, never said much for herself.

The Mayor stared down at her sitting there. She looked back, eyes wide, her mouth open. All of sudden, she jumped up and started wandering around, touching the chairs, the walls, making as if to climb up beside

the Mayor himself. The Constable had to pick her up and sit her down again. The Mayor asks,
"Ye be Mary Trembles?"
The Constable tells the men up at The Arms that Mary had looked up at the Mayor strange-like, her eyes looking him up and down. She nodded. The Mayor told her,
"Speak up, so the Clerk can write it down".
"Write it down. Write it down".
Mary nods again.
"Be ye Mary Trembles?"
"Mary Trembles. Mary Trembles. Mary Trembles. Mary..."
"Yes. Yes. Ye be Mary Trembles".
The Clerk writes it down.
"Ye live with Mistress Temperance Lloyd and Mistress Susannah Edwards?"
Mary nods.
"Speak up"
She nods again.
"Speak up so Mr Hill can write it down".
"Temperance and Susannah"
"Ye live with them?"
"Live with them, live with them", she nods again.
"And ye make potions with them for the healing?"
" 'Ealin'. 'Ealin' ".
"Dost make healing potions?"
" 'Ealin' potions. 'Ealin' potions. 'Ealin' potions".
Mayor Gist looks at Alderman Davie. Alderman Davie takes a breath,
"Dost make the potions, or dost not?"
"Dost not. Dost not".
"So ye dost not make the potions. What dost ye?"
"Dost, dost ... Us dost th'herbs in garden".
"Ye tend the garden".
Mary nods.
"Like all do".
"Yes. Yes. But dost pick and make potions?"
Mary looks puzzled.
"Dost pick and make potions?"
"Make potions ... Make potions ... Can' do that".
"Why can ye not make potions?"
"Don' make potions. Can' do it. Must'n touch nothin'. Temperance say".
Two hours pass, with more and more questions but very few answers. Mary becomes increasingly confused. The Mayor and Aldermen look at

each other, time for a repast. They leave the room and head down to the Rose of Torridge, turning the proceedings over to the Constable.

"Ye do tend the garden?"

"Like all folks".

"Ye don't make potions?"

"Dunno 'ow. Temperance, 'er knows. An' Susannah 'er knows too".

"Why do 'em make they potions?"

Mary is really puzzled now.

"Don' 'ee know?"

"Not for me to know. For ye to say".

"Why?"

"Why? Why do 'em make potions?"

"For they sicknesses. For they sicknesses".

Mary rocks back and forth, repeating it over and over and over.

Sion smiles,

"Constable says twas like prayers on Good Friday, same over and over".

The sun moves to the south-west, the room darkens. The Mayor and Alderman have still not come back. The Constable, not knowing what else to do, continues his questions. Mary continues to repeat whatever the Constable says. The Mayor returns.

"Constable says he told the Mayor as Mary is too simple to do harm to folk. No matter".

The Mayor tries to explain to Mary how serious things are getting for her. If she is a witch, she'll be sent up County, could be hanged for a witch. Mary-Mary nods off to sleep. The Constable had to prod her with a cane to wake her. She jumped and asked,

"Where be us?"

Another Constable comes in. Mary nods off to sleep again while the Mayor, the Constable and the Clerk talk quietly. The evening fades into night. The questions keep on. Mary is tired and hungry, but she admits nothing. John Hill's notes become illegible which doesn't matter. Mary attests to very little. She doesn't make any potions, doesn't know how. She works in the garden. Temperance and Susannah make the potions. The potions are for making sick folk well. She never saw any Devil. Susannah did say as the Devil stayed up by Parsonage in the trees.

"So what dost ye?"

"Us beg for food. Us be starvin'. Us be starvin' now".

Finally Mary gets up and stumbles towards the Constable,

"Want go 'ome, tired".

"Constable says it was after sunset when he dragged Mary Trembles over the bridge to the lock-up. All the while she kept crying that she wanted to go home. Even in the dark, some folk saw the sad sight".

So it was that as Bideford woke to the sounds of the seagulls calling over the fishing boats that tied up at the quay with their night catch, the whispers became open, the talk in the town loud. The three women were evil. They brought all sorts of bad luck to the town. Those storms that took the fishing boats just before Michaelmas past ... That Appledore seaman who had gone crazed and murdered his good wife in her sleep ... And poor William Hebert's father, dead these past twelve years after the witch had treated him. That Temperance, she must have bewitched the jurors up in Exeter so they didn't see the truth from Bideford.

Sure, William the son had done well since the untimely death. His father's wealth coming to him as it did let him replace the boats his drunken crew lost in a calm sea off the rocks at Lundy. Of course it was odd the witch, Temperance Lloyd, that killed his father didn't overlook him with her evil eyes — despite that he had caused her to be arrested, charged and taken up county. You can never know what they'll do and won't do.

"Constable says tonight as Mayor Gist be losing patience. A busy man he be. Little time left for his own business on account of the business of them witches. How much longer will it take to rid Bideford of them three the old women whose keep would surely soon fall on to the Parish rolls? Temperance Lloyd be already in Exeter. Mary Trembles be gone to the lock-up. She'll be off up County soon. The statements already made against Temperance and Mary be sound and true, the number of witnesses growing".

Thomas and Elizabeth Eastchurch had spoken in the matter of Grace Thomas, John Coleman of Dorcas Coleman, Thomas Bremincom confirming their stories. John Barnes had said for sure his good wife's sickness came from her bewitching by Mary Trembles. The list of offences was getting longer, the incontrovertible evidence growing. And the talk ... That Susannah Edwards must be in on it too. She had been right there beside Witch Trembles begging.

"Constable be in with more news. Today John Coleman, respected Mariner, was in the Town Hall to report on the matter of Dorcas, his good and faithful wife, she that been treated by Susannah Edwards".

Mistress Dorcas said she'd been helped more by her than by the doctors, but what would a woman know of healing? Doctor Beare, a trained physician, had been unable to get her healed. He had declared to all Dorcas was bewitched.

Susannah was alone in the cottage when the Mayor sent the Constable to arrest her. The Constable told Sion she had locked her door and gone with him quite calmly.

"Us weren't too bothered by Constable comin'. Temperance been took in twice. Din't take 'er up County one time. Took 'er up an' sent 'er 'ome again dozen year since. Twill be same now. Temperance, 'er'll be let go again. And Mary-Mary, any fool can see 'er's simple, too simple to do nought wrong, nought right neither. Justices bain't foolish folk. Made sure to fasten door 'gainst bad folk us did".

The Constable took Susannah down Lower Gunstone and over to the Town Hall.

"Said 'e did'n go down High Street case us was to overlook any folk. Overlookin'. Foolishness tis. Foolish folk do think it".

Susannah still believed they could not be harmed by mere gossip.

"Justices bain't foolish. Best not to say as us can read 'erbals like Temperance do. Could 'ave learned all us know from Temperance. 'Er knows all bout th'ealin'. Great dark place this Town Hall be. Mary-Mary must 'ave been real afeared. Don't like big dark places, 'er don't".

The Constable tells her to sit. Alderman Davie starts,

"Thy name be Susannah Edwards, Widow of this Parish?"

"Us be sir".

She curtsied as she said it to be respectful.

"Ye live with Mistress Temperance Lloyd and Mistress Mary Trembles?"

"Us did so. They'm took away now".

"Just so. Just so. And you make potions with them for healing? Mr Hill shall write down what ye say".

"Make us potions with Temperance. Mary-Mary 'er's too simple to 'elp. 'Elps with th'herbs in garden".

"She do tend the garden?"

"Said it, us did".

"Thou dost pick herbs and make potions?"

"Aye sir".

"What be these remedies ye use?"

"Same as any do. Lily of valley flowers with wine for memory of dumb palsied, willow bark, feverfew, groundsel... Same as good Doctors do".

Alderman Davie starts to nod. Mayor Gist looks at him sternly,

"Folk all knows that. No need to write it down".

The Mayor looks down at Susannah.

"Tis the Physician, Doctor Beare and other good doctors as say ye do bewitch folk".

"Them do say it only if us 'eal and them do fail".

The men sitting behind Susannah start to laugh. Mayor Gist raises his hand to silence them.

"Master John Barnes doth say ye did bewitch his good wife, Mistress Grace so she did fall sick. Twice that did happen. How say ye?"

"Us spoke not to Mistress Barnes. Mary 'er did only beg 'er maid for a bit o' food".

"Did she give to thee?"

"Nay. Nor did many good folk".

"So be they good folk?"

"To best us knows".

"Didst ye bewitch Mistress Barnes?"

"Nay. Us did not".

"I ask thee again, Didst bewitch the good Mistress with the stomach sickness?"

"Nay. Us never been near 'er, save when us begged of 'er".

"Didst go in to 'er house?"

"Nay. Us never did go therein. Neither me nor Mary. Went to door down stairs for to see maid. 'Er that said 'er'd give us somethin'. Didn't get nought. 'Ow could us 'ave brought on 'er stomach sickness? Us never touched 'er. Never seed 'er".

"Be this true?"

"True tis. Never done 'er no 'arm. Mayor Gist, does 'ee not see us a Christian woman in Saint Mary's Sundays and 'Oly Days?"

"What dost say on Mistress Coleman? Dr Beare and Master Mariner Coleman do say ye did bewitch 'er".

"Truly us did attend Mistress Coleman when 'er did send for me. Ask 'er maid, Abigail. Come for us day and might, winter and summer. Weren't there when Mistress Coleman first took sick. Master Coleman weren't there neither. 'Er got sick when 'e were at sea. Couldn't stand for 'e to be away. Made 'er sick 'is gwain off did. Us tried t'elp 'er. Best for 'er was when 'e comed back. Got a bit better 'er did. Us went to 'er when 'er got sick. Us stayed 'ome when Master Coleman come 'ome. 'Er got well when 'e sailed back 'ome".

"A witch don't have to be around when evil happens. A cat was seen there. Canst ye not make thyself into a cat to enter windows?"

"Nay sir. None can".

Alderman Davie says something to the Mayor.

"A cat was seen in the chamber of Mistress Barnes when she been sick. Knowst of that?"

"Nay sir. Us never been in the chamber of Mistress Barnes".

"Ye weren't in the form of a cat there?"

"Nay sir. In no form".

"There was seen a magpie bird, black an' white, fly in Mistress Coleman's window. Wast that ye?"

"Nay sir. Us b'ain't neither cat nor bird".

"Master Coleman testifies you harmed Mistress Coleman".

" 'E been off at sea when 'er took sick. Makes 'er sick when 'e stays at sea, it do. 'Er gets better when 'e's back. Master Coleman don't know nothing 'bout his poor wife".

"Master Bremincom testifies the same".

" 'E weren't there neither. Jes know what 'e be told be Master Coleman".

Mayor Gist put his hand on Master Hill's arm. Stopped him from writing any more.

Susannah thinks,

"Reckon 'em done they writin' ".

The sun was setting up Bridge Street when the Constable took Susannah over the bridge to the Church lock-up. Mary-Mary was glad to see her. She doesn't know the trouble they are in.

CHAPTER ELEVEN
JULY 19, 1682

"If thou dost not believe the Being of Witches, study the Sacred Writ; consider that the Wisdom of Nations have provided Laws against such persons". Relations of the Informations against Three Witches (1682)

"Sun come in so bright twixt 'oles in walls us could see round th'ole lock-up. Them two rats be lookin' at us nasty 'em be. Guard give us two bits o' bread and water. Said twas for the journey."

They ate it quickly to keep it from the rats. Then they heard the shouting outside.

"Must be 'underds of 'em out there. Waitin' for us. Mary-Mary, 'er eyes got that big us could 'ardly see 'er face. 'Er started to cry. Telled 'er to stop it. Won't do 'er no good. 'Er kep' sayin' 'er wan' a go 'ome, wan' a go 'ome".

Susannah tells Mary they are being taken up County. Mary doesn't know where that is. She asks if it's up by Littleham way. Susannah says it is.

"What 'er don' know won' 'urt 'er".

Seamus tells everyone in The Arms that he was up by dawn and off to see the sight. As he's one to drink the night away he doesn't generally see the day till noon. He was right there walking along behind the open cart that rolled out of the yard on Allhalland Street and turned across the bridge. There were more than a hundred people gathered to see Susannah Edwards and Mary Trembles being brought out of the old church, their feet still shackled so that the Constable had to pick each woman up to heave her on to the wagon. He could have lifted them both at once so small and frail they were. The folk jeered and laughed at the sight of the shreds of loose straw flying up as the thin old bodies hit the floor of the cart.

Such abuse they shouted. Called them "Devil suckers", "Evil doers", "Black witches". They yelled "Good Riddance" as the cart trundled back across the bridge from East-the-Water to head to Torrington and the Crediton road over the moor.

Outside the Town Hall, there was a much larger crowd. Some had come running down Bridge Street, afraid to miss seeing the cart. It was as if they were on their way to see a pageant or a parade. The show was shorter than the wait for most. The cart went quickly along the road and was soon out of sight in the trees past the bend in the river.

Mayor Gist, Alderman John Davie and Clerk John Hill were up to watch. Seamus told everyone about it later up at The Arms, how he saw the Borough leaders peering from the sides of the upper windows of the Town Hall window as befitted their official dignity. He caught sight of Master Coleman beside them with his uncle, Thomas Bremincom. Masters Barnes and Eastchurch and the good Doctor Beare were also at the Town Hall window, standing back so as not to be noticed.

"Not much gets past Seamus. He noticed the Mayor and Alderman nod to each other. With Bideford thriving now as a port, the town don't need rumours of witchcraft putting a curse on its proud new coat of arms. They'll be in Church on Sunday making their prayers that t'will all go right at Exeter, asking the Lord to turn the pages so the book be closed on the happenings for good, forever. As long as … Mayor had Clerk send the testaments all on the Coach up County. Coach will o'ertake the wagon by the Inn at Holsworthy".

Mayor Gist and Alderman Davie waited for the crowds to disperse before they walked down to the Rose of Torridge for their breakfast of ale and cakes, the Clerk scurrying behind.

"Seamus don't take breakfast most days. Today he took himself and his eyes and ears straight over the Rose. The women were gone,"

"God be praised", said Alderman Davie.

The Mayor was still worrying,

"The testaments are all complete?"

John Hill nodded,

"All writ, clear and truly sworn".

"And Rector Ogilby did state his piece?"

"As well he must, according to the Statutes".

"So the Statements go by Coach today".

John Hill was getting bit testy.

Temperance Lloyd: Hanged for Witchcraft in 1682

"Twill all be there by nightfall. Put direct in the hand of the Sheriff".
"And the witnesses be summoned to appear?"
"All by name and by their houses".

Susannah is glad the cart is soon far away from the screaming mob.
"Mary-Mary, 'er was that afeared by 'em. Kep' tryin' to 'ide, as if 'er could".
Even though they are now alone on the road, Mary's puts her head down in Susannah's lap. As they drive towards Torrington the road twists around the river. They pass by the big farm where ale and spirits come into a cave at high tide on dark nights, and the Littleham road. Susannah doesn't tell Mary-Mary that. It would only make her cry again.
"Road be so rough. Cart's bumpin' 'long in ruts from all the coach wheels. Not much straw under us. Bumpin' round like a load o' swedes us be".
They have to hang on to the sides of the cart to keep from sliding off.
"Mary-Mary ain't got much of a stomach. 'Er starts to retch up the bit o' bread guard gived 'er. Watchin' and 'earing 'er gets us gwain too".
Once they were out of the trees and on the hill up to Torrington the sun beat down mercilessly. The driver stopped to give water to the horses and to drink some ale. He gave some to the women, said it would help them to sleep, which it did. It was cooler once the cart was back under the trees that sheltered the road out of Torrington. They slept and woke, slept again. The cart stopped with a jerk and they were wide awake. They were in a yard the carter told them was at the back of Holsworthy Cross Inn.
The ale-house keeper came out to look at them He seemed frightened at first till he saw they were only poor old women, not likely to do harm to anyone. They asked him to spare them a little food. Mary-Mary said if it should please him. Susannah wondered if he might think them to be truly witches that could overlook him if he spurned them.
" 'E wouldn't wan' a be witched. Good soul that 'e be, fetched out bread, bit 'o scrag end o' mutton. An' a pot of ale. Smiled at 'im us did".
"Bless 'ee sir, Blessed be"
Mary-Mary's mouth was too full for her to speak. She nodded to him. He let them be to eat in shade of the oak trees, coming back for the empty ale-pots.
"Blessed be", Mary-Mary smiled at him.
There was no word of them round the village so no one came to see. Then cart was off back on track to Crediton.

Sion heard it was a different story there.

"They say bad news finds its way to spread fast. Just takes a word or two to become twenty. Twas that way with word of Bideford witches and witching up Crediton town. Carter up from Plymouth in here tonight, come by way of Exeter and Crediton. Said our witches nearly had a warm welcome, Crediton folk tried to set fire to the cart".

The trouble for the women began in Bideford when Rector Ogilby told his good wife of his meeting with Mistress Lloyd.

"Well he would wouldn't he? None else much to talk to if he want to keep his living. Seems he had his doubts about any bewitching, but he had to stand by the judgments of the Church. Be on good terms with the town's justices these days, he be. Seems Mayor be ready to forget how Ogilvy knocked him down a while back. And the women would all be on their way up County soon. Rectory maid, Janna, another sister to our Beatrice, heard it all. Would've stopped there, but then didn't Mistress Ogilby give her leave to see her mother who was troubled by the falling sickness over East Crediton".

Janna took such a grand tale with her to Crediton, to Holy Cross. On the Sunday, past the whole congregation heard the Bideford witches were coming by. There was a lot of whispering with the hymn-singing, and talk in the churchyard. Janna had so many offers of a ride home in the carts and coaches. Some folk offered to add miles to their journey by going off in the wrong direction to take her. They all wanted to know when the wagon would pass through town. Janna didn't know just when the cart would stop to water the horses at the Inn, but it would be soon.

The Innkeeper said nothing. He didn't want any disturbance in his yard. That didn't stop the serving maids keeping lookout not to miss such a show. No sooner did the wagon stop behind the Inn than they were out in the yard to look. They saw the ankle ropes and knew right away the women in the cart were the Bideford witches. They rushed outside and told the first passersby they could find. Word spread. Crowds filled the yard, folk jostling to get closer and closer to the cart.

"When Janna came back she told Beatrice the whole story. Well, the whole story save the part her tongue took in the making of it".

Susannah pulled the sack over their head. She told Mary-Mary,

"Bide still. Don' 'ee move".

Mary was too frightened to move. She gripped Susannah's arm so tightly that her nails pierced the skin till the blood came. She was crying in fear. Susannah told her,

"Shhh. They'm close".

They lay shivering in fear under the sack. The crowd got louder, shouting out,

"Show us 'em. Pull they sacks off 'em".
"Don' touch. Could witch 'ee".
A farmhand got a stick to try to poke back the sack.
"Mind 'em don' overlook 'ee".
He hooked his stick on to the sack. The women tried to hold on to it but lost their grip. The man waved the sack over his head like a banner in a parade with the crowd cheering him on. Susannah remembers how she'd told sick folk to breathe slowly to calm themselves. She starts to breathe calmly herself, telling Mary-Mary to be still. She thinks of Temperance.

"Nought for it, Mary-Mary. Us'll 'ave to stare 'em down. Collect what Temperance did say".

Susannah pulls herself up and looks slowly round the crowd. She looks straight at them, right into all the tormenting eyes, one by one, by one, by one. Those who meet her eyes stop shouting, one by one, by one. Some who had pushed their way to the front stop moving. They stand still holding back others who were trying to push their way closer to the cart.

The Innkeeper sees his chance to send the cart on its way. The crowd is there only to gawk. They aren't buying any ale or meat. He pushes bread and ale into the carter's hands, walks through the crowd making a way for the cart, and tells the carter to be on his way. People in the crowd realize there isn't going to be a show. They try to stop the cart and run behind it shouting,

"Set em afire. Burn they witches".

The carter knows the straw will catch fire in a moment. He cracks his whip and the horse speeds to a canter. The crowd start running behind the cart. Susannah grips the rail and maintains her gaze. She makes the sign of the cross over them, as Temperance would. The shouting dies down. The man with the stick tosses the sack back on top of Mary. They are back on their way. The carter tells them it's not that far now to Exeter.

It was dusk when they approached Exeter. Susannah was amazed.

"My they walls be so 'igh. Red like as to blood with the sun on 'em and all. An' great 'uge iron gates. Cart went right through 'em".

Mary-Mary put her head down between her knees, thinking the cart would get stuck. Susannah told her there was room enough for a coach to pass through the gates, never mind a little cart. They expected to be taken straight to the lock-up. That didn't happen. The carter was hungry and told them he was going to the Ship Inn. He tied them tightly to the sides of the cart and tethered the horse in the great square at the back of a Church the carter said was the Cathedral. He spread sacks over them to hide them from prying eyes. After he'd eaten his fill, he came back and drove the cart up the street to the Gaol. Word of their arrival was spreading through Exeter, and a few people were watching for the women's cart.

Though there weren't too many of them, they made a lot of noise as they ran alongside the wagon shouting,

"Kill they witches",

"Show us they evil doers".

"Shame on 'em".

"Shame on they".

Susannah and Mary let go the sides of the cart and held on tightly to each other. Soon they were at another great gate set in high red walls. It was the castle. The gates creaked and clanged shut behind the cart leaving the crowd outside. The women pushed away the sacks and looked up at the walls in the moonlight. The carter banged on the door with his whip. The gaoler came out and dragged the women down from the cart. He pushed them inside. It was too dark for them to see where they were going and they half slid, half fell down the slippery steps and stumbled along a narrow passageway. He took the rope from around their legs and kicked them through a doorway. They heard the heavy door slam behind them. The gaoler took the lantern with him so they could see nothing. Then they heard a voice calling from the darkness.

"Susannah, Mary-Mary ... Be it ye? Be it ye?"

It was Temperance. Mary-Mary calls out,

"Temperance, Temperance".

Susannah and Mary were glad to see Temperance. She didn't seem too pleased to see them. She asked over and over again exactly what they had said to the Bideford Justices. Told them they must be careful to say nothing about each other, to stick to speaking of themselves. She told them,

"If one said to be a witch accuse another, both will be hanged".

In the morning the gaoler tells them prisoners have to pay for their food. Susannah tells him,

"Us got no moneys. 'Ad to beg for food up Bideford once Temperance was come 'ere". Temperance tells them they won't be allowed to starve before they go to trial.

"Wants us to die be hangin' not be starvin' ".

The gaolers did throw them just enough bread to keep them alive. There were just the three of them in the cell. Temperance told them that's so the gaoler can keep an eye on them in case they changed into a cat or bird and escaped. Temperance says,

"Pray God us could. A cat'd chase off the rats that be runnin' round all night. 'Ard to sleep for 'em climbin' on us, tis".

During the day, crowds of people keep up a steady shouting and caterwauling outside. The women can hear them through the small windows high up in the wall. They can tell there are more of them arriving by the shouts that get louder and louder. Mary is so frightened she huddles in a corner, her head between her knees. She can't sleep until the crowds leave for the night. When she does, the nightmares come. She shouts out in her sleep to let her out, let her out. Her shouts bring the gaoler down to tell her to shut up.

Susannah knows Mary is having the dream she used to have at home. It's a dream of being stuck in a place underground and she can't find a way out. She didn't know what the place was. Susannah knew it was the coal cellar Mary had lived in back in Littleham.

"Us knowed that. Us was there. 'Er don't collect much from when 'er was a child. Too simple 'er be to collect".

They all had nightmarish dreams, day and night. Susannah's take her back to lying in the grass wet with dew behind the stone wall in front of Temperance's cottage.

"I sees 'er door open. Twere'nt Temperance opened it. T'were me cowherd man come to beat us back th'Abbotsham road, draggin' us to barn to fetch poor dead baby, that same baby 'e'd beat out o' me".

Back at The Arms it seemed quiet after the three women were gone, too quiet. There was no more gossip. They were gone and good riddance, folk said. Forget them, folk thought. Sion knew the three of them would have a full month lying in the dark in Exeter gaol. It took that long for all the indictments against them to be drawn up to prepare for the Justices at the summer Assizes.

"A month. Would seem like a month of Sundays to them held in that Castle up County. Seems the Bideford women folk need a month of Sundays for all they have to do, such a great fuss they be making. Mistress Wakeley and Mistress Barnes off to buy a new bonnet to go to Exeter. Don't want to look like country folk up there in the County. Mistress Wakeley had Master Jakes, Milliner, make such a fine bonnet, yellow straw as tis still high summer, trimmed with all manner of fruit. Mistress Hearne said twas more like a picnic feast than hat. Exeter folk would know she was country soon as she alighted the carriage. So ... Mistress Wakeley had Mr Jakes take the fruit off and put silk roses in the stead. And wouldn't you know it, Mistress Barnes, who's friend to Mistress Hearne, right away had Master Jakes use the lovely cherries and apples on the bonnet he was making for her".

Their husbands are hiding up at The Arms to be away from the arguing all day and half the night.

"Stayed for a lock-in they did to give the women time to pack for the journey. Not that the wives were any way mollified by their men's thoughtfulness. Their tempers got the worse for waiting up to rage at them. Still angry they were when the carriages started out for Exeter. What with the

Mayor, the Alderman, the Clerk, the Rector, all the witnesses, and any other folk that could pay the fare, every carriage in Bideford, Appledore and Torrington was took. And the arguments over who would travel inside, well ... And Mistress Coleman tis said didn't want to go at all. Said she had no quarrel with Mistress Edwards. Master Coleman had a carriage come right up to the door. Helped her, more like dragged her into it, I hear from Master Pridham, with Master Bremincom taking one arm".

Temperance is very worried by the arrival of Susannah and Mary.

"Twas good to see the two of them, bad in a way too. May mean the worst for us all. Alone, I can acquit myself. With them, specially poor Mary, twill be another matter altogether".

She knows she must keep herself calm. She tries to comfort the two of them, helps them to pray. Mary likes it when Temperance sings softly to her. She can lull them both into calmer sleep with hymns in her Welsh tongue, sung as sweetly as she can.

The gaoler never lets it last. He pokes them with his staff when he finds them resting. Of long experience he knows that sleep can heal prisoners' minds so they may no longer be willing to admit to the crimes they are accused of. Temperance can see how Susannah is reacting. The sleeplessness is breaking her mind that's already troubled by hunger and the questions the Bideford Justices kept asking. She grows open to the gaoler's fanciful suggestions. He comes each hour to ask if she be a cat. Or be she not a hare? He tells her that if she admits her crimes she could get respite from the Sheriff when she stands before the Justices at the Assizes. Temperance tells her that isn't so. If she admits to being a witch she will surely be hanged. Susannah understands that when she talks to Temperance, but forgets as soon as the gaoler awakes her again.

"Hunger, rats, dark. Our gaol be almost as dark be day as be night. We sleep when he lets us. We are coming more confused. Be this day? Or night? What day is it? How long have we been here? How much longer will it be?"

They lose all count of time. Their past is fading. Temperance knows she must keep her wits about her, for them and for herself. Her questionning is all done. Susannah and Mary have witnessed to the Bideford Justices. The gaoler has no right to ask them more. Temperance knows he has no cause to ask. Yet if they say anything to him, he will surely add to the evidence.

"Been here afore I have. Been here afore, and been let free afore. Different then, me being full in charge of my own fate".

She fears that Susannah is now losing her mind, and no longer knows what's real and what she's imagining. Sometimes she can't remember well, sometimes she remembers nothing of what she must tell the Jurymen and Justices when she stands before them. Temperance tells her over and over,

"Tell only what ye telled Bideford Justices. What they have wrote down".

And then there's Mary ... Mary-Mary.

"Poor thing never knowed her own mind — if she have one".

She tells herself the City Jurymen must see Mary is too simple to do evil.

"Or the Justices from London will see it for sure, they will. Oh Good Lord help us for we cannot help ourselves".

CHAPTER TWELVE
AUGUST 13, 1682

> "Sir Francis North dreaded the trying of a witch... it fell out that [Sir Thomas] Raymond sat on the Crown side there, which freed his Lordship of the care of such trials". (Roger North, brother and biographer of Justice Sir Francis North who was in Exeter for the trial).

A deep dip in the road sends the carriage travelling to the last stop on the Western Circuit summer assizes lurching almost into the ditch. The passengers, Sir Thomas Raymond of the King's Bench and the Lord Chief Justice of the Common Pleas, Sir Francis North, are thrown almost into each other's arms.

"This road shall have our bones broken before we rest tonight".

This is the first time Sir Thomas has travelled to Exeter on the road rutted by Spring rains, hardened to rough rock by summer suns. Sir Francis sighs,

"Brother Raymond, just be grateful we go not to Newcastle upon Tyne. The road to Cumberland is truly hideous. On my journeys there, just ten years since, I had to be provided with arms and guards against the prevailing lawlessness of the North countrymen. We were beset by highwaymen on the road, by thieves in our lodging, by threats in the Court. Though I too shall be glad to reach Exeter today".

He does not mean to show his seniority by reminding Sir Thomas of the long years it takes to become Lord Chief Justice of the Common Pleas.

Sir Francis is so exhausted by the sittings in Wiltshire, Hampshire, Dorset and Somerset, he can barely endure the heat in the coach that bumps its way onwards to Exeter.

"Sir Francis, I did not mean "...

"No, no. I should not have spoken so. The August heat leaves me so weary".

Sir Thomas nods and smiles. He knows Sir Francis has been in poor health for some years now. He thinks,

"Sir Francis North, the Senior Judge for these sessions... He has many years of experience with Quarter Assizes. Working with him will teach me much".

Sir Francis smiles again. Brother Raymond has shown himself to be a pleasant fellow, eager to be at his side, eager to benefit from his long years on the Bench.

"Too many a long year, my dear wife would say. Today I would agree with her. It has been too long. The road to Exeter seems rougher and longer as each Assize is called. Some days it seems life, at least this part of my life, goes on too long".

There have been small victories. He has seen some of those most obviously wrongly accused acquitted. Some murderous highwaymen have been taken off the road. It's frustrating that many juries of the common folk seemed unable to understand the clearest of flaws in the evidence, to remember from morning to early afternoon what a witness had said. At times though he has to admit to being glad he has to leave London, especially to be gone from Westminster.

London had been a scene of confusion back when the Generals and the Rump parliament politicked over the return of King Charles II from Holland. It wasn't much better now with the King's propensity for all things pleasurable. Sir Francis knows it's best for a Justice to stay aloof from the gossip of the coffee houses and watches that his family is not seen to be entertaining those whose politics could be dangerous. He feels blessed that his closer friends understand that a man who must be away so many months will want private time with his wife and children at his London home. The years have been busy, too busy he feels as he grows older.

There had been the horror of the plague years, the Mortality Bills increasing in size by the week, over 2000 at the worst of the sickness. He recalls hearing the bells tolled at night as the bodies were removed. By day the streets were deserted. Death was all around. Fear of death took hold of everyone. Even the King's Court was not immune. Then the red crosses appeared on doors in the neighbourhood of Sir Francis North's own house. He had been loathe to move, but finally had to agree with his wife that it was necessary. Their friends to the north helped them find a suitable residence for the family outside Bedford.

Only shortly after their return to London the following year, the Great Fire destroyed much of the City. With so much turmoil and distress, back then it had been a relief for a while to travel the countryside, no matter how rough the roads. Today ...

"Truth be told, Sir Thomas, I shall be glad to reach Exeter today. But let us leave the morrow to the morrow".

The carriage is soon surrounded by the crowds in the streets calling loudly for the deaths of the witches that they expect the Justices to offer them. Justice Raymond seems surprised at the number of people. The Sheriff had warned them by letter to Wincanton that the crowds have been gathering in strength and noise since those named as witches were brought in to stand their trial. The mob that had started to gather with the arrival of the women was now larger and louder, milling around the private coach as it entered the city gate from the London Road. Sir Thomas was truly surprised by the excitement the trials of the old women had generated, further fomented by the gossip in the ale-houses. Sir Francis had anticipated it. He knew only too well how the influence of the mobs on the Jury would be enough to convict those named as witches on the flimsiest and most fantastic evidence.

There had been similar disturbances in the North over the past month. Sitting mainly on the King's Bench in the City, Sir Thomas has been sheltered from the wilder fantasies of witchcraft. Sir Francis, being older, can remember the 200 executions forty years ago in the Southeast of those accused and sent to trial by Mathew Hopkins, the self-appointed Witchfinder General.

The clamour of the crowds around the coach impedes their progress to their lodgings. One of the horses starts to dance between the shafts. The heat warms the refuse and excrement under the mare's feet on the narrow street. The stench seems to embody the distaste Sir Francis feels for continuing to try witches under the old Statute of King James. He knows that anyone with any scholarship, as have his brother Justices, cannot help but be skeptical of what is written about witches, including the ramblings of the former Monarch in his "Daemonologie". Yet these works are still the accepted basis for judging the crimes of sorcery. And when he thinks about the Reverend Joseph Glanvill's definitions of the "Attributes of Witches" having recently been published in a new edition...

"How could any reasonable man believe in people anointing themselves and flying out of windows to remote places, or transforming themselves into cats, hares and other creatures? And the idea that one person could cause pain in the body of another by magical thinking, and then feel that pain in her own body... Such ideas are truly preposterous. We know from the study of metaphysic that tempests arise in nature. They do not come, as the Reverend Glanvill wrote, from the 'uttering some nonsensical words or performing ceremonies alike impertinent and ridiculous' ".

Two years before, Sir Francis had been able to gain the acquittal of alleged witches. But now? The times are more confused. He sees that he cannot sustain his opposition to the witch trials. To express his views, though anyone who thought about it would accept them, would put his own life at risk. He thanks God that Sir Thomas is willing to take the trial of witchcraft and the other serious felonies, leaving Sir Francis to deal with the Civil cases.

At last they reach their lodging with nothing worse than bumps and fatigue from the journey. They bathe and rest a while. The evening air comes cool through the open window as they talk over a dinner of roasted chickens in a private room at the Ship Inn close by the Guild Hall.

"Another sessions-day tomorrow. It seems to me that one fades into another," Sir Thomas sighs. Sir Francis nods,

"Or worse they do repeat. I could expect to see our brother Robert Hunt reflect back from my mirror, his discoveries in Taunton do so reflect our calendar this week. This new enthusiasm for witching comes on the courts like a second plague upon the City".

"But still the Statute is the Statute. Tis said that to affront it is to admit to witchcraft, or worse, tis to deny our Christian faith".

Sir Francis has recovered a little from the our journey. He sits by the fire, lapses into a reverie, talks of the past.

"My father was seated in the Palace of Westminster when good King James watched his Statute become the law. He told me of it. How the King had been so convinced of politic acts by witchcraft that he became obsessed. He seemed possessed of such a passion to find and punish those who claimed to work evil by magical powers, that he sat trembling through the reading of his Statute. And far away in Scotland, there was in truth such superstition abroad as would support claims that reason would not".

Sir Thomas nods. He is glad to be in the presence of such a learned man.

"Scotland. Such a wild and lawless place I hear it was. Still be, according to our brothers that travel there to preside on Justice"

"Indeed, though in dangerous times, it can seem prudent to believe in the most fantastic feats of magic, unsafe to blame any true criminals. A witch be thought to injure simply by looking at her victim, cause pain and death by pricking a wax doll, or by an evil gaze. Up there in the North, and now even here, she is thought to kill or maim when absent at the time of the death. Tis even commonly held such women can transform into a cat, a bird or a frog, and go unseen into the victim's home".

Such wild beliefs had led to hundreds of crones being hunted and found, to be found to be guilty, and sent on their way to the gallows in Scotland.

"I collect my father saying that the King's Statute stirred little interest in London. The King and his Parliament were soon busied with other affairs of State, navigating the seas of religious conflicts in the fragile new Union. The country folk believed themselves well served by all manner of superstitions. And then as now there were those with a liking to see themselves as authorities, but with neither liking nor any talent for higher learning of the system of laws. Such folks saw for themselves fine opportunities to find favour in the Court of King James by enforcing the law out in the farther reaches of the kingdom. It was a matter of the security of the King, of the nation. Witchcraft might seem a superstition in London's coffee-houses, but after what had happened to the King himself... The trade of witch-finding could only be honourable".

Sir Francis sinks further into his chair.

"My father had his doubts. To be politic, he spoke of it only at our family table. He asked us, was it possible that dozens of old women, who had always soothed minor ailments with their use of herbs and rubbing of limbs, had suddenly become Satan's servants? Or was it more likely the new law offered an easy way for country parishes to avoid payment to the almshouses? Certainly no witches seemed to be plying their trade around the Palace of Westminster. My mother listened to the tales told by the wives of the Chief Justices who travelled out into the distant counties, even to the borders with Scotland, but she said little".

"And so today, with so strange a twist of what shall be taken for evidence, we could deny the very commandment on which our justice rests — 'Thou Shalt not Kill'. Oh Brother Francis, you best keep such thoughts within these walls".

"I will. But be you skeptic where skepticism is in order. I'm too tired for more of witches. So I thank you for judging it".

"Skepticism you say. How so in our cases here?"

"What think you of our host's cat that lies there by the fire, Brother Raymond?"

"The cat? She will keep the mice from us. She is harmless, warming her fur against the flames".

"Maybe thou should think on that the morrow when you hear the evidence that would convince you that if a cat leap in at an old crone's window at twilight, verily said cat be the Devil. And if the same cat jump out the crone's window, it be the crone herself. As well, the poor wretches brought to trial upon account of witchcraft have, as usual, a popular rage that does demand them to be put to death ... and if a Judge declares against that impious vulgar opinion, the countrymen that try them will cry out that this Judge hath no religion, for he doth not believe in witches; and so, to show that they have some, they will hang the poor wretches. Which tendency to mistake requires a very prudent and moderate carriage in a judge, to convince by detecting the fraud rather than by denying authoritatively such power to be given to old women. If thou stay passive thou wilt let those poor women die".

"The Mayor and Alderman of Bideford brought forth the informations against the women, duly noted by the Clerk. Can we deny all this? The Jurymen will surely accept it. Unless they put it down to mere country ignorance".

Sir Thomas points to the papers that now lie piled beside them.

"Tomorrow they shall learn from the good burghers of Bideford all that has been witnessed".

"Witnessed or believed. The eyes see only what the mind expects. There has been such a fever of accusations. Such a babble".

Sir Francis picks a paper from the top of the pile and reads,

> "Information of Dorcas Coleman, Wife of John Coleman, Mariner, Taken before Thomas Gist, Mayor and John Davie Alderman, Justices of the Peace on the 26th of July, 1682 That on or about the end of August 1680 she was taken in tormenting Pains by pricking in her arms, Stomach and Heart, upon which she asked Thomas Bremincom to repair unto Doctor Beare for some remedy. And very shortly afterward Doctor Beare upon view of her Body did say that it was past his skill to ease her of her Pains for he told her that she was Bewitched, and further that at the time of her tormenting Pains she did see Susannah Edwards in her chamber and that she would continue so every week, and that when the said Susannah was apprehended concerning Grace Barnes that she (Dorcas) did go to see Susannah and that when Susannah was in Prison she did confess unto Dorcas Coleman that she had bewitched her "...

> "Information of Thomas Bremincom, Gentleman, Taken before Thomas Gist, Mayor and John Davie Alderman, Justices of the Peace on the 26th of July, 1682 That about two years ago Dorcas Coleman was taken very sick, and this informant did repair unto Dr Beare ... who did say ... that she was bewitched "...

"You will note that Master Bremincom be uncle to Master Coleman, and Master Coleman and Master Bremincom heard all from Doctor Beare. But let us continue..."

> "*Information of John Coleman, Mariner, Taken before Thomas Gist, Mayor and John Davie Alderman, two of his Majesties Justices of the Peace on the 26th of July, 1682 The said Informant upon his Oath saith, That Dorcas Coleman, his wife has been a long time sick in a very strange and unusual manner; And he hath sought far and near for Remedy, and saith that one Doctor George Beare being advised with concerning her Sickness, in this Deponents absence (whilst he was at Sea) the said Mr Beare, (as this Informant was told by his said Wife, and his Uncle Thomas Bremincom, at his return), said that it was past his skill to prescribe directions for her Cure, because that the said Dorcas Coleman was bewicht. [And] that about three months last past, his said Wife was sitting in a chair, and being Speechless, he this Informant did see Susanna Edwards of Biddiford aforesaid Widow, to come into the Chamber under a pretense to visit her. Whereupon this Informants Wife did strive to come at her the said Susannah, but could not get out of the chair. Upon which this Informant and the said Thomas Bremincom did endeavour to help her out of the Chair, and the said Susannah did go towards the Chamber door. And further saith, That when the said Susanna was come at the Chamber door, she the said Dorcas (remaining speechless as aforesaid) did slide out of the Chair upon her Back, and so strove to come at her the said Susanna: but was not able to rise from the Ground, until the said Susanna was gone down the Stairs. And further saith, That the said Dorcas hath continued in such a strange and unusual manner of Sickness ever since unto this day, with some intermissions*".

"So the Doctor tells the Mariner tells his Uncle tells the Justices. And do we know more about these intermissions? When did they occur?"

"Yes. Indeed these are questions that needs must be asked".

"If you be so inclined as to ask them. But there is more of the same nature".

> "*Information of Grace Thomas, Spinster, Taken before Thomas Gist, Mayor and John Davie Alderman, Justices of the Peace on the 3rd of July, 1682, That on or about the*

> 2nd day of February, 1680, she was taken with great pains in her head and all her limbs, which continued until the 1st day of August and then began to abate and she was able to walk abroad to take the air; but in the Night season she was in much pain, and not able to take her rest, and that on or about the 30th day of September now past, she was going up the High Street where she met Temperance Lloyd, Widow, [who] did then fall down on her knees saying Mrs Grace I am glad to see you so strong again, and that in that very night she, this informant was taken very ill with sticking pains ... And that on Friday night, the 30th of June, she was again in pain. And that upon the first of July, as soon as Temperance Lloyd was apprehended and put into prison in Bideford, the pricking pains ceased and abated".

"So this woman is taken with pains from time to time, the pains abate while the supposed witch is free. Yet on another time, abatement of her pains are occasioned by the imprisonment of the Witch?"

"It would seem so. And then her sister also testifies..."

> "Information of Elizabeth Eastchurch, Wife of Thomas Eastchurch, Taken before Thomas Gist, Mayor and John Davie Alderman, Justices of the Peace on the 3rd of July, 1682, That on the 2nd day of July, she had been with Grace Thomas who was lodging with Thomas Eastchurch and had observed nine places in her knee which had been pricked, whereupon she did demand of Temperance Lloyd whether she had any wax or clay form where by she had tormented Grace Thomas, upon which Temperance said she had not wax or clay but confessed she had only a piece of leather which she had pricked".

"And may we know the reason a woman would prick a piece of leather? Surely tis most likely she mended her leather slipper".

"I must have the Sheriff be sure to ask the witch that".

"The Witch, you say? And we can be sure of that from other reasonable testimony?"

> "Information of Anne Wakely, Wife of William Wakely, Taken before Thomas Gist, Mayor and John Davie Alderman, Justices of the Peace on the 3rd of July, 1682, That on the 2nd day of July, by order of Mr Mayor, she did search the body of Temperance Lloyd in the presence of Honor

Hooper and several other women, and did find two teats hanging nigh together like unto a piece of flesh that a child had sucked, whereupon she asked Temperance Lloyd if she had been sucked in that place by the Black Man, whereupon Temperance did acknowledge that she had been sucked there often by the black Man, the last time being on June 30th last, And that Temperance had been attendant on Grace Thomas about six weeks past, and that on Thursday past, the 29th of June in the morning, Anne Wakely did see something in the shape of a magpie to come at the chamber window where Grace Thomas did lodge. She demanded of Temperance Lloyd whether she did know of the bird and Temperance did say it was the Black Man in the shape of the bird and she, Temperance was at the door of the house where Grace Thomas lodged".

"Information of Joane Jones, Wife of Anthony Jones Taken before Thomas Gist, Mayor and John Davie Alderman, Justices of the Peace on the 18th of July, 1682, That on the 18th day of July, she had been with Susannah Edwards when John Dunning of Torrington came in to see Susannah. He asked her how and by what means she became a witch. Susannah did answer that she had told no one before, but she would tell him. She was out gathering wood when she did see a Gentleman, whereupon she was in good hopes to have a piece of money of him. This informant further saith, that the said John Dunning did demand where she did meet with the Gentleman, Susannah said it was in Parsonage Close. John Dunning then left. Then on Sunday July 16th she heard Susannah confess that she and Mary Trembles with the help of the Devil, did prick and torment Grace Barnes. And the Informant saith that she did hear Susannah Edwards and Mary Trembles say and confess that they did this present day, being the 18th of July, torment and prick Grace Barnes again. And further saith that she did hear Mary Trembles say to Susannah Edwards, "O thou rogue, I will now confess all. For tis thou that hast made me to be a witch, and thou are one thy self, and my conscience must swear it". Upon which Susannah replied to Mary Trembles, "I did not think that thou wouldst have been such a Rogue to discover it". And that Susannah Edwards did say and confess that

> the Devil did oftentimes carry about her spirit. And that she did hear Susannah say that she did prick and torment Dorcas Coleman wife of John Coleman, and that Susannah confessed that she had lain with the Devil in the shape of a boy lying in her bed. ... Hearing this her husband and the Constables were sent to bring Grace Barnes to the Town Hall to testify upon which Susannah Edwards looked at Anthony Edwards who forthwith leapt and capered like a madman and fell shaking, quivering and foaming and lay there half an hour. Joane declared her husband had never had a fit before there".

> "Information of Anthony Jones Taken before Thomas Gist, Mayor and John Davie Alderman, Justices of the Peace on the 19th of July, 1682, "...

"How doth John Dunning collect this confession?" Sir Francis asks.

"John Dunning. John Dunning "... Sir Thomas rifles through the pile of documents.

"His testimony seems not to be among those presented here. There is here a confession..."

> "Information of Temperance Lloyd, being brought by some constables upon the complaint of Thomas Eastchurch and charged on suspicion of having used some magical Art, Sorcery or Witchcraft upon the body of Grace Thomas, and to have had discourse with the Devil in the shape of a black Man, Taken before Thomas Gist, Mayor and John Davie Alderman, Justices of the Peace on the 3rd of July, 1682. She said that on the 30th day of September last she met with the Devil in the shape of a black Man in the middle of the afternoon in Higher Gunstone Lane and that he did tempt her to go with him to the house of Grace Thomas ... she confessed to seeing a Grey or Braget cat that went into Thomas Eastchurch's shop. And that the following day she came again to Thomas Eastchurch's house invisible, and the cat did leap back into the shop; and she said she was at the house on Friday the 30th of June and that the Devil was there with her and that he was about the length of her arm and that his eyes were very big..."

Temperance Lloyd: Hanged for Witchcraft in 1682

"Information of William Hebert, Taken before Thomas Gist, Mayor and John Davie Alderman, Justices of the Peace on the 12th day of August, 1682, That on the 4th day of July, he went to see Temperance Lloyd in the Prison to ask whether she had harmed his Father in 1670 that she had been accused of and acquitted and that Temperance had answered, Surely I did kill thy Father, and that she had also confessed to the deaths of Lydia Burman and Anne Fellow at about the same time".

"Yet was she not accused and acquitted of these same crimes ... ".

"So against the fanciful nature of the evidence I agree. But as well, they have confessed their crimes".

"As well they would. The old women are surely in a sort of melancholy madness, not possessed of their full wits, thinking in pain and want of spirits, and so contract a false opinion of themselves. Such confessions must be weighed against rational and sensible evidence".

"Yet wast it not a good Doctor that did declare the bewitchings? I find no information from him".

"The good Doctor Beare is an important and busy man, too busy to be called to witness, too important to be questioned".

"Aye. That means much. Yet, what is evidenced is much repetition of the tales of others absent. As should be evident to our good Exeter Jurymen".

"That's for you to have them consider. Have them look at the destitute crones they see before them, to see them as the helpless women they surely are, not as the empowerful tools of the Devil. Tis the women not the crime of Witchcraft that ye try".

CHAPTER THIRTEEN
AUGUST 14, 1682

"Atheism is begun in Saducism: and those that dare not bluntly say, There is no God, content themselves (for a fair step and introduction) to deny that there are spirits and witches". (Joseph Glanvill, 1681)

Susannah and Mary had been with Temperance in Exeter Gaol for almost a month. Monday, August 14 was a clear, warm day. The gaoler brought bread to the women and mashed vegetables to go with it. Temperance recalls being given better food on the day of her previous trial.

"Well, they won't want for us to faint from hunger in the Court, will they. This must be the day".

She's right. The Gaoler soon comes back. He leads them through the door, out of the dark into the courtyard. They stumble in the chains round their ankles as the bright sunlight half blinds them for a moment. The gaoler hands them over to a constable at the bottom of the steps outside the door. The great walls of the Castle of Exeter had glowed red in the setting sun when Temperance was first brought there.

"Tis redder from the sun this morning. Red sky in morning ..."

She asks the Constable what day it is. He says it's Monday. There was a huge crush of people all around them as the Constable led them through the courtyard. Temperance knew the courtroom must be full already. The people shouted loudly at them as the Constable pushed the women forward.

"Witch, Witch, Witch".
"Filthy witch".
"Blasphemer. God-hater".
"God hated Filth".
Temperance shakes her head sadly,
"Do they know the Lord, they that be taking his good name in vain?"
Mary-Mary is so frightened she can scarcely move her legs. She snivels quietly as she shuffles along, eyes on the ground ahead of her. Temperance tries to walk calmly through the crowd, looking around her as she believes is her right. As she had told Susannah and Mary in the cells,
"If ye looks guilty to them, ye art guilty to them",
" 'Ee was none guilty last time. For sure", Susannah said.
Mary just muttered over and over, "For sure, for sure, for sure..."
Temperance told them again they must remember that they are not guilty, not now, not ever.
"We none of us be witches. Healers we be. We must think on that. Think on that. We must hold our heads high no matter what".
Susannah keeps trying to hold her head up till the shackles make her trip over her own feet. She falls against the Constable who holds her upright. A man in the crowd calls out,
"See 'er be drunk".
Mary has her head bowed so low her chin almost pierces her breast.
"Poor thing, she'll be deafened by her own fear. Still, she won't be hearing the calls of the crowd".
As they reach the stairs up to the front door, the boldest in the crowd push forward, making as if to follow them through the heavy doors. The doors clang closed behind them and they can no longer hear the calls of the mob outside once they're inside. They pass through more huge doors into the high-ceilinged court room. Temperance recalls it from her trial in 1670.
Then they hear more shouting and see there's a whole great crowd seated up in the gallery, eating, drinking, laughing, playing cards.
"Twas quieter when I was yere for William Hebert".
Sir Thomas Raymond looks around the courtroom.
"Such a fine day for such a terrible prosecution", he thinks to himself.
Bright sunlight streams through the mullioned windows to show a scene like a pageant in the London theatre his good wife, the Lady Raymond, likes so much.
"Would she like this play", he wonders. "Here we all are dressed for the occasion, me in my velvet robe and periwig, the Jurymen in their Sunday best, and three dusty, bony, old women".

Temperance Lloyd: Hanged for Witchcraft in 1682

The bright sunlight exposes every wrinkle, every patch of dirt on the women's faces, every tear in their skirts. As they pass by the public, kerchiefs and pomanders are pressed to noses against the stench rising from their unwashed bodies. Sir Thomas cannot smell them as strongly from his place high up on the bench. He stares at the three old women who have been accused of witchcraft. He sees standing there, the most old, decrepit, despicable, miserable creatures he has ever seen.

"A painter would have chosen them out of the whole country for figures of that kind to have drawn by. There are no artists here".

The Jurymen look at them with curiosity. They think they see, in the life, depictions of what surely evil must be, the very opposite of the clean, white-clad angels from the paintings of heaven recently returned to the walls in their churches. Sir Thomas speaks to the Jury, his voice echoing back from the wood panelling,

"Gentlemen Jurors, today you are called on, and it is your solemn duty, to find the truth about the women who do stand here before this court. Are they indeed witches, or have they been accused wrongly for various and sundry reasons? Witnesses, the good citizens of the Borough of Bideford, have sworn to their statements. And the Law is clear".

He clears his throat to emphasise the point he is about to make.

"Since the time of good King James himself, we have known about the crime of Witchcraft. Learned men have reasoned and written great books on the subject. The former King himself, may he rest in peace, had written so in a learned treatise near a hundred years past. The attributes of witches are set out clearly now, that we should know them, by very learned men at Cambridge that have also shown that truly witches must exist. To deny their existence is to deny God himself".

Some of the Jurymen start fidgetting. Of course they know there are witches. Everyone knows that. They want to get on with it.

"The question today is not whether or not the activities of witches occur in general. This is established and cannot be denied. The question you must deliberate and decide is whether these three particular women that stand before us today have performed Witchcraft. Have these women done the work of the Devil? Have these women through his powers caused harm and injury to their fellow citizens?"

The Jurymen have already heard the statements sworn in Bideford. What more do they need to know?

"Ye must listen to the witnesses. Ye must listen to the accused. Ye must weigh the case. Ye must consider each of the accused separately, though they are companions to each other and they stand all three here today. Ye must make your judgments without fear nor favour. There is nothing to fear. God himself will protect you. So we shall begin. God be with you and God bless our country. Sheriff, call the first accused to the bar".

The Sheriff calls out,

"Temperance Lloyd, hold up thy hand".

She raises her hand to let everyone in the court know they are dealing with the right prisoner. Sir Thomas nods to the Sheriff to continue. He reads,

"Thou art here indicted by the name of Temperance Lloyd, late of Bideford, Widow, for that thou didst bewitch Lydia Burman unto death and that thou didst by witchcraft consume the body of Grace Thomas. How sayest thou, Temperance Lloyd, art thou guilty of this felony as it is laid in the indictment whereof thou standest indicted, or not guilty?"

Temperance seems about to plead guilty. Sir Thomas raises his hand to have her think before she speaks.

"So long and hard have I prayed on this time. I collect my acquittal more than ten years past. Guilty or not guilty? Every week we pray, so we do, Almighty and most Merciful Father, We have erred and strayed from thy ways like lost sheep ... we have done those things which we ought not to have done, and there is no health in us; ... Spare them, O God, which confess their faults; Restore thou them that are penitent..."

She pauses to look at the Jurymen, some of whom are passing around a pomander. She sees before her a Jury she hopes are as God fearing as she herself. If she pleads guilty they will surely offer her lenience. She looks up at the Judge. He nods at her slowly. Temperance thinks what to say. This time, the Jury may be carried by the mob and will take a guilty plea for the truth, even if it is not true. She waits a moment. Then, as if in a dream, she hears herself say it,

"Not guilty".

She tells them she did nothing to Lydia Burman, and Mistress Thomas is still as well as she has ever been. The Sheriff is speaking again,

"Temperance Lloyd, Did ye bewitch a child with an apple?"

"I sold apples and the child took the apple from me, and the mother took the apple from the child. She refused to pay, for which I was angry; but the child did die of the smallpox".

She's telling the truth but it's obvious the Jurymen do not to believe her. She can hear them murmuring to each other,

"That may be truth".

"Truth maybe. Collect though what we be told by the Sheriff".

"This child became sick after he be given an apple. He died by witchcraft for sure. The witch must hang. She be a witch".

The Sheriff asks her,

"Mistress Lloyd, ye did offer potions to one, Grace Thomas?"

Everyone knows she did. Temperance replies,

"Indeed sir. She did demand of me to come to her when her poor legs and back were aching so".

"You gave her potions?"

"I did so, Sir. And rubbed her legs to ease the stiff joints, I did".

"These potions what are they?"

"The same physic the Doctors offer. The same I read in Master Gerard's writing if it please thee sir".

Sir Thomas is leaning forward to speak,

"Canst thou read, old woman?"

"Since a child in Welsh Wales, I have had the reading. Learned from the Hallowed Book in Church School up the Valley. Welsh I did read first. English only a little back then. The Holy Bible, God bless King James for his gift, has been my tutor in England".

The Jurymen start to murmur again.

"Must be a witch to read a book".

"Witches be known to turn the Holy book to evil".

"Say the words backwards to spell evil".

"Valley 'er be come from, Valley of Evil dare say".

"That Temperance Lloyd speaks a foreign tongue. Evil tongue".

"One witch can call another. That Susannah, 'er said 'er was taught by this one. 'Er can be 'anged for that with nought else agin' 'er. Sheriff, 'e did tell us last night in The Ship".

"Sheriff did tell that".

Sir Thomas tells them to be silent. Later talking to Sir Francis, he sees he should have asked why the Sheriff was with the Jurymen before the trial. The Sheriff continues,

"Temperance Lloyd, Didst thou confess to consort with the Devil to bewitch?"

"I did think that for a time. I mind I said it. Now I doubt my mind. Perchance I dreamed it, though it seemed true real. I live with my friends, Susannah and Mary. We drank too much of the potions for to sleep away the cold and hunger. Terrible cold twas in the bad years. Now my mind is clear I canst not well collect what was dreams and what waking real. They say it was my dreaming. My friends did tell me that, Sir. They swear I lay between them the night long when I thought me flying in the night. For myself I know not".

The Jurymen are talking again,

"Devil could come to 'er at night, like a dream. The Black Man 'as 'is own ways".

" 'Er be guilty. Mark my words".

"Don' make no difference, guilty or not. Folk all round be angered. Won't stand for nought but they'm guilty. Want for 'em to be 'anged. 'Ang they or 'ang us, jest 'ee see. 'Angins be good sport for Saint Bartholomew".

"They witches could bewitch us from the 'angin".

"So stay 'ome".

"An' miss the sight. No fear".

"Afeared 'ee be one way or tother", he laughs loudly at his own joke.

Sir Thomas glares down at them, "Be silent".

They leave the Court to eat. Sir Thomas fears the Jurymen will talk more superstition as they take their food. When they return to the courtroom, the Sheriff calls Mistress Susannah Edwards.

" Susannah Edwards hold up thy hand".

A woman who appears to Sir Thomas even more frail than Mistress Lloyd stands and raises her hand.

"Thou art here on the charge of bewitching Dorcas Coleman. How dost thou plead?"

"Not Guilty, Sir".

Poor Dorcas. Susannah recalls treating her with all kindness, and even more patience.

"For sure 'er be not witness to this. Could be 'er good man that was always off to Banks. Or did 'e go just to Bristol tellin' 'er twas the Banks, could be 'im as said 'e witnessed 'arm". The Sheriff is speaking again,

"Did ye visit Mistress Coleman at her house in Bideford?".

"Indeed sir, up on th'ill over East-the-Water. Many times 'er called for me".

"How did she call you?"

"Sent 'er maid, Abigail, for me, 'er did. Kep' on sendin' 'er for me 'er did. Summer an' winter time. In all weathers,' er did come to us door".

"She sent for ye often?"

"Day and night that Abigail 'er come".

"Why did she send for thee?"

"For the sickness. 'Er got sick when 'er man went to sea. 'Er sat waitin' for 'ee to come 'ome. 'Er couldn't rest for 'er worry. Worrited sick 'er was".

Master John Coleman leans forward as if to stand up. The Sheriff raises his hand.

"Silence, sir. Thou hadst thy say in Bideford and shall maybe have it again here. Mistress Edwards be under question".

He looks again at Susannah.

"Mistress Edwards, Thou wert called to help?"

"An' 'elp us did, as God can see".

"What didst thee to Mistress Coleman?"

Temperance Lloyd: Hanged for Witchcraft in 1682

"Gived 'er potions for the pains, pains 'er got from sittin' so long watchin' boats go out and come in. Sat dawn to dusk 'er done at 'er window till 'er gived 'erself such pains. Pains in 'er back. Pains in 'er neck, pains in 'er 'ead. Pains all over 'er poor body".

"She did bring the pains upon herself?"

" 'Er din't purpose so. Mistress got so melancholy over the good mariner's being away. 'Er 'ad it set in 'er mind that 'e be gwain a die at sea. Sat so stiff watchin' for 'im as to cause such pain. Betimes 'er went days off 'er victuals till 'er swooned. 'Er stomach closed up so 'er couldn't then eat".

"And the potions you gave her, did she benefit in health?"

"Nought could make 'er well. Only to know 'er good husband safe at anchor down the quay. 'E sail back. 'Er got better. 'E sailed off. 'Er got sickened. Us potions but soothed 'er a little".

"What potions did ye use?"

"The same as Doctors offer. Feverfew, prunes, horse-foot, heartease in Spring, herb twopence, dead nettle, linden in Summer... Seasons all bring they own".

"How did you learn this physic?"

"From Temperance Lloyd, when us come to live in Bideford".

"Did Mistress Lloyd learn from the Devil?"

"Nay sir. 'Er 'ad 'er books. Us can read some too".

"Mistress Coleman has witnessed that you did harm her by witchcraft. How say you of this?"

"Mistress Coleman 'er was glad enough of me 'elp. More 'elp 'an 'er got from Doctor Beare. All 'is cuppin' an' leachin' did make 'er worse, weakened 'er near to death 'em did. Twas Doctor Beare did say as 'er was bewitched".

"Other witnesses said the same".

"Nay sir. They b'ain't witnessed nought. B'aint seed nought. Mistress Coleman 'er got it from Doctor. Mariner Coleman heard it from Mistress Coleman. Us tended 'er only while 'e was off sailing the Banks for Master Gifford, then for 'eself. 'E weren't there. 'Er was sick when 'e was gone. Better when 'e come back. 'Er telled 'e so 'erself. Us weren't there when Doctor said things".

"And what of Thomas Bremincom, Mistress Coleman's kin?"

"Master Bremincom, uncle to Master Coleman 'e be. 'E 'eard it from Mariner Coleman. 'E weren't there neither".

"Three witnesses. All be wrong?"

"If 'ee do say so sir. They jes' were'n around".

"They witnessed when they were absent?"

"If 'ee say so, Sir".

The Jurymen and those in the public gallery all start to laugh. It isn't funny to Susannah. The Sheriff stands up and shouts, "Silence".

He tells Susannah they are finished with her, for now... Then he calls for Mary-Mary.

"Mary Trembles, Raise your hand".

Mary just looks at him.

"Mary Trembles, Raise your hand".

Susannah nods to Mary and motions to her to put her hand up. Mary puts her hand up. The Sheriff says,

"You stand accused to causing Mistress Grace Barnes to become sick. Do you plead guilty or not guilty?"

"Not guilty. Not guilty. Not guilty".

Mary rocks back and forth, her head moving from side to side. Sir Thomas can see that Temperance and Susannah are old, poor, and sick. But Mary ...

"This one seems not have her wits".

Mary stands there looking confused. Her mouth hangs open but she says nothing. She looks across at Temperance who shakes her head.

"Not guilty. Not guilty".

"Mary Trembles, Are you acquainted with Mistress Barnes?"

Mary looks puzzled.

"Mistress Barnes. Mistress Barnes. Mistress Barnes".

"Do ye know her?"

"Know her".

She looks up at Sir Thomas.

"I seed 'er afore".

"When was that?"

"When? When us was beggin' up by market. Starvin' us was".

"Did she give you anything?"

"Nought. Maid wanted to. Mistress stopped 'er".

"So you bewitched 'er".

"Bewitched 'er. Bewitched 'er".

Sir Thomas leans forward to speak to her.

"Didst ye bewitch Mistress Barnes, Or did ye not?"

"Did not. Did not. Did not".

He watches her rocking back and forth. The Sheriff speaks again. He's becoming impatient,

"Didst ye bewitch Mistress Barnes?"

"Mistress Barnes. Mistress Barnes. Mistress Barnes".

"Yes, Mistress Barnes. Didst ye bewitch her?"

Mary seems to have a rare moment of clarity.

"Nay sir. Don' know 'ow. Save if Susannah'd show me. 'Er won't".

"So Susannah Edwards knows how to bewitch".

"Dunno".

"You went to the home of John and Grace Barnes later in the same day".
"Us did go there. Sometime..."
"Why didst ye go to the house? Wast called there?"
"Maid told us come to th'ouse. Fer to get us bread. Us was starvin' ".
"Did ye get bread?"
" 'Er din't 'ave none".
"So then what didst do?"
"Went 'ome, us did".

She said it as if that would be obvious to anyone who thought about it. Mary Trembles was accused of bewitching Grace Barnes. She had no idea why, and little idea of anything else. Some of the Jurymen seemed puzzled. They could see Mary was too slow to do much on her own, probably unable even to follow directions.

By law "the charges cannot be made severally for a crime", the charges must be made to each separately. One crime, one accused. Sir Thomas tries to explain this to the Jury, some of whom look no wiser than the accused. He decides to recess the court for the day. He can hear the Jurymen talking to each other as they leave,

"Be'm guilty or no?"
"Dunno. Gwain a be a 'angin' though".

CHAPTER FOURTEEN
AUGUST 15, 1682

> *"Temperance made answer, that she had no wax nor clay, but confessed that she only had a piece of leather which she had pricked nine times"*. (Informations of Elizabeth Eastchurch taken upon oath in Bideford - 1682)

The first day of the trial over, Sir Thomas rises to leave the bench. The people rise. Sir Thomas muses that he has so much ritual power, but so little power to exercise reason. He enjoys the cool breeze coming through the open door to the Castle garden. The high walls laced with vines keep out the people but not their shouts. The Jurymen leave by another gate to the cries of the crowd.

"They'm guilty, they'm guilty".

"Find 'em guilty. Or ye be guilty".

"Guilty. Guilty. Guilty".

The Constables' boots ring heavy on the ground beyond the walls. They are roughly pushing the three old women through the crowd that swarms around them.

"Devil lovers".

"Devil sucklers".

"Filthy witches".

"Satan's servers".

Those at the front of the mob are spitting on the women, those further back throw gravel and refuse at them. Sir Thomas goes back into the building and up the seven stairs to look out of a small window. He sees Temperance holding her head high, looking straight ahead. Susannah and Mary shield their eyes from the assaults.

The short walk feels like a mile to the women till they reach the doors and hurry down the damp, dark stairs. Their hearts are racing. They sink to the floor.

"Never thought to be glad to be back down yere. Safe we be now, safe in the cells. The shouting mob outside, they can't get in yere, no more than we can get out. Mary-Mary, poor Mary-Mary. Shaking fit to drop she is".

Temperance tells her,

"Be off to the ale-houses soon enough, ye'll see".

It's been a long day for the women.

"So many questions, with so little listening to what we answer. Maybe the Justice did. He tried to hear. So tired... So tired..."

They fall down in a pile in their corner into blessed sleep, a sleep too deep even for the rats to trouble them. Temperance is the first to awaken. She sits quietly, resting against the wall. It seems so long since she was picking her herbs by the river. Without the feverfew tea her back hurts, and sleep comes slowly when she has no seeds of white poppy to blind the knife hurt of hunger in her belly.

"Don't hardly know my own body, no more I don't. And my mind ... No escape from what's real. No herbs that was my friends, and friends to the people I helped. People I helped..."

The growing clarity of her mind produces only an increasing sense of terror. She wonders if she was thinking straight when she talked to the Mayor and to Rector Ogilby back in Bideford. Or was she out of her right mind? Did her own tongue betray her into admissions of devilry? She's tired, so tired, but the thoughts, the doubts, racing in her head keep sleep away.

"Sleep. Sleep. Must sleep. Need me wits about me tomorrow. Must cease the fearful thoughts. Must fix my mind on some object else. The Good Book. Like my Mam said. Say the names of all them books in the great Good Book till you fall asleep. Say them again. And again. Sleep will come. Good sleep. Sleep peopled by visions of the Patriarchs in the Judean deserts. Abraham, Isaac, Jacob. Genesis, Exodus, Leviticus, Numbers, Deuteronomy..."

She's tired from the long day of trial, so tired the words fade quickly into sleep. She wakes again, exhausted, and tries to fix her thoughts on Abraham, Isaac, Jacob.

"Where are thee? No. No. What's this? Who be thee? Who be this man all in black? God help me tis the Devil".

Temperance Lloyd: Hanged for Witchcraft in 1682

She wakes. Susannah wakes up too. Temperance had screamed out aloud her fear of some enormous flying thing, shooting right at her. The Thing, a black bird of prey with a sharp beak, seems to be heading for her eyes. Suddenly Mary-Mary's eyes are wide open. She's frightened. Temperance had cradled her to sleep in her arms. She had rolled away when Temperance pulled back her hand to shield her eyes from the flying phantom. She now awoke realizing she was alone. The phantom disappears. Susannah comforts Mary-Mary. Temperance sits shaking. She lies back down.

"Genesis, Exodus, Leviticus, Numbers, Deuteronomy ..."

Sleep comes. Then she shrieks out again,

"Save me, Lord. Save me!"

She sees the black beak coming straight for her face. But it isn't a bird. What is it? She sees a bird, a bird with face of Thomas Eastchurch. Its lips move,

"Witch, Witch, Witch".

"Get thee away. Get thee gone", Temperance screams at it, then she murmurs,

"Genesis, Exodus, Leviticus, Numbers, Deuteronomy ..."

The spectre fades away. Temperance rolls over into Susannah's arms. Sue murmurs to sooth her to sleep. The phantom returns to hover over Temperance again. Now it has the head of Thomas Bremincom.

"Looks funny, it do. Neck twisted, head hanging down and turned back. Is it his neck is broken?"

She's awake again. She sits up to pray the black visions will stop, then lies down again. It's no good. More and more fantastic apparitions come floating by. One by one she sees them, all the men that witnessed against her, questioned her, hounded her.

"They fly at me, leave when I wake screaming, praying".

Now that their trial is on, they are put in a cell with other prisoners, many of whom now wake and shout at Temperance to hush up and let them sleep.

"Now the Black man-headed bird is my man, dead eyes staring, black stinking river-mud dripping from his clothes".

He speaks to her,

"Killed me, ye did, ye did, ye did do it".

She calls out to him,

"Get back to thy grave".

The apparition fades away, the dead voice gurgling, sinking back into a shroud that floats out with the tide down the Torridge. Then she sees the river throw up other drowned sailors she once knew, Welsh would-be lovers who called out to her from the boats those first few years after her man's death, till the hunger and the cold made her old and wrinkled. They came like an Easter Church procession in good dreams. It didn't last.

"Black devil birds with heads of men flew back. From Wales, from Bideford, came every man into my sleeping mind that would abuse me had I not wounded them first. They infused my mind. Is it God's way of telling me I did whatever I did under Satan's own power?"

The light of dawn wakes the women. The guard is at the door. The nightmares and the dreams fade.

"Dreams do have meaning even after sunlight washes them away. I must confess to gain absolution that was promised us Sundays in Saint Mary's — *yng Nghrist Iesu ein Harglwydd ...* Through Jesus Christ in Heaven ..."

Temperance has come to believes confession will bring absolution.

"We have done those things we ought not to have done, and there is no health in us ..."

The gaolers throw scraps of bread over their heads. A piece hits Susannah in the face. She swears at the guard. Temperance cautions her to be quiet,

"Aisht. Aisht. Ye'm jes asking for his fist in yer belly".

He slops water into the bowls that hang on the walls. Mary-Mary manages to pick up three crusts that fall under her skirt. She swallows them faster than a seagull on Bideford quay. They hear the jangle of iron keys. The Constables arrive and the gaoler pushes the women up the steps. The mob in the yard is even bigger than it was yesterday, and louder too.

They are throwing whatever comes to hand at the women. Small stones hit Mary. She steps back. The constable pushes her on, almost into the arms of a big shouting man. In her fear, she vomits, splashing the skirt of women at the front of the crowd. They step back in horror. The witch has defiled them. They will be cursed. Mary-Mary starts crying loudly. Temperance whispers to her,

"There, there, Mary-Mary. Don't fret thee. Ye did nothing wrong. Ye didst not know how. Collect that, alright?"

She tries to touch Mary's shoulder. The Constable slaps her hand back. She tells him to let her be.

"Thy Constable's duty be to take us, not to chide and chivy us".

She looks him in the eye and he obeys. He motions the mob to stop the stoning and hustles them towards the Courtroom steps.

The Courtroom settles into silence broken only by whispers as Sir Thomas takes his seat on the bench. The Sheriff calls out,

"Temperance Lloyd. Temperance Lloyd".

She holds up her hand and the questions start again.

"Tis witnessed ye did punch and pull at Mistress Grace Thomas till she called out in pain. Didst do this?"

Temperance Lloyd: Hanged for Witchcraft in 1682

Temperance nods,

"Indeed I did rub her legs. Hurtin' she was, see, due to the damp and her rheumatics. Her takin' to her bed did make it worse, it did. But her sister would have it she should lay still there. And hurt it did when I rubbed".

"It is witnessed that thou rubbed so hard it pained".

"Indeed it did. Her sister was just strokin' and strokin'. Doin' no good at all she wasn't. Got to do it hard to get the pain out. Made it better that did. Up out of her bed she was and walkin' up the market the next day. Told all the folk she was well be my hands".

"And did ye make prickings with thy needle".

"Only on the leather I was sewing into a slipper for me foot, so I did".

She looks up at Sir Thomas,

"Image magic. They do believe in it over yere in Dyfnaint, not like in my Welsh Wales. Terrible ungodly superstition, isn't it. 'Thou shalt not make unto thyself any graven image...' The Reverend Ogilby should instruct them of a Sunday".

The Jurymen seem ignorant of the Commandment, though they must have heard the words often. Now they understood. They start suddenly a hubbub of quiet chatter, nodding and shaking their heads and looking at Temperance.

"Silence".

Having done with Temperance and Mary, the Sheriff calls for Susannah. Temperance watches her, trying to support her, willing her to remember their conversation.

"Talked with her over and over in our gaol I did of the power of forgiveness. God will forgive the sinner that repents. But she must only confess to what she have done. False confession is a lie, a great sin. Collect that when they ask thee, I told er".

Susannah looks back at Temperance. She remembers something about confession and thinks about it,

"Confess... Be forgiven... God, Merciful God... Din't us been told in Church? Repentance. Forgiveness. Let us go 'em will, if us confess. Let us go 'ome. Us prayed that in back Saint Mary's Church of a Sunday, us prayed it. Got to confess to what they witnesses say. Justices be learned. They knows".

She sees a woman standing up, not someone she knows. The Sheriff calls, "Joan Jones". Susannah and Temperance listen, puzzled, as she tells that she heard Susannah "confess in full" that she had done witchcraft. She says she heard Susannah say it to John Dunning who was in Bideford from Torrington to go to market. Susannah can't believe her ears. The Sheriff calls Susannah again.

171

"Dost know one John Dunning of Torrington town?"

"Aye, sir. I do know Master Dunning. Us talks with 'im betimes market days. Knowed 'e for years".

"Didst confess to him that ye be a witch? That ye did meet with the Devil?"

"Nay. Us confessed nought to 'im. Why would us? Nought to confess. 'E'll say as much when 'e be come".

She looks all around the courtroom, searching the sea of faces for John Dunning.

"Where be 'e? Can't see 'e. 'E'll put 'em right. Knowed 'e since us was chillen in Littleham. 'E'll tell em, 'e'll say".

The Sheriff's voice startles her.

"Susannah Edwards, dost swear thou knowst not Mistress Joan Jones?"

"Now us sees 'er with light on 'er face … Be 'er the one with 'er shop down the quay? Look different, 'er do, in 'er fancy bonnet".

"So ye dost know the witness?"

"Mebbe seed 'er be 'er shop. Don' know 'er. Where be John Dunning? Where be 'e?"

Dunning is not in the courtroom. The Sheriff speaks again,

"I ask again of Mistress Dorcas Coleman. Ye did declare Master Coleman was at sea when Mistress Coleman was sick".

" 'E was. Off to Avalon 'e was with load of ware from pottery down by river. Like Master Titherley on 'is 'Seafarer' for Master Shapton this May past. Whispers down quay 'bout that. Made poor Mistress worse. Us told 'er tweren't true".

"There were whispers?"

"Folk in Bideford do say as some seamen 'ave tother families cross the sea, in they new lands. Us told Mistress Coleman as t'weren't true. 'Ad to stop 'er worrying. Made 'er more sick worry did".

Mariner Coleman stands up. The Sheriff glares at him.

"Sit thee down, Sir".

"Ye speak of gossip?"

"Tis said some o' they seamen 'ad two fam'lies. One 'ere. One over Newfoundland. Called planters over there they be. 'Ave rooms on quay. Took pots, stayed to drink out of 'em, trying 'em out tis said. Tryin' out more 'n pots o'er there too, tis said up market. Mistress Coleman 'eard of it. Made 'er poorly. Us told Mistress Coleman 'er mus' calm 'er mind. Master Titherley 'e be a God-fearing churchman. Mistress Coleman 'er would'n 'ear as tweren't true as Gospel. Us gived 'er 'erbs to 'elp 'er sleep. Tried all us knowed t'elp er. Went to 'er day 'n night, all weathers, summer 'n winter. 'Eard out 'er worries. Soothed 'er mind an' body. Good mistress 'ad no cause to call us for bewitching. Us 'elped betimes, most times. An' 'er lives still, don' 'er?"

The Sheriff speaks again.

"Tis said by Master Eastchurch, and by Mistress Wakeley, a cat was seen to leap in at your window at twilight. Tis said the cat were the Devil. What say ye of this?"

"Cats do leap in windows. Lookin' for food, us s'pose. Lookin' for warmth. Would'n find neither in us 'ome. Don' 'ave none most times. Twas neighbour's cat. Poor mangy creature twas".

"And what say ye of the magpie that flew in Mistress Coleman's window?"

"I did see un. After ring Mistress left by 'er window, twas. Shooed un out us did. No 'arm done".

The Jurors whisper to each other.

"Cat there be'ed. 'Er be a witch for sure. Tis proof".

"Cat an' a magpie. Black both".

"Silence".

Sir Thomas stands and the Sheriff calls,

"All rise".

Sir Thomas walks slowly out of the Court. The Jurors leave quickly today, but they cannot avoid the yells of the crowd,

" 'Ave 'em 'anged. 'Ave 'em 'anged".

"God 'elp 'ee if 'em go free".

At the window on the stairs Sir Thomas watches the Constables push and drag the three women out into the blinding sunlight. After all the noise and commotion yesterday, extra men have been called in to clear a way through the crowd gathered in the courtyard. They hold the mob back, but nothing can stop the insistent cries for the women's execution.

Mary-Mary is too frightened to speak, even to repeat what Temperance and Susannah say to her. Susannah just keeps saying, "John Dunning. John Dunning". Temperance tells them,

"T'will all be done the morrow. Only three days in the Court. Three days last time for me twas".

She tries to speak calmly. She doesn't feel calm. Only three days. Susannah is confused. Mary is frightened. Three days — three months it seems since they left Bideford. The gaoler comes in to tell them,

"Tis well tis nigh done. Can' give 'ee no more'n 'alf a crust. Got to pay for thy food in 'ere. Free bed at the King's pleasure ye be gett'n' ".

"Half a crust, even less than we did have by begging in Bideford. Makes them days seem good times, it do".

Some of the other prisoners are getting bolder as they don't seem to have been bewitched yet. Others urge caution,

"Don't go by 'em. Witch 'ee they can. Stay clear. Don' let 'em look on 'ee".

Temperance talks softly to Mary,

"They be feared of us. Take care not to look to them. They do think we can harm them by looking".

They huddle closer together in the darkest corner of the dark room. By lying together in a circle they can keep away the rats that grow more and more bold in their runs towards them. Temperance tries to keep Susannah and Mary calm,

"Let us pray. Good Lord, Whose power knows no bounds, look on us, Thy humble servants. Grant us Thy Peace. Good Lord deliver us".

To herself she whispers, "By death or by acquittal".

CHAPTER FIFTEEN
AUGUST 16, 1682

"*The Attributes of Witches: "their transformation into cats, hares and other creatures ... their being sucked in a certain private place in their bodies by a familiar"* (Philosophical Considerations Touching Witches and Witchcraft, Joseph Glanvill, 1666)

The sun shines down brighter and hotter than ever as Sir Thomas walks into Court for the third and final morning of what he now calls "this benighted trial". Still he's thankful that the air in Exeter stinks less than the fetid Thames. Out of the sun's blinding glare, the courtroom seems dark as night. Sir Thomas sighs,
"Dark as the tales told by these darkened minds".
He knows the people inside the Court and outside hunger for a hanging to celebrate St Bartholomew's Festival. Three hangings at Heavitree will bring the crowds to the City. The merchants will be paid.
"The thieves will take home gold and silver pieces to last till Christmastide. The barrows will roll in heavy with good country fare and roll home heavy with all manner of goods".
Silence falls on the Courtroom when he enters. He can still hear the calls for vengeance against the poor women. He hears too the vengeance against the Jurymen should they acquit,
"Though heaven knows acquit they should with such a fanciful pack of tales spun out as evidence. And more of it to come this day I expect. The

man bringing our supper to table said one John Dunning was found in a drunken stupor behind the Shippe. No sign of him this day".

The sun travels across the August skies shining a changing light on a parade of witnesses, most of whom had neither seen nor heard anything for themselves. Their names are on the calendar. They have the right to the pay they get to appear, the right to say their piece, to repeat the witness they had sworn in Bideford. They tell of cats running past houses, magpies flying in and out of windows, confessions overheard of carnal knowledge of the Devil, and belief in a witch's power to cast ships away at sea. At last all have been heard. All has been heard.

"Tonight my Brother Justice Sir Francis will remind me again of the dilemma of the Statute. It is I, not he, that must charge the Jury".

The jurors are silent, their whispering ceased.

"How well they listened up to now only they and their God do know. How well they understood ... God only can know that...".

The Jurymen look serious as if they sense at last the gravity of the decision they must make.

"Whether they see the three women as witches, as poor women, may they see them as living beings".

Sir Thomas looks across at the Jury and takes a breath.

"Good masters, ye have attended here at the County Assizes, in this City of Exeter, in the County of Devon, in the year of our Lord, 1682. Ye have knowledge of the Law of the Land in this case. The Statute against Witchcraft that was duly passed into English law on the Ninth day of June in the year of our Lord 1604 still verily remains in effect. Under that Statute it is an offence to use, practice or exercise any Witchcraft, Sorcery, Charm or Enchantment whereby any person shall be killed, destroyed, wasted, consumed, pined, or lamed in his or her body or any part thereof".

He pauses.

"Ye have heard many persons that appeared here testify to their knowledge, or to the knowledge of others of their ken, of acts the women before ye are believed to have enacted. It is now time for ye all to consider what ye have heard, so that ye may render judgment to the best of thy abilities, and with the help of the Lord. It is my right and duty to try to help ye as Jurymen to use your judgment to adduce how likely it is that these women's confessions were true, and that said confessions were given without fear or favour and without undue inducement by any persons. Above all, ye must try to set thine own judgments apart from the call of the rabble gathered for this trial. It is usual for such a rabble to want the entertainment of a hanging. These desires cannot be cause for the hanging of three old women".

Some of the Jurymen move in their seats.

Temperance Lloyd: Hanged for Witchcraft in 1682

"As Jurymen ye must ask thyselves, Where did the confessions come from, from reality, from dreams, or from fear and desperation? And if there be some truth to the allegations, has any man of this Jury personal knowledge of anything brought forth in the Court? Has one man among you ever sat at a deathbed where life was ended except by cause of sickness or of known injury by fall or by assault? Has one man of you seen with his own eyes a cat or a hare transform before you into a woman or a man? Or witnessed a woman change herself into animal form? Hast seen any woman or man to fly aloft through the heavens by day or by night? Hast known of thyselves the power of any person to make to happen anything to any other person by only thinking it? How possible, how real, dost think what has been told to the Mayor and Alderman in Bideford and reported again in this Court?"

He knows he must be careful not to suggest there is no such thing as witchcraft, only to question the credibility of the evidence against the three women.

"Ye must ask as well, Did these women truly bewitch their fellow townsfolk? Or in their hunger did they eat the only food they could grow, herbs and roots of great power. And did these medicines take hold of their minds so they did come to think themselves possessed of magical power? Could the poverty of their existence weary these three poor women of their lives and wishful of death, but fearful of the curse of heaven on the sin of ending their lives by their own hands?"

Sir Thomas himself had wondered this.

"If their miserable lives be the reason for their ill-considered confessions, ask in Christian spirit whether their lives could be bettered without benefit of execution. Consider if their oppressing poverty has constrained them to wish for death, and to confess to sins they did not commit that the might find death. As a Justice, there would seem to me to be another means to help this case. It would be proper for them to be carried to the Parish from whence they came, and that the Parish should be charged with their maintenance".

He stopped and bowed his head to the court.

No sooner had he finished speaking than the Courtroom echoed with the roar of the crowd calling for execution. The good citizens of Bideford who sent the so-called witches to Exeter for trial were not ignorant peasants but educated Merchantmen and Master Mariners. They came here themselves as witnesses, and now in the public seats they hear the Judge's words with displeasure. Even in London people believe the most incredible stories of witchcraft, or if they do not, they keep silent for fear of offending the Church.

Justice Francis North had said to Sir Thomas just the evening before at supper that the strange tales were not told by witnesses who were illiterate country folk. Even in Exeter, where people are accustomed to County trials, miracles were attributed to the women. Sir Francis had said himself that a Judge must bear in mind that 'the level of unrest now in the city is like that seen elsewhere before uprisings or revolution'. He was afraid that,

"If these women are acquitted, the country people may rise up to commit some disorder".

Sir Francis had already written this advice to the Lord Chief Justice. Sir Thomas wishes the letter had not been delivered to the London coach.

The Jurymen huddle together to decide their verdict, clearly very afraid. They keep their eyes lowered to the ground so as not to catch the eye of any in the crowd. Theirs is a hard dilemma. If they admit the evidence against the women is at best fanciful and at worst purposely false, they themselves will be thought ungodly. It is not just those who read the words of Glanvill in the Latin that understand their influence. The Jurymen know this from the testimony of Reverend Ogilby, a man whose posture was so confident he might have had God himself at his side. To acquit a witch will be seen as denying witchcraft. To deny that there is witchcraft is to deny God himself. Sir Thomas can see too that some, most, of the Jurors feel threatened for their own lives by the crowd that calls for a guilty verdict.

The Jurymen talk for almost half an hour, with much gesturing and hand-wringing, before they turn back towards the Court. The Sheriff asks,

"In the matter of the charge of Witchcraft against Mary Trembles of Bideford in the case of Grace Barnes?"

"We find her guilty".

"In the matter of the charge of Witchcraft against Susannah Edwards of Bideford in the case of Dorcas Coleman?"

"We find her guilty".

"In the matter of the charge of Witchcraft against Temperance Lloyd, Widow of Bideford in the case of Grace Thomas?"

"We find her guilty".

The crowd cheers at each verdict. When all three women stand convicted, hats fly in the air. Someone starts to lead the people in a tuneless hymn.

As is the practice when a trial ends, Sir Thomas remains on the bench till the Constables remove the accused from the court. The public follow. The room is quiet, only the dust dancing in the sunlight tells of the frenzy that was raised at the verdict. Sir Thomas listens to the sounds of derision from the assembled public outside as the three women are taken back to gaol.

Temperance Lloyd: Hanged for Witchcraft in 1682

The Constable tells the women they are to be hanged the day after the Feast of Saint Bartholomew.

The crowds have left the yard outside the gaol. They and a lot more people will be back for the real spectacle, the public hanging. It will be a Saint Bartholomew Feast such as they haven't seen in the past five years. Their trial done, the women now wait.

The gaoler takes them clean straw for a bed and blankets to cover them. He gives them dripping with their bread, and strong ale to wash it down. They gain some strength. Susannah now seems to understand their situation,

"Us be doomed, us be, Mary".

"Doomed. Doomed. Doomed. Wast that?"

Mary had thought she and the others were going to be acquitted. Susannah had believed that too. And Temperance?

"I did hope for it too. Confessing didn't help neither. Confessing to man brings no forgiveness, no mercy neither. Me, I should have gone back to my Welsh Wales stead of going back to Bideford after the last Assizes. Maybe after my man died. Could've married that Minister of the Church that thought I had the face of Mary Magdalen. Still had that face then. After that first trial I should have gone, Minister or no. Too late now".

Susannah looks at her wide-eyed,

" 'Ad 'em no mercy?"

"Fear kills mercy. Only God can help us now. Let us pray".

They knelt, huddled together, repeating over and over the prayers they had said weekly at Saint Mary's in Bideford,

"Almighty and most merciful Father, we have erred and strayed from thy ways like lost sheep ... But thou, O Lord have mercy upon us, miserable offenders ..."

For Temperance it wasn't the same praying in the English. She preferred to pray in Welsh, to sing the hymns of her childhood. No one minded that in Bideford. They were used to hearing Welsh, with the boats going back and forth from Swansea.

"Scarce a day went by but I'd see a collier moor at the quay. Exeter be a big place, but folk here know little of the world".

When she prayed to her Welsh God the other prisoners called to the guards that she was casting spells. The visiting Clergy could not admit they knew no languages but English and the Latin liturgies so they said she was indeed speaking Welsh. Temperance told Susannah and Mary,

"The Lords up there in London can save us yet".

179

No breeze stirs through the open window of the Justice's dining chamber. Even in the dusk, the air is warm. The roasted chickens were tasty but the meal too hot and heavy for the day. Sir Thomas had little appetite. Sir Francis was still feeling little better than he did on the journey to Exeter. Fortunately there had been few civil cases for him to try. He was glad to stay in the lodgings.

With all the noise and anger about the trial of the three old women, Sir Francis was no more surprised than was Sir Thomas at the verdict. While Sir Thomas sat on the Bench, Sir Francis had considered what they should do whether they were declared guilty, or whether, by some trick of fate, they should be found innocent. Through the open window of the lodgings, Sir Francis had listened to the intermittent calls of the crowds in the streets below. As soon as the verdict was declared, he heard the runners begin their calls,

"Guilty. Guilty. Guilty. 'Eavitree 'anging for the Festival".

The crowd outside the Castle had turned as if ruled by one shared spirit and jostled up the lanes to the Heavitree Square. There they pitched their poles to save a wagon space in the meadows for their return for Saint Bartholomew's Fair and the hangings that will follow.

As had been agreed before the two Justices left London, Sir Francis penned a letter to Sir Leoline Jenkins, Secretary of State, the only man with the power to offer a reprieve to any convicted at the Assizes. He wrote,

> "The evidence against them was very full and fanciful, but their own confessions exceeded it. They appeared not only weary of their lives, but to have a great deal of skill to convict themselvs. Their description of the sucking devils with saucer-eyes was as natural that the Jury could not choose but believe them".

Sir Thomas agrees,

"Fanciful. To a thinking man, that's what it was. How much thinking occupies the minds of the carters who even now fight each other up at Heavitree to gain a patch of meadow close by a straight path to the gallows square the next week? The good citizens of Exeter do not think it right to pardon, to reprieve. We must consider the politic of England in this year of our Lord 1682 that finds our country alive with political intrigue"

They both know the King is well-liked by the people, for his pleasant demeanour if not for a mindful administration. Remnants of republican sympathy still live down in the West Country. In London the Whigs and Tories still argue over the Church's sway, though Parliament has not been in session for over a year past. Sir Francis was well aware of the mood of the people.

"This instability doth make any unpopular verdict the provocation to widespread riots in those with no shared discontent save a liking for disorder. Further, in the Established Church, the Saducists still hold sway over the minds of the Clergy. These men of God whose hearts might favour Christian mercy now needs must attest that to acquit any person accused of witchcraft on any grounds is to deny the existence of witches, and thereby deny the existence of God Himself".

Sir Thomas knows that Sir Francis truly wished the Jury could have been able to reason, but he understands the politics. They had both heard the mood of the people shouted out at every Assize between Exeter and London. Any rational people would see that the old women were likely delusional and depressed from a life of penury. The mob is not rational. So Sir Francis had good reason to advise the Secretary in his letter that,

> *"I find the country so fully possessed against them that although some of the virtuosi may think these the effects of confederacy, melancholy, or delusion, and the young folks are altogether as quick-sighted as they who are old and infirm; yet we cannot reprieve them without appearing to deny the very being of witches, which, as it is contrary to law, so I think it would be ill for his Majesty's service, for it may give the faction occasion to set afoot the old trade of witch-finding that may cost many innocent people their lives which the justice will not prevent".*

Sir Thomas had to agree with his learned colleague's view of the matter. If the three women were to be reprieved there would be anger and hatred greater than that stirred by Master Witch-finder Hopkins himself. The people will have their witches, no matter how. The witch hunts like Newton's theory of gravity are something the people 'have accustomed themselves to and grown to love'.

"At dawn tomorrow we shall ride the coach home to London, God willing".

In her ignorance, Temperance is still hopeful,
"The Lords up in London can save us".
She knows this is true. She tells Susannah and Mary. They look at her as if she were a mad woman. Susannah will have none of it.
"If'n 'em save us from noose, us'll be stoned on us way 'ome us will".
"Or home in our bed, Susannah".

The gaolers come and go, bringing them food. They let them sleep soundly at night. A Clergyman, Mr Hann, comes to them. His mission is to have them confess so they will depart their lives in the grace of the Lord. Over and over he keeps asking them to confess. Temperance tells him they did enough confessing in the Court, and much good did it do for them. She tells Mr Hann that it would be evil to lie to God to please His servant.

"His other servant, the Reverend Ogilby, lied in Court of his questioning of me though he swore to tell the truth".

The Clergyman came again, this time to teach them the prayers for the gallows. Temperance told him that they, well, she and Susannah, already knew their prayers well, being in Saint Mary's every Sunday and Holy Day. Mary-Mary just said along with them whatever words she could.

"Didn't know the meaning she didn't. Said the words wrong. Used to finish the last words a bit behind on account she was trying to repeat what Susannah and me had said".

The servants in the seats in front of us would turn and look at her. Temperance would just look right back at them. Mary was too busy watching what to do next to notice them looking. God, he wouldn't hold that against her, "God of mercy that he is".

Mr Hann would not leave them be. Temperance asked him to leave Mary-Mary alone. There was no point trying to get her to remember any words.

"Heard our Lord's prayer every week she lived with us in Bideford but can't say it for herself, save when ye do say it slow in her ear".

Temperance asked him for a Bible. He gave her one and a candle to read it by. Mary-Mary just cried and cried till she fell asleep. She spent most of that last week sleeping as she would later sleep on forever.

Susannah prayed for her soul, for God to speed her to heaven. Temperance prayed the Lord might spare them. She prayed the Lord would have the Lords up in London spare them.

So their days passed. They could hear the carts passing outside on their way to the Saint Bartholomew's Day Fair.

"We die tomorrow unless the Lord, or the Lords up in London, show mercy".

CHAPTER SIXTEEN
25 AUGUST, 1682

"gwared ne rhag drwg" - "Deliver us from Evil" (The Book of Common Prayer - 1587)

No. There was no mercy. The Lord did not hear our prayers. Or has He a different plan?

Not for us to question Him. The grand lords up in London heard not neither. A quiet night we had of it. Gaoler took us to a different room after our supper. He called it our last supper. Laughed he did. I said to him twas close to blasphemy. He only said twas not for me to know that. He left the lamp so we could read".

Mary ate her bread and dripping, then lay down to sleep. Susannah and Temperance had no need to talk softly. Nothing would disturb her.

"Saint Bartholomew Day today, 'And I appoint unto you a kingdom that ye may eat and drink at my table in my kingdom ...' Sunday past, the twelfth Sunday after Trinity".

Temperance asks Susannah to say the Collect with her,

"Almighty and everlasting God, Who art always more ready to hear than we to pray, and art wont to give more than either we desire or deserve; Pour down upon us the abundance of thy mercy: forgive us those things whereof our conscience is afraid, and giving us those good things which we are not worthy to ask, but through the merits and mediation of Jesus Christ, Thy Son, our Lord".

Mary-Mary, suddenly awake, calls out, "Amen. Amen". Susannah jumps. Then she asks Temperance to read to her,

"Jes want 'ear 'ee say they words".

Temperance opens the Bible at random to read whatever is there.

"My Mam said as that's a way to get the word of God from His mouth to our hearts,

"And God shall wipe away all tears from their eyes; and there shall be no more death, neither sorrow, nor crying, neither shall there be any more pain..."

Temperance stops. Tears run down Susannah's face and on to her frock. Temperance has Susannah lay her head down on her lap where she sobs quietly. Temperance strokes Sue's hair till her breath comes soft, even. Then she leans back against the wall and relaxes. Genesis, Exodus, Leviticus ... Temperance falls asleep. They are wakened by the sun shining through the high window making a pattern on the wall.

"The twenty-fifth day of August, as full a summer day as I ever saw. Our last bed chamber must be facing east".

The gaoler brings them food, dark bread, dripping, strong ale, and apples. He tells them to eat up, the wagon waits outside. He walks them out through the door and bids them farewell. A Constable lifts them on to the cart. He covers them and the three wooden boxes with a blanket. He tells them to stay low, then he drives out through the far gate. The women can hear a mob at the public gate.

"So disappointed they will be to miss our departing".

They can see the closed back doors of the houses through the side slats of the wagon and soon they hear the crowds at Heavitree. So many people are there in such a boisterous gathering. So much trade for the hawkers who have stayed on after the Saint Bartholomew's Fair.

"Can hear the bakers calling fresh bread. Lying they are. Must be yesterday's leftovers. No time to bake this morning".

Barrows stand loaded with blackberries, early apples and whinberries. The hawkers are calling "Protection against the Devil and his Covens". They brandish masks on sticks, be-ribboned and decorated with oak leaves and wild daisies. As the Constable hands the women down from the wagon, the masks wave like a forest in a windstorm above them.

The Sheriff stands beside the steps up to the gallows platform. Mr Hann in his black robe and the purple funeral stole stands by the Sheriff's side.

They take Susannah first. Mr Hann asks her in a loud voice if she be guilty of the offences they charged her of. Susannah shakes her head.

"Say out loud, dost deny thou did harm by the power of witchcraft and sorcery?"

"Nay. Us did no 'arm".

Temperance Lloyd: Hanged for Witchcraft in 1682

"Let us pray for thy soul, for without confession will come the fires of hell for the guilty".

Susannah knelt and bowed her head. Then she asked Mr Hann to sing with her the fortieth Psalm. Mr Hann looks startled and fumbles through his Prayer Book. Temperance sings with her to give her the tune.

"Withhold not Thou Thy tender mercies from me, O Lord; let Thy loving-kindness and Thy truth continually preserve me. For innumerable evils have compassed me about, mine iniquities have taken hold upon me, so that I am not able to look up; they are more than the hairs of mine head; therefore my heart faileth me. Be pleased O Lord to deliver me. Make haste to help me..."

Temperance could sing no more. Tears choked her voice.

Susannah walked of her own accord up the steps. She put her head through the noose and spoke her last words,

"The Lord Jesus speed me; though my sins be as red as scarlet, the Lord Jesus can make them white as snow".

A gust of wind swung the rope. The crowd shrieked out with delight. Mary-Mary's finger-nails pierced into Temperance's hand drawing blood. Then she turned and leapt higher than her own small stature, right back on to the wagon. She clung fast to the wagon side slats. Her skirts were dripping. The Constable lifted her back on to the ground. She dragged her feet refusing to walk. The Constable held her while the Sheriff's man fetched a horse. They tied her to the horse and led him to the gallows. By now Mary-Mary knew she was beaten. She gave in, climbed the steps and stood quietly.

The Sheriff called out loudly,

"Dost be a witch, or a sorcerer? Confess now."

"Din't do nought of it. Dunno 'ow."

Then it seemed approaching death made her remember the prayers she had never said properly in Saint Mary's of a Sunday.

"Jesus, take me soul, Speed me..."

The noose barely snapped under her bony form as her legs swung from under her. Another roar went up from the crowd.

The Constable went to take Temperance's arm. She stopped him, said she could walk well enough. She took the apple from inside her frock and bit into it.

"Still have a few teeth left I do. Lovely it tasted. The juice was sweet. Mother Eve knew that".

She held her head high as she walked up the steps to the platform. While the Sheriff set the noose about her neck, she prayed,

"Lord Jesus speed me well, forgive all my sins ..."

The Sheriff opened his mouth. Mr Hann raised his hand but the Sheriff would have his say.

"Ye are looked on as the woman that had debauched the other two. Didst thee ever lie with devils?"

"Nay, I did not".

"Did ye know of them coming to ye in gaol?"

"Nay. Why would ye think that indeed?"

"Have ye anything to say to satisfy the world?"

"The world. Ye do mean they that lied to the Justices? They that had me said a witch?"

His questions go on. She admits she did believe that she had been approached by the devil. Could it be a dream? Could her dreams be false?

"Nay, I did not get help from the devil. I would always rather rely on the Lord my God. I affirm truly my belief in God and Jesus Christ, I pray to Jesus Christ to pardon all my sins".

As the noose snaps around her neck she hears the people cheering loudly. Then they turn and run to buy the trinkets on the stalls.

EPILOGUE
FACTS AND FICTION

What do we know for sure about the lives and times of Temperance Lloyd, Susannah Edwards and Mary Trembles? We know about the times and what led up to their execution, but little or nothing of the lives of the three women.

The minutes of the House of Lords for June 9, 1604 document the passage of the Statute against Witchcraft. We know who was there, and what they discussed. We know that King James VI of Scotland and I of England was convinced that witches had the power to cause storms at sea, like the one he believed his cousin Sir Francis Stewart had roused by witchcraft to try to assassinate him. He described his beliefs in his Daemonologie to build a case for the 1604 Statute that was the first to associate witches with the Devil. Before that there was no witch cult in England, unlike in his native Scotland. Did his near-death experience lead to what we now call Post Traumatic Stress Disorder? It would account for the curious obsession in the man we know better today for commissioning the Bible that bears his name. But did the deaths of hundreds of his citizens finally end his Odyssean voyage through in a traumatized world?

The pamphlet about the trials of the Bideford witches is a sensational account written to sell well to the gullible, like many such publications of the time. Sir Francis North, one of the two Justices in Exeter for the trial, dismissed the accounts of the women's confessions in letters he wrote at the time. The pamphlet describes the acceptance of hearsay evidence even third hand descriptions of the women's activities. It also documents the more bizarre beliefs of the time, that people could transform themselves into cats, or hare, or birds.

Joseph Glanvill, and other leading theologians, made such bizarre beliefs integral to Church dogma — to deny the existence of witches was to deny the existence of God. This left Bideford Rector, Michael Ogilby, little choice but to testify against Temperance Lloyd. As to Ogilby, his testimony is his only claim to fame, that and his name on the list of Rectors on the wall in the Parish Church of St Mary in Bideford.

Apart from their involvement in the trial, we know little of the women's accusers. The trial transcripts do offer other hints about the ailments of the women's "victims". Dorcas Coleman tended to become ill when her husband was at sea. Damp weather affected Grace Thomas. Grace Barnes probably felt guilty for refusing alms to the women begging on the street. According to the "Informations", the women confessed — under torture and starvation. It's also obvious that Mary Trembles was "simple", an unlikely miscreant.

The women were likely herbalists, using the knowledge of the time. Gerard's Herbal
describes many remedies the active ingredients of which are now supported by medical research. The physician, Dr Beare, with his training in Discourse, would have had few tools to treat the sick, but his accusations of witchcraft would have carried great weight.

Weather records of the time document poor growing conditions and we know there were crop failures. Shipping records and archival information from Newfoundland and Virginia show increasing trade with Bideford over the seventeenth century. The export of pottery to the New World was so prolific that archaeologists identify sites by finds of North Devon ware with its glossy ochre and terra-cotta glaze and unique designs. Trade between South Wales and Bideford began in the fifteenth century and continued for 500 years.

Seventeenth century Bideford was a thriving port with grand buildings and a bridge dating from Roman times. In other respects it was like many country towns in Britain. By the mid-twentieth century, very little had changed for the poor in 300 years. Many of the houses like the ropewalker's cottage that still stands, had been updated with a cold water tap to replace the well that dried up. Otherwise they were like Temperance's Old Town home. Local dialect had not changed significantly in 400 years. So much for the knowns.

The unknowns are three women who are now on-line exhibits in the cult of the occult. Was Temperance Welsh? Did she use the Welsh Book of Common Prayer? She was a widow but how was she widowed?

One more thing we do know. No one could have committed the crimes of which they were accused, to which they confessed. And is there *A hope of an end to persecution and intolerance* — anywhere? Is it just human nature to hunt down and punish those who are different from us?

THE PETITION

Please join me in signing a Petition asking the Government of the United Kingdom to pardon Temperance Lloyd, Susannah Edwards and Mary Trembles of Bideford, Devon, who were hanged as Witches on August 25, 1682 under the 1604 Statute against Witchcraft passed into Law by the British Parliament on June 9, 1604.

To find the Petition, Please go to: http://epetitions.direct.gov.uk/petitions/37616

ACKNOWLEDGEMENT OF SOURCE MATERIALS

House of Lords Journal Volume 2 9 June 1604 www.british-history.ac.uk

The Trial of the Bideford Witches (1982) Frank J. Gent

History of Witchcraft in England 1558-1718 Volume 5 The Later English Trial Pamphlets Wallace Notestein

A True and Impartial Relation of the Informations against Three Witches Temperance Lloyd, Mary Trembles and Susanna Edwards Freeman Collins 1682 http//dlxs2.library.cornell.edu

Bideford History http://www.bidefordtown.co.uk

History of Roads http://www.highways.gov.uk/knowledge/

Old Bideford and District Muriel Goaman, Bristol: E.M. and A.G.Cox, 1968

Shipping and Cargo Information - Special thanks to the staff at The Colony of Avalon Museum and Archaeological Site - Ferryland, NL

The Boke of Common Prayer 1547 Schoenberg Center for Electronic Text and Image

Llyfr Gweddi Gyffredin http://justus.anglican.org/resources/bcp/Wales/

Leaves from Gerard's Herball - Arranged for garden lovers by Marcus Woodward - London: Gerald Howe and Boston: Houghton Mifflin 1931 based on The Herball or General Historie of Plantes John Gerard 1597

Homeland Defense Corps http://www.homelanddefensecorps.org/quotes.htm

Weather Records - http://booty.org.uk/booty.weather/climate/1650_1699.htm

Daemonologie by James VI of Scotland - http://www.sacred-texts.com

Lightning Source UK Ltd.
Milton Keynes UK
UKOW041626140313
207633UK00001B/32/P